# THE
# RED
# TOWER

# THE RED TOWER

a novel by

## J.B. SIMMONS

This is a work of fiction. Names, characters, and incidents in this book are products of the author's imagination or are used fictitiously. Any resemblance to actual events, locations, or persons is coincidental.



ISBN 978-1949785029

Published in the United States by Three Cord Press
www.threecordpress.com

www.jbsimmons.com

*On life's vast ocean diversely we sail,*
*Reason the card, but passion is the gale;*
*Nor God alone in the still calm we find,*
*He mounts the storm, and walks upon the wind.*

Alexander Pope

THE FIVE TOWERS
RED
BLACK
GREEN
THE SCOURING
BLUE
YELLOW

# 1

THERE IS NO BLUE when I wake up. Dark, heavy furs wrap around me like a bear's coat. Two torches light up the rough stone walls of the cramped cave, giving it a reddish glow. I sit up and feel something at my neck. Inch by inch my fingers prod around the smooth metal band. There's no clasp. My throat clenches.

I stand slowly. My legs ache and my head throbs as I stagger to the cave wall where there's a wooden door. It doesn't have a handle and doesn't budge when I push it. There's no window or other hint of where I am. My stomach churns. My hand wipes parched lips and comes away covered in crusted blood.

Blood.

Red.

It hits like a wrecking ball: *this is the Red Tower.*

I've come from the Blue Tower, memories intact. A smile lifts the corners of my bloodied lips. *Memories!* Red could have wiped my memories away but didn't. I fought in the Scouring. I lost Kiyo, but got her back. I captured Emma from Yellow. Abram let me look into the Sieve. I saw who I was before, Paul Fitzroy, the doctor. My Mom should be somewhere in this tower. I'm a prisoner, apparently, but the people here might know who I am. They will want me to fight for them.

Someone will come.

The pile of furs invites me to lie down again. The torches make shadows dance along the craggy wall. The warmth lulls me back to sleep. I curl up, ignoring my rumbling belly, and sleep again.

A knocking sound wakes me.

My eyes open just as the door does. A woman strides in, with long auburn hair and amber eyes that sparkle like jewels. Her red dress has slits cut at the sides and fits snugly up to her neck. It looks like it's made of flecks of metal, glimmering in the torchlight.

She leans against the open door and crosses her arms. "Welcome, boy."

Abram had said the exact same thing when I arrived in Blue. She must be the leader. She's nothing like Abram, not even like Sarai. She's younger and…stunning. "Who are you?" I ask.

"Presumptuous," she says, looking down at me.

"That's your name?"

Her red lips stretch into a faint grin. "No, that's what you are. I'm the leader of this tower. Rahab."

"So you know me?" I ask.

"Cipher. Dr. Fitzroy. Doesn't matter. You're a lump of coal here. You're not even lit yet."

She tosses some clothes on the floor, then holds out

her hand. A small flame flickers above her palm. There is no candle, nothing to burn. She can summon fire.

"How do you do that?" I ask.

"The same way you can put it out," Rahab says. "Give it a try."

Her words remind me of my power over the wind and the air. I try it, just like before. I focus and pull at the wind. It doesn't obey. Before, I could gather up the air in my mind and weave it, but I can't see it anymore. I try one more time, harder. Still nothing.

I shake my head.

She looks amused. Her palm closes and her fire disappears.

"Get dressed," she says, as she turns her back to the room and to me.

Emerging from the den of fur, I hold up the clothes to the light. The pants are reddish brown leather—smooth but not as soft as the robes of the Blue Tower. It's tougher. Like armor. The shirt has leather laces to draw tight at the top of the chest. The shoes are sturdy boots up to the calf, with the same kind of laces.

Rahab keeps her back turned as I slide on the clothes and pace a couple times across the tiny room, getting a feel for the tight fit. These clothes are not made for sitting in a classroom or going sailing. They are for hiking across a desert or up a mountain. Maybe for battle.

"Okay, I'm ready."

She leads me out. The hallway has rough red rock walls like the cave where I woke up. The floor has been worn smooth. Bright flames flicker from torches every twenty steps or so. Everything glows like lava.

Just like my beginning in Blue, I do not see anyone else. But now I know they're here. I know what's outside. The Scouring and four other towers. I also know where I came from, and why I came here: to find my Mom. It was not easy to leave Emma, Kiyo, and Hank, but Abram said my Mom would be here.

"I'm looking for someone," I say.

Rahab doesn't slow down or look back. "Everyone here is."

"But this is different. It's my Mom."

"What's her name?"

"Rose Fitzroy."

"She's here," Rahab says. "Do what you're told and you might see her."

Her red dress swishes back and forth as she walks quickly down the hallway. Unlike Blue, we are heading down, not up. And it gets warmer, not cooler; redder, not bluer.

By the time we reach an iron door, there are no more torches on the walls. The only light comes from the flame hovering an inch above the woman's hand. It reflects rubies set into the door, forming an intricate flame pattern. The woman holds her hand to the pattern, then nudges the door slightly. It swings open without a sound. A rush of air comes from inside and fills my nostrils with a suffocating smell. It is hot, dank, and noxious.

"Go in," she says.

But there's no way I want to do that. "It smells like burning sewage."

She glares at me. "You're not in Blue anymore."

For some reason, her tone makes me angry. I *know* this isn't the Blue Tower. I'm not a novice. I have risen to the top of Blue. I have captured from Red in the Scouring. I came here by choice, not just as a captive. Doesn't she know this? And why does she want me to go in this door? Some kind of punishment? Fear and anger are a potent mix. My mind clenches like a fist and I manage to grab something, just a little—the air. I funnel it into a small wind that blows into the woman's flame, flickering over her palm, and douses it.

*There, still got it!*

My satisfaction does not last long. Rahab overpowers me, shutting down my control of the air and bringing her flame back.

"Not bad," she says, "for Blue. Now you will enter."

I stand up straighter. "What's in the room?"

"You'll see." She motions me forward, flames now hovering above both of her hands to light the way.

I inch ahead, hesitantly, then I glance back at her. I try once again to seize the air. But I can't.

She shakes her head, and I swallow in fear. It seems I have little choice. I could trust Abram and Sarai. Maybe I can trust this woman, too. I take two more steps.

The iron door suddenly swings shut behind me.

It's pitch black inside. I snap around and bang on the door. I shout for Rahab to open it. But I know she won't.

*Calm down*, I tell myself. *It must be a test.*

My heart thuds quickly. My back presses against the door. Between my breaths, I hear another sound. It is deep and terrible. It is growling.

It can't be more than ten feet away.

A sliver of light appears in the darkness. At first it runs parallel to the ground, but it grows into a round, yellow eye. The eye is as tall as I am, with a vertical black slit like a snake's.

# 2

A DEEP RUMBLE comes from near the yellow eye. The sound is terrifying, like rock grinding against rock at the heart of the earth. "Cipher…" it says.

*It knows who I am?* I cower back against the door, still sealed tight.

"You are…cold," the creature rumbles.

Maybe I should be comforted that the beast is talking instead of eating me. But the horrible sound and smell and the complete darkness suffocate me. The only thing I can see is the giant eye, staring at me. An eye like that means a mouth that could swallow me whole in one bite. I want to ask: *what are you? A monster? A snake? A dragon?*

Instead I'm frantically searching the door for a latch or handle but feel nothing. I bang against the iron, slamming my fist over and over. I start to shout. Maybe Rahab will show mercy.

Over my own voice, I hear a surprising sound: laughter. I look back and the yellow eye blinks. "Get out," it says, sounding amused. "You're not ready…"

*Ready for what?* I think, just as the door starts to open. I slide through as soon as I can. The door closes immediately behind me, sealed as it was before. The stench of the dark room and the creature lingers.

Rahab waits with flames hovering above one hand. "That was quick," she says.

I rise to my feet. "What *was* that?"

"It depends on what *you* are. Let's see." She takes my right hand and studies the back of it. The scar is still there, the one from the Blue Tower with a long vertical line crossed by a shorter horizontal one. She runs a finger along the scar, then releases my right hand and takes my left. It has no scar. She glances at it only briefly before letting go. "It also depends on what you will become."

"What's that supposed to mean?" I ask.

She just smiles and starts walking, leading me back the way we came. I ask her more questions but she ignores me. I'm left wondering why she took me there, what the beast's words meant, and how they held such terror.

Eventually my thoughts turn to Emma. I hope she won't try to follow me here. But I miss her. We had connected, joined our powers. Maybe it was a mistake to leave her.

When we reach the cave where I first woke up, I hesitate before going in. "Will I be locked inside again?"

Rahab nods. "Someone will come for you."

"Who?"

"One of the boys, task fourteen."

"What's task fourteen?"

"You ask a lot of questions."

Which, apparently, she's not going to answer. "Can you tell me just one thing?"

"Try me."

"Is my Mom okay? Rose?"

Rahab smiles down at me. Her lips are thick and red. "You sound like a boy from Blue. They like you to believe the past is so, so important. Here, in Red, what matters is *passion*—right now, in the present. What do you feel, Cipher? Are you cold? Lonely? Afraid? Want someone to lay with you? Warm you up?"

"I…no, I'm fine." I blush, unsure of what to say.

"Always so cold," she sighs. "No wonder Blue's survivors need us. Ice has to melt."

*I'm not a survivor.* I came here by choice. Besides, I thought the towers were supposed to show past mistakes that could be scoured. "Will the Red Tower show me something about the past, about passion?" I ask.

"You think passion is a vice?"

"I guess so."

"Oh, Abram, you've frozen another one…" She motions to the pile of furs. "Lay down, warm up, sleep."

I move forward, but turn back. Rahab distracted me from my real question, and her dismissal of the past suddenly makes me worried. "Does my Mom remember me? Does she want to find her son?"

"Ah, always good to care what a woman wants," Rahab says. "Rose has passions as we all do. When ice melts, it makes a useless mess, unless it is properly contained. We will teach you how to use your passion, to harness it as it was meant to be. We have no use for ice here."

She turns to go, but I still want an answer. "So what about my Mom?"

"Someone will come to bring you to the Feasting Hall," she says. "By all means, ask around while you're there. You'll meet plenty of girls. But you should know, you get only one in the Pairing."

# 3

ANOTHER KNOCK AT the door wakes me. This time I'm on my feet fast. The two torches still flicker on the cave wall. There's no way to tell whether it's day or night.

The door opens a crack. "Hello? All good in there? Mind if I come in?"

It's a boy's voice, high and squeaky like an excited mouse.

"Anyone there?" he asks. "Helloooo?"

"Yes," I say. "Come in."

The door swings open and reveals a boy built like a bathtub. He's about my height and three times as wide, with huge freckles dotting every square inch of his pale pinkish skin, like someone splashed him with mud. He wears a band around his neck as I do. It's gleaming silver, like the band Emma and the other servants wore in the Blue Tower.

"Morning, morning!" he says cheerfully, holding out his hand. It's hard to believe the squeaky voice comes from a boy so large. "I'm your new best friend, Seymour."

We shake hands. His palm is sweaty.

"I'm Cipher."

"Oh, I know all about you!" His eyes linger on the scar on my hand before he releases the handshake. "The boy wonder from Blue. The boy with the wind. The boy who waltzed right into the Red Tower. Gotta admit, I thought you'd be bigger!"

"Why?" I ask.

"Not everyone *chooses* to come to Red. Kind of crazy, really. But I don't mind. We're all a little crazy here. We feast on bacon. Our girls summon fire and tell us what to do. Yes, ma'am! What'll it be? More bacon? Right away! That's just how it goes, but I'll tell you everything you need to know. You just listen to me, Seymour, and you'll be just fine, boy wonder. Or would you prefer Cipher?"

*This is…different.* His rapid-fire words leave me feeling speechless. They must all know about me here. And this boy has told me more about Red than I learned about Blue in days.

"Cipher's fine," I say.

"You got it, Cipher. I see you already put your jerkin on. Nice work. Some people forget to tie their laces." He fingers the leather string pulled taut at his rotund chest. "Can't forget that! Unless you want to be burned, of course. Lots of burning here, I'll tell ya. But I'll keep you out of the fires if I can. And don't worry about that little collar. Nothing special. All of us boys wear one. Like pet dogs! But we're free enough. You'll get used to it. You ready for the best time of the day?"

"What's that?" I ask.

"The feast! Bacon and beans. It never gets old as long as you have the right spices." He pats a little pouch hanging at his waist, then turns for the door. "Come on, follow me, good old Seymour, and let's get to the food."

He waddles out the door and starts down the hall, with me following. He never stops talking. I manage maybe seven words, and he spews forth information like a geyser. He hardly seems like the discerning type, so who knows how much of what he says is true. But at least I learn some basics about the Red Tower as we make our way through the cave-like tunnels. I learn that boys in Red do not have any powers but get paired with the girls. The girls can summon and control fire, like Rahab. Apparently each girl gets her own nice room, with a fireplace, while the boys all sleep in a big room called the Barracks.

"The Barracks is boring," Seymour tells me, "except for the training ground, if fighting is your thing, anyway. There's lots of weapons. The boys spend most of their time there, fighting and hanging out. After we finish our tasks, of course. The sooner you finish, the sooner you get to come back to the training ground. Better to get back as soon as you can!"

"Why's that?" I ask.

"Because in the Barracks, you are safe and free. No girls allowed. Not even Rahab comes in there. We do what we want as long as we report to meals each day and finish our tasks."

"What happens if we don't?"

"Don't what?" Seymour asks, as if he'd never thought

of disobeying.

"Don't report for meals, don't do our tasks." My fingers slide smoothly over the collar at my neck. "Whatever it is they want us to do here."

"It's not *they*, my friend. It's *her*. Rahab. She's the leader here. Don't mess with her." Seymour wipes his hand over his eyes and his forehead, where there's a thin layer of sweat. "She'll wipe you quicker than paper burns. Then you start back at the bottom. It's happened to most of us. But let me tell you, it sucks. That's the place with the monster that smells like death. Rahab took you there, right?"

"Yeah."

"Then you know what I mean. Heck of a way to wake up. The boys tell me I've been there more than anyone. I don't mind too much, since I only remember the last time, but that's still enough. I'll do anything to avoid that monster."

The memory of the creature makes me shudder. "What *is* it?" I ask.

"Maybe a dragon. I don't need to know more."

Seymour moves on to another topic, spewing more information about the tower. He explains that most meals have some form of bacon or pork, because the Red Tower has hundreds of pigs. They also harvest onions and beans and herbs from the surrounding mountainside. Seymour lists herbs like they're his best friends. He gives categories. He describes flavors. I start to zone out, wondering why this tower would make the boys and girls so different. We were treated like equals in Blue.

As we round about the thirtieth turn since leaving my little cave room, we reach a larger hallway. It is made of the same red rock, but here the walls are polished smooth. The hallway is straight, flat, and at least three times as wide and as tall as the other tunnels that weave through the tower. Dozens of blazing torches make the walls look alive.

Seymour leads me into the hallway and we fall into step with a group that has just emerged from a doorway on the opposite side. The boys are wearing reddish brown leather like me. But the four girls with them all wear sequined red dresses that glitter in the torchlight. Two of them wear ruby rings. Their fingernails look painted red.

"Hey Pig," one of the boys says, eyeing Seymour before he glances at me with his hard, narrow eyes. He has a scraggly black beard, deep voice, and the same kind of collar around his neck. He looks very familiar. "Who's your new friend?" he asks.

"He's Cipher," Seymour says. "And he's not just a new friend. He's the boy wonder from the Blue Tower who can control the wind, so you better watch what you say."

The boy laughs as he steps closer to me. "Pigs have spines after all. Cipher, I'm Axe."

He holds out his hand. As we shake I look into his eyes and remember. I force myself to hide my shock. The beard and the clothes masked it at first. But it's Max. The same Max from the Blue Tower, the one who mocked Kiyo, the one I blasted out of his chair and beat in the boat race. After that he showed up in the Red Tower and attacked me, without remembering me. Why did he change his name? He clearly doesn't remember me now. So we get a fresh start. Sort of.

"Nice to meet you," I say.

"I heard about you," he says. "Wind won't help you much here. It's not allowed, and anyway—" he flexes his bicep and smiles—"it can't break iron or stone."

"Take it easy on him," says one of the girls. She walks forward to my other side and slides her arm into mine like she's my escort. Her fingers warm my skin. She smells like cinnamon and cedar.

Seymour falls into step behind us, quiet for once.

"I'm Boleyn," she says, sounding almost as refined as she looks. "We're always glad to have new boys in Red, especially ones who have brought a little intelligence from Blue."

"Wait, there's no intelligence here?"

She laughs. "You're funny. I like that."

I murmur thanks but my attention is stolen by the room ahead.

"The Feasting Hall," Boleyn says, releasing my arm and walking forward into it. She holds out her arms and spins, her dress twirling above the ground. "Dazzling, isn't it?"

It is. The room looks two hundred feet long, with a ceiling a hundred feet high. Flames burn in midair halfway up, suspended by nothing and burning bright red. Three boys bang three huge drums on the opposite side of the room, making a steady bump, bump, bump that makes the hairs on my arms stand up. A long table runs down the center of the room, stretching the entire length and leading to a raised dais on one end. Two thrones are on the dais, one larger than the other. Both thrones look chiseled straight from the red rock of the hall. Behind the thrones there's a view of mountains. The bright blue sky above the peaks makes me think of the sun. Maybe I'll see it here. Maybe I could like Red.

A huge dark shape soars into view over the mountains, then descends behind a ridge. Too big to be a bird. I watch breathlessly for it to appear again, but it doesn't. My gaze settles onto the larger throne, where Rahab sits. The smaller throne to her right is empty. Her auburn hair radiates in the ruby red light from the suspended flames above. Seeing the flying shape, and now her, reminds me again of the creature below. Okay, maybe I won't like Red. Blue was calmer, cooler. There were no monsters there, only a few sharks and sea creatures that we could watch peacefully from the underwater dining room.

"Come on, Cipher." Seymour pulls at my arm. "I'll show you your seat. It's probably beside mine."

He leads me away from Max, Boleyn, and the others. There are open seats halfway down the long table. I remember the latest tally of the towers' numbers that I saw in Blue. Red was in third place. It looks like there are almost a hundred boys and girls in the room. That's well short of the equilibrium that Abram wanted—144 for each of the five towers.

"This is your spot," Seymour says. "See, there's your name."

There's a black rock the size of my fist on the table.

The rock is shaped like a flame and has the word Cipher carved into it. In front of the seat to the left there's another rock with Seymour's name. There are no rocks to the right. The table and the benches to my right are empty. Dozens more could fit.

"So I get the last spot?" I ask.

"For now," Seymour says. "But you can work your way up, no doubt."

"How?"

"Oh lots of ways. There's the Arena, where you can fight. There's journeys out of the tower to get things that we need. There's…well, I don't even know all the ways."

"What's the Arena?" I ask.

"Where we compete for girls. You'll see soon enough."

"Have you fought there?"

Seymour's freckled cheeks flush pink. "I'm not much of a fighter."

"How long have you been here?"

He laughs nervously. "As long as I can remember. Hey, I gotta go serve the food now, okay? Just sit tight. I'll be back."

He lumbers away, leaving me alone.

I look down the length of the table. The boys all sit on one side, and the girls on the other. I scan the faces, hoping to see a girl who looks like a younger version of my Mom. None of them look familiar. Most of the others are talking and laughing loudly. The crowd's noise echoes along with the drumbeat through the hall. Seymour and a few others are serving bowls and spoons to everyone, starting at the top of the table, nearest to the throne.

After a while a girl sits across from me. She's wearing a glimmering red dress like all the others. She waves and says hi. It's hard to hear her across the wide table, and over the noise of the room. She keeps her bright green eyes on me.

When Seymour returns with his bowl and mine, he tells me he's starving after all that work and digs in. Beans with strips of bacon fill the bowl. It's not bad. I'm halfway through the food when the drummers suddenly increase their rhythm and finish with a loud crescendo. For a moment there is silence. The room feels hollow.

"Welcome to the Red Feasting Hall," Rahab announces. She stands in front of her throne, but it sounds like she's standing right beside me. She must have some power to project her voice. "We have two new members since our last Scouring. Cipher and Henrietta, stand."

I stand, and so does the girl across from me. There's a round of tepid applause and we sit again.

"This brings us to 90," Rahab says. "We remain near our lowest numbers. There was a time when we filled *two* tables like this. Now we have grown weak, as Black has grown strong. Even Blue has passed us. We must do better. Girls, you may choose your pair any time. Choose wisely. Only with strong pairs will we win. Boys, your assignments are on the bottoms of your stones. There are two days until the next Scouring. Let passion burn. Thrive like fire."

Rahab sits. The drums thump back into life, and a murmur of voices spreads again through the room. Seymour picks up his flame-shaped stone. He lifts it with two hands above his head, eyeing the bottom of it.

"I'm seventeen," he says, turning to me. "You?"

I pick up my stone. It's as heavy as iron. Underneath there's a number written in chalk white. "Seventeen."

# 4

THE FEASTING HALL bursts into action as the crowd rises from the long table. People move toward the far wall, where a chalkboard is covered in writing.

"Come on, Cipher," Seymour says, tugging at my sleeve. "Let's go see what task seventeen is. It could be anything! I don't remember seeing it. I know all about the others. Fourteen is the best number I've gotten. Guess I got demoted..."

"So the lower, the better?" I ask, following him. "What's fourteen?"

"It's serving food and bringing newcomers like you to the Hall. But I've never had a boy with memories before. How'd I do?"

"Good," I say, though I hardly feel qualified to judge. "What's number one?"

"The Scouring," Seymour says. "Twelve people get that one. It's a high honor. Six boys. Six girls. All of the strongest. We want to win, you know?"

I nod along, but that's not how it was in the Blue Tower, where we were organized by classes and trained as teams. Blue may have been cold, but at least it maintained order.

Seymour tells me about the other assignments he's had since the last time he was wiped. His favorite is pig duty, number sixteen, which he usually gets. There are four pig-duty assignments: feeding, cleaning, butchering, and cooking.

"The best is feeding," Seymour says. "The pigs love it."

As we join the crowd gathering in front of the board, boys are calling out numbers.

*One again!*

*Hey, any fours?*

*Who else is a six?*

*I got nine.*

These announcements lead to constant shuffling as the boys maneuver around to find each other and form groups with their numbers. The girls add to the chaos. They are interspersed everywhere, watching the boys, like they're sizing us up, like we're cattle.

"You," one of the girls says, pointing to a tall boy in front of me. "You're group number four?"

The boy bows before the girl like she's a queen. "Yes. Drums."

"Good. I like drummers." She reaches down and touches the silver link at the back of his neck. The boy rises and takes her hand. He has a spring to his step as the two of them walk away together.

This happens over and over as we press our way through the boys. Whenever a boy gets picked, the next boy just steps into his place.

None of the girls picks me. I shouldn't care. I don't even know what it means. But there's something demoralizing about watching dozens of others get chosen while I keep trudging forward with the other boys. No one wants to get picked last.

I finally get close enough to see the list of assignments on the board. Each one is written in big block letters.

1. SCOURING
2. BEHEMOTH
3. SIGNAL FIRE
4. FEAST DRUMS
5. WEAPONS
6. ARENA GUARD
7. RUNNERS

My eyes scan over the others and see a bunch of boring chores. Cleaning, laundry, dishes, and pig duty. They are not too different than what we had to do in the Blue Tower. But the last task is:

17. DRAGON TEETH

At first it seems like some kind of joke, making me smile. *Dragon teeth?* What, like brushing them? Drawing them? My smile fades as I look over the list again and remember the creature. Number two is "behemoth"—and I remember that's a word for a mythical beast. Is that what Rahab made me see under the tower? It's ridiculous, but the idea of doing anything connected to that monster makes me shake a little in fear. It's like the beast has gained some kind of power over me.

"Oh no. No, no, no," Seymour is saying. "Not fair! I make it all the way to number fourteen, newbie welcome, and now this? I feed the pigs, that's what I do. I don't leave the tower!"

"What do you mean?" I ask.

He looks at me startled, like he'd forgotten I was there. "Oh, Cipher, this is bad news. I'm sorry you had to start with this. It's not fair, not at all. *Now* I remember this assignment. Haven't seen it myself, but you know how rumors get around. People say, occasionally, a group has to leave the tower for the mountains, and to bring back…dragon teeth."

"Seriously?"

A hand clasps my shoulder firmly. It's Max, or apparently Axe as he's known here in Red. A stunning blonde girl in a long red dress stands beside him, with a finger running idly over the silver link at his neck. She wears a large ruby ring. She looks like she belongs at a royal ball. He looks like he belongs in a gladiator's arena.

"Oooh, tough luck, boys," he says. "The last ones who had number seventeen were killed. Eaten, actually."

"I— I don't want to go," Seymour whimpers. "I can't fight a dragon…"

"That's life, or whatever," Axe laughs and gives Seymour a friendly—or maybe not friendly—punch in the shoulder. "Here's your chance to toughen up, Pig." He holds out his stone, flipped over so the number 1 shows. He puts his other arm around the shoulder of the girl, who looks at us like we're children. "Maybe you'll get to pair with a real girl someday and go to the Scouring," he says. "Maybe your new grunt friend will help you bring back a tooth. But hey, in case you get eaten, we'll tell you your names after you're wiped!"

He and the girl walk off toward another group. Seymour's hands cover his face.

"Hey, don't listen to them," I say. Max's name change doesn't seem to have changed anything else about him. He's still making everyone around him feel small. He doesn't remember that last time, in Blue, I was the one who blasted him out of his desk…

"But he's Axe!" Seymour says. "He's the strongest boy here. He could even be the next Alpha!"

"What's that mean?" I ask.

"The Alpha is the first boy. He gets special privileges. He's the only one who doesn't wear a collar. The rest of us boys, you know, stay in the Barracks and serve the girls."

"So who's the Alpha now?"

"We don't have one. The last Alpha got captured by Black, probably after he captured you. The only way we get another Alpha is if a boy captures someone else in the Scouring."

"So…Axe is no different than the rest of us."

"Of course he is! Just look at him. He's strong. He even has a beard! He must have been here for ages without getting wiped. Aaaannnnd, he's paired with *Melissa*. Everyone knows she summons more fire than any of the others. She's…beautiful, perfect, whatever you want to call it. You saw her ring, right? That's the Red Tower's crown jewel, for the strongest girl. And she picked Axe. So yes, he *is* one to talk. And he's right, we're…"

"No. He's wrong," I say, more confident than I feel. I've beaten Max before, so I'll do it again. "We're going to get a dragon's tooth." I glance around and see mostly clusters of boys and girls together, but a few boys still wander alone through the crowd.

"Any seventeens?" I ask, but my voice is swallowed by the room's noise, the drums. I focus and pull on a little of the air and use it to project my voice, like Rahab did. "SEVENTEENS?"

The drums stop. Silence snaps over the room, like the air was sucked out.

I just pulled a little of the wind. Still, every eye is suddenly on me. I must have been…loud.

The group around me begins to part. Rahab walks through them, straight toward me. Heads swing from her to me, and from me to her, as she approaches. Her dress looks like a million tiny rubies glued together. The room is unnervingly quiet. I can hear my own heart thumping.

Rahab stops before me. She has faint lines by her eyes, and the way they press together shows anger—not some young impassioned fury, but like a mother scolding her child. "You're the one who said *seventeens*?"

I look down at my feet. "Yes."

"Look at me, boy." Her finger reaches under my chin and the point of her bright red nail is like a dagger at my neck, lifting my gaze. Her other hand rises to her side, palm up, and a flame suddenly appears above it. The metal band around my neck feels hot, almost searing my skin. "Boys may not use powers in *my* tower," she says. "You understand?"

"I don't understand."

Rahab's eyes narrow. "But you will obey."

In the Blue Tower anyone could use whatever power they have, but this woman could set me on fire, or feed me to the giant creature down below. I have to be able to use my power.

"I'm new here," I say, sounding more defensive than I wanted. "I don't know the rules yet. How am I supposed to bring back a dragon's tooth without my power?"

Her lips curve into a smile. "Boys must be brave. Sometimes the most audacious tasks are given to the weakest. Then you can prove yourself."

It's not hard to catch her meaning. I'm small. I'm weak. And apparently so is Seymour. But I'm not afraid.

I'm angry.

And when I'm angry, my power grows. I begin weaving the air around us, channeling it like streams of water through the red light. The streams merge and grow. All this happens in an instant. I set a wall between Rahab and me. Then I gather a huge gust above us in the air and send it flailing through the room, as hard and as fast as I can. The torches above blow out and darkness falls, except for the flame above Rahab's hand.

Screams fill the Hall.

People start to scramble over each other.

I ignore the sounds. I focus the gusting air to target

Rahab's flame, but it doesn't budge. Instead she steps forward, right through the wall that I've made, and she holds her hand up so that the fire flickers inches from my face. The power is yanked out of my grasp. The band burns at my neck. The flames burst back into light above.

The Hall is bright again. Everyone goes still.

"Enough," Rahab demands, her face aglow. "Did you try to resist Abram?"

I hold her stare but don't answer.

"I didn't think so," she says. "And why not? Because he's a man with a staff, and because I'm a woman in a dress?"

"No, because he's reasonable and—"

"Silence!" she shouts. "You are in the Red Tower now. This is my domain. You think you are special because you bring some power from Blue, but hundreds of other boys have been where you are now. Here you must earn the Pairing before you can be scoured."

"And if I don't?"

She shrugs. "You will be taken to the bottom of the tower. You will be devoured. Your memories will be wiped clean, over and over, as many times as it takes. So…you understand me now?"

I nod, and the meek expression on my face doesn't take any pretending. I couldn't bear losing all the memories and starting over, not after what I went through to get here.

"If you so much as blow a hair off your forehead," she says, "I will know. This is your last warning. Understood?"

I take a deep breath. I have no choice. "Yes."

"Good." The fire disappears from above her hand. She spins off and heads back toward her throne.

Murmurs spread through the crowd. The drumming resumes. People go back into motion, but everyone stays away from me, like I'm a plague. It doesn't take a genius to see that I don't fit in here. How am I going to have a chance without my power? Boys like Axe are so much stronger. The girls get to summon fire and pick their pairs. No one will pick me. I miss the Blue Tower.

A tall, skinny boy approaches me. He has a somber face but hard, bright eyes under a mop of sandy hair. "Hey Cipher," he says, "I'm Marcus."

"You're not avoiding me like the others?" I ask.

Marcus shrugs and glances at Seymour, who has joined my side. Then he holds up his stone. The number 17 is scrawled on the bottom. "Looks like we're together."

# 5

RAHAB ANNOUNCES THAT it's time to go to the Arena. Everyone begins moving toward the front of the Feasting Hall. A line forms before a small open doorway and a stairway leading down. Rahab stands by the door and watches as the crowd enters and disappears from view.

Seymour, Marcus, and I are at the back of the line. Last place. I guess it makes sense. We're the number 17s. Number 6 was assigned to guard the Arena, whatever that means. Seymour keeps talking about how much he would have rather gotten number 16, pig duty. He says the pigs don't judge him or call him names. He says you get used to the smell.

I interrupt his monologue. "You said we fight in the Arena? How does it work?"

"Oh, it's dangerous, very dangerous," Seymour says. "A girl will perform, showing her power, and the boys fight to get to her. I suggest you stay quiet and watch. That's what I always do. No matter how much you like one of the girls, just sit still and you can leave without getting hurt. Because if you go into the Arena…" Seymour eyes me up and

30

down. "Boys like us don't fare well, okay?"

"So no powers?" I ask.

"No way," Seymour answers. "You heard Rahab's warning. The Arena is just one way the girls decide who to pick, you know, for the Pairing. Better to stay solo if you ask me."

"Speak for yourself," Marcus says.

Seymour laughs. "Oh, I do, but I speak for you and Cipher, too. You've seen the other boys. They'd knock us out with a single punch." He pauses, eyes on Marcus. "Hey, I remember you now. You've entered the Arena before, haven't you? Yeah, I definitely remember it. I've seen you fight, and last time you got hit in the head by an axe and…" Seymour's face goes pale as his voice fades.

Marcus scratches his head casually. "Guess so. I don't remember."

I'm glad all over again that I managed the keep the memories that I gained in Blue. "So you were wiped clean?" I ask Marcus.

He shrugs. "Don't remember."

"Oh come on," Seymour says. "Tell us what you do remember. I'm always hoping to compare. Last time I woke up under furs in one of the deep, cave rooms that are warm and close to the creature. Those rooms are kind of nice. Kind of like wombs, I guess. Better to stay inside than come out into this harsh world. I wish they'd let us stay there longer. But Rahab came and got me. I guess it's always like that. Is that how it was for you? You just woke up and now you're here?"

Marcus nods.

Seymour asks more questions, but Marcus doesn't say much. We move closer to the doorway, where Rahab still stands like a sentinel. Her fiery stare silences me. What does she have against me? Just because I'm from Blue? Or because I tried to put out her fire? Okay, that was a bad idea. I definitely don't want to end up like Marcus. I want to remember Kiyo and Emma, and my Mom and my wife and my son from before—at least, the few memories that I have of them. The Red Tower must have something like the Sieve, some way to get our old memories back.

"Seymour," I say, interrupting him again. "How do we get our memories back?"

"From the fire," he answers. "They can come back clear as day, usually when it's dark and you're staring into flames. But sometimes they don't come. I don't know why. I don't…like to think about it much…"

For once Seymour falls completely quiet. He doesn't volunteer more. I want to ask him more, about who he was before, but he keeps his eyes away, like he doesn't want to talk about it.

Rahab eyes the three of us silently as we go through the door beside her. Inside is a stairway going down, like a rough-hewn tube, almost as far as I can see. Flames hover just below the ceiling, giving a faint reddish light that dances along the cave walls.

"Go on," Seymour whispers behind me. "We have to keep up."

I begin the descent, counting the steps to keep my

mind occupied. At number 144 the stairs end and open into an immense, round room. It must be the Arena. It's not as big as the Feasting Hall, but it is somehow more intimidating. Several rows of stone benches rise from a wall that surrounds a large, circular pit filling most of the room. The pit has yellow sand as its floor, and in the center there's a cube of reddish stone—about five feet on each side, and five feet high. There are a few weapons scattered around. An axe lays half-covered in the sand below us.

Seymour tugs my arm and I follow him around the circle to a seat on a stone bench, three rows back from the edge. My guess is it's fifty feet from the center of the pit to the wall surrounding it. I look up at a large flame hovering in midair and burning directly above the cube in the center.

A flash of memory comes to me. I held a green plastic protractor against paper, studying the degrees and angles of a circle. The memory is narrow and tightly bordered, like something seen at the opposite end of a long tunnel. But it is from before, on earth. While I see the protractor and the circle, memories of numbers and formulas flood into my mind. I remember Pi.

If this pit in the Arena has a radius of 50 feet, then the circumference would be 2 times Pi times 50. Pi is 3.14159… So that's a 314-foot circumference. The thought makes me smile. I feel more comfortable. Maybe there's no time in this place, but at least there's Pi. I have to believe, or at least hope, that Pi can't change, even here in the Five Towers.

The sound of cheering brings my mind back to the

Arena. Boys and girls line the edge of the ten-foot stone wall that encloses the pit. There are three rows of benches, but only the first is full and the second is only half full. The room could hold many more of us.

Rahab stands on the opposite side of the Arena from us. Her voice echoes in the vast room: "The performance begins!"

On cue, a girl steps out of a small gateway in the wall just below us. She walks toward the center of the pit, with honey hair flowing over her glittering red dress. She swings up onto the cube of stone and stands in the center. Arms raised, she turns and gazes around at the cheering crowd.

When her eyes pass over mine, my heart almost stops.

# 6

YOU COULD LINE UP a billion sets of eyes. You could choose only the eyes that are brown and olive-shaped. You might get down to four hundred million sets of eyes. It wouldn't matter how many eyes there were, or how similar, because I would go straight to these eyes and know them as the ones that matter. They are the eyes that first looked deeply into mine, that fed me, bathed me, loved me. I would know these eyes in any universe or tower, at any time or age.

They are my mother's eyes.

I learned something once about penguins. On the frozen tundra, where the sun rises only half of the year, a mother penguin would lay a giant egg and let the father penguin scoot it up under his blubber and feathers to stay warm. The egg would incubate in that safe space, with thousands of father penguins huddling close to share warmth and deflect cold, while the mother penguins went out searching for food in an icy ocean. The mothers would be out there for weeks, swimming and diving and catching fish and storing them in their guts. Then they'd return in flocks. Hundreds and thousands of mother penguins, looking like an army of identical waddling tuxedos, would press through the frigid air back to the huddle of fathers with their football-sized eggs ready to hatch.

And here's the thing: the mothers knew, and the babies knew, exactly who belonged to whom. As soon as that little puff of feathers would lay eyes on its mom, all the ice and the ocean and the distance no longer matter. The penguins get by with their supernatural sense of family in their little bird brains.

That hasn't changed in the Five Towers. I'm like one of those baby penguins. Except, instead of crossing the tundra, my mother apparently died like me and came to this place where I instantly recognize her eyes as she stands on a platform in the middle of a pit of sand.

The Arena. The crowd cheers for her. She looks like she's my age. But it doesn't matter. I love her like I did the day I hatched.

"Oh man, you're going to like this." Seymour nudges me in the side. "Last time this girl performed, she drew nineteen boys. Nineteen! Can you believe that? I've heard only one other girl drew that many—Melissa—and she's been in group 1 ever since."

Group 1. That means my Mom's at the top. She goes to the Scouring. Was she ever there when I was there? Have we fought without knowing it?

She raises her arms and the crowd falls silent. Then she starts to sing.

The words are soft at first, the melody gentle, like I'm a

little boy back in a bed with Mom singing a lullaby. But then there's a flash of flame and above her head fire begins to coil like a crown a few feet above her as her voice rises and the tempo quickens.

I feel myself pulled forward. I need to get to her, to tell her that I'm here.

"Whoa!" Seymour says, holding me by the shoulder. "Don't move, man. You'll get smashed by the boys. Just stay in your seat. Quiet. Watch."

The fire above her expands and rises like fireworks in slow motion, pulsing to the rhythm of her song. She spins and dances seamlessly as she sings. My eyes can hardly take in all the bright movement.

She ends on a long, delicate note. There is a moment of quiet, and then the crowd erupts. Everyone stands and cheers. Boys are shouting, pressing against the edge of the wall around the pit.

"Now," Rahab announces. "Let the race begin!"

It's like a floodgate opens. Boys begin sliding over the wall, dropping to the Arena. A few of them rush to pick up weapons.

I can't wait anymore.

I fling off Seymour's arm and in one quick motion I step over the wall, holding tight to the edge as my body drops on the other side. I glimpse Seymour's shocked face, his head shaking, mouthing "no, no, no" as he looks down at me. Marcus is coming over the wall like me.

My hands release. The sandy floor is soft as I land.

I spin toward the center. Other boys are charging

forward. I take off at a sprint.

Two boys in front of me collide and drop to the ground, wrestling. I veer around them and keep my eyes on my Mom. Her back is to me. Flames still dance above her hands. Metal clinks from skirmishes around me.

Twenty feet away from the center I'm hit from the side, hard. I never saw the boy coming. He sends me flying through the air and crashing down. At least he didn't have an axe. He stays on his feet and charges ahead. He must be twice my size. I stagger to my knees, head spinning. There's no way I'm going to catch him, and there's no way I can let him get to my Mom before I do.

I shouldn't do it, but I see no other option. From my knees, I summon the air. Just a little. Wind snaps like a whip around the boy's ankles. He tumbles to the sandy ground.

Marcus sprints past me, wielding a sword.

*Sorry, Marcus*, I think, as I trip him with wind, too.

I move forward, weaving the air into a wall that blows the other boys back. A few get up and charge again, only to be flung back. I feel the power coursing through me. Mom has turned to me, her eyes open wide in shock as she stares at me. She recognizes me. She must. I smile, so close, when a fire bursts into life before me, out of nothing.

The flames burn violent orange and red. But in an instant they fade.

Rahab stands there. Her lips form a severe line. She reaches out and places her palm to my forehead. My power is gone. There's only heat.

*So much heat. Burning.*

But still I look up, past Rahab and through the pain. The last thing I see as I collapse is my Mom's eyes.

**7**

SOMETHING STROKES MY CHEEK, soft and gentle and warm. The strokes are in rhythm with my breathing. They bring me a memory, or a dream—it is hard to tell which—of when I was young, lying in bed with my mother coaxing me awake for the day. It is the kind of memory that has no time or place, because it was repeated so many times at such a young age that it is forged into my being.

This is why, when I open my eyes, I am not surprised to see my mother sitting by my side. She gazes down at me, stroking my cheek, as I lie in a bed. I half expect to see my childhood sheets, but this is not a memory. There are no sheets, only furs. The walls around us have a reddish glow from torch light. This is the Red Tower.

"I can't believe it," she whispers. "You're actually here."

"You remember me?" I ask.

"Of course. You're my little Paul."

The name feels odd, like a shirt that has shrunk and no longer fits. I sit up and rub my eyes. We are in a simple but large room with a low, domed ceiling. A fire burns in the hearth and three round windows line one wall. It's dark outside. A fur rug lays in the center of the smooth stone floor. There's a small table with two wooden chairs by the windows, and two leather chairs face the fire.

"You like it?" she asks. "This is my place."

"It's nice," I say, meeting her calm eyes. She is a young girl, about my age. She looks so innocent, so…un-aged. There's no trace of a wrinkle. All of her hard work, all of her cigarettes, are wiped away. But she remembers me.

She takes my hands into hers. She wears a ruby ring, like the other girls I've seen. "How did you get here?" she asks.

"I woke up in the Blue Tower, without any memories."

"I'm sorry," she says, as her finger traces the scar on my hand. "I've heard Blue is cold. How did you get the memories back?"

"I looked into the Sieve. It's a pedestal of water at the top of the tower, and it shows memories. I saw you there."

"Do you remember…everything?"

"No, only little bits," I say. "But it turned out okay."

"Really?" She eyes me doubtfully.

*Well*…Some of it was okay, like becoming a doctor and getting married and having a son, but other parts were not okay, like me and my pride and dying, however that happened. But we're both here now, and Abram said this place wasn't the worst option.

"Maybe it depends on what happens next," I say. "We found each other, didn't we?"

"Yes. How did you get here?"

"Abram—he's the leader of Blue—he told me that you were in the Red Tower. So I came."

She smiles. "You were always so brave."

I squeeze her hand and lean my head on her shoulder. Her words make me feel better than I have since I woke up in the Blue Tower. It feels so good to be close to her, to a living and breathing part of my past. "I'm glad I found you," I say.

"Me too." She sighs softly before continuing. "When you were seven, you decided you could do a flip on your bike. You didn't practice, you just tried it." She rubs a slight scar on the side of my forehead. "Twenty-three stitches. And now, on your first day in the Red Tower, you charge into the Arena without even knowing what it is. It could have ended a lot worse."

"How did I get here from the Arena?" I ask.

"Rahab was very upset. You disobeyed her. She was going to send you to the bottom, to be wiped clean. I asked her to give you another chance. She said no. Then I begged, on my hands and knees. She eventually relented, but she told me to keep it quiet. She didn't want this to be an example to the others. You were lucky. As the Arena performer, I get to choose which boy wins. I chose you."

"Thank you." I imagine what it would have been like to be that close to my Mom, only to have my memories of her wiped away. I wouldn't even have remembered that she was here, in Red. I would have started from zero again. The few memories that I have feel all the more precious. "I'm sorry about...rushing in like that."

"You're sorry?" She grins, her eyes lighting up. "Now that is a surprise. *Sorry* used to be the hardest word for you to say. I couldn't believe how many tears it took sometimes to draw that one little word out of you. But now you're here, with me. There's no need to be sorry, Paul."

"I go by Cipher here."

Her brow rises. "Why?"

"A cipher is a code—a way to unlock something. The name came to me when I first arrived in Blue. I'm still desperate to understand this place's secrets."

"Maybe that's why you started in Blue," she says. "Most of us in Red are not so curious. We are passionate. Passion doesn't want explanations. It wants action. But please, tell me about your life before. I want to know everything."

"I saw some of our time together. I saw where we lived when I was a boy, after…after my father left." I swallow. It's hard to talk about this, especially with her. "Not many details."

Her body has gone stiff, as if gripped by my words. *What is she thinking? What does she remember?* Maybe her memories could fill my gaps. Or mine could fill hers.

"What's wrong?" I ask.

"I've gazed into the fires many times," she says, looking away, "for as long as I could bear. You were so smart and so brave. You were quiet and focused. Maybe you had to be, since you didn't have a father and I was gone working so much. I wasn't there for you like you needed me. But I tried…I really tried." She takes a deep breath. Her face falls into her hands and her young body shakes again, as if the past haunts her. "I wanted to give you a better life. But…" Her voice breaks as she turns back to me, tears in her eyes. "I could have done better. I've wanted to say that for a long time. I've needed to say it. I'm sorry, Paul. I'm so, so sorry…"

I pull her into my arms as she cries. It's the only thing I can think to do. We look the same age and sit in the same room. Our past will forever tie us together, but this equal ground makes me feel further apart. We're crammed full of our own pains and memories and regrets. Familiar questions that I had in Blue come back to me. Why have we come here in these young bodies? Why do we have to remember the past like this?

"It's okay," I say, holding her tight. "You did your best."

"Sometimes, but not enough," she sighs, "and it hurt you. I know it hurt."

I want to tell her again that it was okay, that I turned out fine. But the words will not form on my lips. I didn't turn out fine. But that was more because of me than her. The right words come to me: "It wasn't all your fault."

A fire comes to her eyes. Her lips press tighter. "No, it wasn't. And the man who takes most of the blame burns for it."

"What do you mean?" I ask.

"Your father. He left us. He never came back. He never said sorry—not to me, not to anyone. I have seen him in my visions, in the flames. He will burn forever. He will always feel the pain that he caused you and me."

I want to share her anger, but I don't. Instead her words make my stomach turn, because from the little I remember, I was just as absent to my son as my father was to me. "Why was he punished like that?"

"It is justice," she says.

"How do you know?"

"Because even though we are broken, we are here together. The fires of the Red Tower burn away the darkness and leave light. The fires where he burns leave nothing but pain. That is what he deserves."

"You must have loved him, once."

"I'm not sure anymore." She gazes into the fire burning in the hearth. "Love is not so simple. It's not just a feeling. It's a commitment. Love uncontained is wildfire. It destroys everything around it. We didn't understand that. We chased the wrong passions. I have learned a lot since then. I have been here a long time."

We are quiet again, sitting close and staring into the fire.

In the flames an image emerges. It is a picture, from my life before. I remember finding it, tucked away in my Mom's closet. The photo fit in my young hand. Its edges were bent. It showed my Mom, younger, and my father. They were happy together, smiling. It was before I was born, before he left. I'd kept that picture, never telling my Mom. I'd tucked it into my wallet as I grew older. It went wherever I went, a reminder of what life would have been like for them if I'd never been born.

Mom's soft voice brings me back into the small room in the Red Tower, out and away from the image in the flames. "My last memory of you was in the summer," she says. "I had saved up just enough for us to have a weekend at the beach. You were reluctant to leave your friends, and your computer, but you came. We had dinner one night on the sand, just the two of us. We built a fire and I brought a large pot and we boiled two whole lobsters and corn on the cob. Do you remember that?"

I swallow, thinking of the picture of her with my father, and now this. I can't stop the tears. Her words bring it all flooding back. I'd been a teenager. I'd told her the trip was a stupid idea, but she'd insisted and we'd eaten the lobster as the sun set and it had been beautiful.

"I remember." That's all I can manage to say. Had she died soon after that? And if so, how? The memories come in isolated bits. I still can't see the whole.

"I must have missed so much after that," she says. "Will you tell me? Did you grow to be a man? Did you marry, have kids?"

My cheeks are wet. I don't want to answer. Shame locks my lips. Shame squeezes me like a vice. She doesn't deserve a son like me, not after how hard she worked to raise me. But she's my Mom. Of all people ever to grace the universe, maybe she alone could still love me despite my mistakes.

"I became a doctor," I say. "I was married. I had a son."

"What's wrong?" she asks. "What happened?"

She sees right through me, just like she did when I was a child.

"I was not a good husband, or a good father," I say, steady as I can. "I worked too much. There was so much stress…and success and pride…there's still so much I don't remember. Sometimes I don't want to remember. I don't want to know how I died."

She blinks away tears. "I know how you feel."

"I'm…I'm sorry, Mom, that I didn't do better."

"No, no," she says. "I'm sorry. I was gone so much."

"You loved me. That's what mattered."

"I tried…" She looks down at her hands, folded over mine, covering the scar that I got in the Blue Tower.

I stand and she stands and I wrap my arms around her and we cry. We hold each other close for a long time. Our past hurts. But now we hurt together.

# 8

MOM AND I talk for hours, maybe an eternity.

I tell her more about the Blue Tower, and what I have learned about my life before. She has many questions. They make me realize how much I still don't know. My memory is like a few pieces of a shattered stained-glass window. Huge shards are missing, like how I met my wife, my own son's name, or the city where we lived. My Mom cannot help with those facts. They came after she died. But she assures me that it is okay, that the memories will come. She says she wants to meet her grandson.

We also talk about her memories. She answers my many questions patiently and gently. She tells me I was the son of Paul Fitzroy Jr. and Rose Gallaway. She was born and raised Chicago, the youngest of a family of seven. She played the french horn and studied psychology. She met my father at a rock concert in college. He played lead guitar in a local band. He had freckles and long sandy blonde hair. They married when she was twenty; he twenty-four. It didn't last a year, but that was long enough to bring me into the world.

My birthday was July 12, 1978.

My father left Mom and me without a dollar or a goodbye. Mom's family never forgave her for marrying a guitarist instead of a respectable man. They thought she deserved it when he left her, because they'd warned her it would happen. She endured a decade of burnt pink hands from doing dishes and waiting tables to keep a roof over our heads and microwave meals on my plate.

"While I worked," she says, "you drew inward."

She tells me about the days and weeks and months I spent immersed in books and computer games, and my deeper self knows that this is how I hid the pain of growing up without a father. I traversed other worlds and shoved my own feelings way down. I made myself hard as iron. After Mom died, the last hope of any softening was gone. I was a hammer, and the world was an anvil. Anything caught between us had to be beaten into the shape that I desired.

At some point I lay down on the bed, exhausted from these thoughts. Mom pulls the furs over me. The fire in the hearth burns with the same warm orange glow without any wood being added. Mom tells me that she keeps it going. She says it's not so hard with a fire this small, especially since she's been in Red for so long. It sounds like her power over the fire is a lot like my power over the air. The more fire she tries to hold, the harder it is to maintain and control.

I ask her about why only the girls get to use powers here in Red. She tells me it's just how it is, that she doesn't make the rules. She lectures me, like only a mother can, about how I should obey. "I'm not sure I'll be able to save you again," she says. "Rahab is fair, but she's easy to ignite…"

I learn that the tasks are like the different levels in the Blue Tower. The longer someone is in Red, the more they can move up. But if someone disobeys or dies, they go back to the bottom tasks, like some form of pig duty or, on occasions, bringing back a dragon's tooth. She doesn't know much about this task. It's very rare. But whenever teeth are brought back, they are taken to the top of the tower and placed around the fire that always burns there. She's heard that the more teeth the tower has, the more power the girls can control.

"Can I use my power outside the tower?" I ask.

"Maybe." She tells me that the rule, as she's always heard it, is that no boys can use their powers *in* the Red Tower. That's enough of an opening for me.

When the windows let in the first light of day, I rise and stand tiptoe to see out. The sky looks lavender. The Scouring is far below. The flat grey battleground, with the white circle in the center, makes me queasy. Across the open space a dense wall of clouds obscures the view, except for the tip of a structure jutting out at my eye level. It's the top of the Blue Tower. And to the left is another one: the tip of Black. They look similar aside from subtle differences in shape and hue. The clouds billow higher and higher until they completely block any sight of these two towers. But the other two towers are still visible to my right. There are no clouds around the giant tree that is the Green Tower. The Yellow Tower sparkles like a golden castle in the morning light. I watch it, mesmerized, when an even more stunning thing happens: the sun peeks over the horizon, directly beyond the Yellow Tower. It never appeared when I was in the Blue Tower. I saw it only when I went to Yellow's walls with Emma, and later to Green. Now the sunlight shines on my face through the window, and the warmth of it almost makes me cry.

"The sun," I whisper.

"Keep watching," my Mom says beside me. "Here."

She has slid a chair for me to stand on. I quickly step up on the chair and look out again. Far to the right of the rising sun, almost directly behind the Green Tower, another source of radiance emerges. It's another sun. This one is larger, redder, and breathtaking. But before there was only one sun. Suddenly, another shining orb rises between the other two. The three of them rise slowly in tandem, casting their brilliant light over the Scouring and the Yellow and Green Towers. Black and Blue remain hidden behind clouds, receiving none of the warmth. The sky above shifts from lavender to orange to blue. The three suns are too bright to keep staring.

I step down from the chair. My Mom sees my confusion and answers before I ask: "It's been a long time since I've seen all three suns," she says. "It happens rarely. Usually there's only one."

"What does it mean?"

"I'm not sure. It's how things work wherever we are in

the universe."

I shake my head, trying to understand. "So we're on a planet?"

"Seems like it. Orbiting a sun, or three suns."

The explanation makes as much sense as any other. But how can a planet orbit three suns at the same time? Or do the suns orbit the planet? My mind recoils from the questions, like a child dipping a finger into a tub of freezing cold water and then yanking his hand away. Better to just enjoy the sunlight streaming through the windows.

Mom retrieves a few slices of salted bacon from an alcove in the room and cooks them on a pan above the fire. It smells delicious.

"If you succeed with the tooth," she says, over the sound of crackling in the pan, "we should be able to pair."

*The Pairing.* Rahab and Seymour talked about this. "Why wait?" I ask. "Can't we pair now?"

"I am in the Scouring group," she says, "so I must pair with a boy who can enter the Scouring as well. You will be gone, hunting a dragon tooth. But if you bring one back, you will be able to rise in the ranks. We can pair then."

"How does it work?" I ask.

"No one knows for sure." She touches the silver collar at my neck. "These links hold the power. A girl chooses a boy, and they pair through the link. The girl can control the boy through it, but also feel whatever he feels. Together they can access new memories. The Pairing unlocks more of the past. The boy and girl also combine their powers. It's the only way a boy with powers is allowed to use them."

*The only way?* The rule doesn't make sense, though it fascinates me that Pairing reveals more about our pasts. "Wouldn't the Red Tower be stronger if boys could use our powers any time?"

"Maybe not," she says. "Two are stronger than one. Our performances in the Arena help determine our rankings. The girls who are strongest can pick the best pairs. They can fight together. And Rahab usually gives the six strongest pairs the highest ranking and task: the Scouring."

"Sounds fair, I guess." The Blue Tower had its own sorting methods. It used the links for servants.

Mom finishes cooking the first batch of bacon. It tastes as good as it smells. We eat peacefully as the light grows brighter outside, until a sudden bellow of horns interrupts us. The deep sound makes the walls tremble.

"Time to go," Mom says. "The horns announce the start of the day's tasks."

We leave together and she leads through passages and stairways to the main hall. To the right is the Feasting Hall, where we were the night before. To the left is a doorway leading outside. She tells me that's the way and embraces me.

"I love you, Paul," she says. "And I always will."

I manage to hold it together, eyes barely dry, as I head toward the doorway, where Seymour, Marcus, and Rahab stand waiting.

# 9

"HERE COMES THE LUCKY BOY," Rahab says as I approach. She has a hand on her hip, wearing the same red dress.

Seymour and Marcus, like me, are in drab brown leather. Seymour says hello but is unusually quiet. He and Marcus stare at me in wonder. I survived the Arena. My Mom saved me. Of course, they don't know she's my Mom. They also don't know the turmoil inside me, after so many new memories. Maybe Rahab doesn't know, either.

I stop in front of her. "I heard what you did."

"Thank the one who chose you." Rahab looks past me to the hallway where my Mom dropped me off and said goodbye. "Most boys don't get picked on their first try, especially not by Rose. She's one of the tower's top girls."

"How long has she been here?" I ask.

"There is no time here." Rahab shakes her head. "Didn't you learn anything in Blue?"

"There are days and nights."

"Countless," Rahab sighs. "Rose has been here long enough to have paired with many more talented boys than you. But, who knows, maybe you will surprise me. Your entry into the Arena showed more passion than I expected. Maybe you will control that passion and bring back a dragon's tooth."

*Challenge accepted.* My Mom said if I get the tooth, we could pair. Then we could fight in the Scouring together. It seems like that's the only way to get into the White Tower and out of this place. "I'll do whatever it takes," I say.

Rahab steps close to me, looking straight into my eyes and emanating heat. "You have come to me *cold*. You are frozen by your past. You have power, but you have no idea *why* you should use it." She holds out her pale, sleeveless arms out, motioning to the tower around us. "What's the point of these towers? Have you figured it out?"

These were the questions I was never supposed to ask in the Blue Tower. "To be scoured," I say.

"Oh, if only it were so simple. The Scouring will scrub you of your flaws, yes. But then what? Are we to become clear vases, holding nothing but air? What a shame! The Blue Tower leaves you hollow. But don't worry, we can fill you up here. You will learn that we are made to be full of life, of passion." She puts her hands back on her hips. "What would Abram do without me?"

*Abram.* He wanted me to learn about my pride, to have it scoured. But he never talked about passion. So, do we get scrubbed and then filled, moving from tower to tower? Or is it different for each of us?

I glance at Seymour and Marcus. Not even Seymour has said a word. He gives me a confused shrug.

"I needed Abram," I say softly to Rahab.

"Most do," she replies. "You need me, too."

"What do you mean?"

"You will see," Rahab smiles. "Bring me a tooth from a dragon, and you will see."

She claps her hands and summons fire overhead. The flames spin into a large, vertical circle in midair, like a gateway between us and the open doorway.

"Go forward and seek passion," she says formally, as if this is a rite of passage. "The wind blows wherever it pleases. You hear its sound, but you cannot tell where it comes from or where it is going. So it will be with you, in time."

*The wind?* The words don't make sense. The fire doesn't make sense.

But Rahab motions for us to leave. She doesn't look like she's taking any more questions.

Marcus goes first, and Seymour and I follow. We step through the circle of fire and the doorway. Ahead there's a bridge that arches high above a chasm. We are only a few paces past the door when there's a loud grating sound. A solid iron gate lowers steadily behind us, closing the doorway, as Rahab turns away.

The three of us stand at the edge of the bridge, with nowhere to go but across. It is long and thin, made of the same red stone as the tower. Beyond the bridge there are ranges of rust-colored mountains with snowy peaks, stretching as far as I can see. A valley with a river cuts through the middle of the mountains. Far to the left the mountains meet the vast forest of the Green Tower's land. To the right the mountains rise to a steep and rocky ridge, with pockets of snow clinging to the cliffs. I do not see any dragons.

"Let's go." Marcus leads the way onto the bridge. He walks steadily, even though the bridge is two feet wide and impossibly high. The jagged ravine is hundreds of feet below us.

Seymour goes next. His body is wider than the bridge. He holds his arms out on either side, balancing like a tightrope walker. He starts talking as if oblivious to the height. He says something about a type of berry that grows in the mountains, and the kind of bush we should look for. He says the berry goes well in tarts. I tune him out and focus on my feet.

I've taken two steps onto the bridge when I go to my knees. The height makes my head spin. With my hands gripping the edges of the narrow stone platform, I glance back at the closed iron door. There's nowhere to go but forward. I start to inch my way across, crawling, clutching at the smooth stone, and trying not to look down.

The Blue Tower had nothing like this. Water is dangerous, but even stormy seas are gentler than these mountains. One slip and I'm dead. Even if it's only temporary, it's got to hurt. And then my memories would be wiped. I would lose my Mom all over again. I'm more afraid of falling than drowning.

"Come on!" Marcus shouts.

He and Seymour wait at the end of the bridge. I'm over

halfway there.

"Stand up!" Seymour says. "It's better to walk."

I keep crawling, eyes fixed on the red stone under my hands. The going is slow, but safe.

"What, are you scared of heights?" Seymour asks.

*Yes, apparently...* But I don't respond, or speed up. I remember the first time I walked up the path inside the Blue Tower, following Abram and hugging the outer wall. The view down the tower's hollow center scared me then. This bridge is worse.

When I finally reach the other side, Marcus and Seymour laugh a little as they clap me on the back. At least they waited.

"I hope you like dragons more than heights," Marcus says.

We begin descending down a narrow path along the side of the rocky slope. Seymour is back to his talkative self. He tells us that he's seen a dragon fly over the distant ridge, so that's where we're headed. My focus is on the landscape, and keeping my footing. A valley opens below into a broad, bowl shape. There is a twisting river at the bottom. It must have carved this valley over ages. I wonder again about how old this place is, where it is, and what it is. It could be another dimension or on some other planet in the far reaches of the universe. With three suns. There are familiar things from earth—mountains and sea, towers and people—but everything here seems more surreal.

I interrupt one of Seymour's monologues about varieties of bacon. "Hey, do you guys think we're in a different universe than earth?"

"Oh yeah," Seymour says. "I've been thinking about it ever since we got this task. I was scared at first, but I'm over it now. If we all died on earth, then this is some kind of afterlife. It's not that bad, really. We get to discover our old memories and have these nice young bodies that can't be destroyed. It's some crazy magic. Burn me up, toss me off a cliff, whatever—I'll just wake up in cozy furs in the Red Tower and start again. I mean, I guess I feel trapped sometimes but there are worse places to get trapped. I was telling you guys about all the kinds of bacon I can make. And here I can eat as much as I want!"

Seymour doesn't stop talking. Marcus and I are quiet as we walk. We trek further toward the edge of the river. The three suns beat down from directly overhead.

It feels like we've been going for hours when we reach the river. Steep cliffs rise from either side of it, at least twenty feet high. A few trees cling to the rock walls. The water below rushes over and around boulders, churning into frothy rapids. We won't be able to wade across it. There's no bridge in sight.

We decide to head upstream, believing the river will be narrower that way. The path becomes more difficult, with huge boulders to scramble over and around. We pass a forty-foot waterfall and have to climb almost straight up to keep going. My hands and knees collect scratches and scrapes from the rocks. Seymour huffs and puffs behind me, no longer talking.

"Look," Marcus says, pointing ahead. It's his first word

in hours.

There's a fallen tree. The roots are wedged under a large stone, and the bare branches grab the opposite edge of the ravine like a person's hand holding on for dear life.

"A cypress!" Seymour says, rushing ahead of us.

"A bridge," Marcus mutters as if annoyed.

We follow after Seymour and see him kneeling down by the roots. He gathers up little berries from a bush growing by the tree's uprooted base, putting them in a small leather pouch.

"Those the berries you wanted?" I ask.

"One of the varieties, yes," Seymour says. "These are no good in a tart, but if you drink the juice, it gives you energy."

"How'd you learn so much about berries?"

He glances up at me, and for once he hesitates before he answers. "From before."

"Before the Red Tower?"

"Yes, I was a chef." Seymour doesn't say more. He steps up onto the tree that stretches over the river.

Marcus stops him with a hand on his shoulder.

"What?" Seymour asks.

Marcus pulls Seymour back with surprising strength, then he moves to the tree and dangles his long legs around it. "Watch me. Like this."

Marcus starts scooting across, his front hands fixed fast on the slick wood, his legs wrapped tight around it. The fallen tree is so narrow, and his legs are so long, that his feet almost touch underneath the trunk. He does not hurry, but he does not pause. His lean frame steadily slides across.

"He's just showing off," Seymour says to me.

"You want to go next?" I ask.

"Sure. But after this, let's get some rest. I'm ready for a campfire and dinner." Seymour clambers onto the tree and begins sliding across. His round body's grip does not seem nearly so tight, even as he tries to follow Marcus's form. A couple times he wobbles, but manages to keep his balance. At least his center of gravity is low.

"Hug it closer," I shout out to him. "Lean down more."

He does as I say, inching forward. The river rushes along twenty feet beneath him. He's about two-thirds the way across when we hear a distant but terrible roar.

Above, silhouetted against the slate gray sky, is an honest-to-god dragon. It is pitch black with a long, sinuous body and vast wings shaped like a bat's, but flapping slowly and smoothly like an eagle's.

It roars again, louder, as it swoops toward us. It passes over my head so close that I can feel the air as it flaps its wings and soars past. I don't have time to duck, or to think, before it is flying away, toward the mountains rising from the opposite side of the river.

A loud shout pulls my gaze down. It's Seymour.

His large body hangs, one hand gripping a branch, the other swinging wildly to try to take hold of something. I start to dash forward, but it's too late. His grip gives and he falls. He drops like a rock and splashes into the water below.

His head bobs up. He shouts again, arms flailing. White rapids churn around him, carrying him quickly downstream.

Before I can even think of what to do, Marcus jumps off the opposite cliff and into the water after Seymour. I sprint along the bank, remembering what's ahead: a waterfall that no one could survive.

I race past Marcus and Seymour and grab a long branch from the ground. A quick scramble brings me down to the river's edge, just before the waterfall. I reach out, extending the stick over the water.

"Seymour! Marcus!" I shout. "Grab it! Grab it!"

Seymour is still ahead of Marcus. He reaches out of the water as he drifts toward me. His hand connects with the wood, clinging fast.

"Hold on!" I say, as I start pulling him in.

Then I hear a crack, followed by the split of wood. The stick couldn't hold him. The water rushes him ahead, broken stick still in his hand. Marcus is swimming closer now, but Seymour is out of time. I charge to the cliff and watch in terror as Seymour floats toward the edge. This is his last chance. A few last rocks to cling to.

He grabs at a rock but the current is too fast. He slips past it. He goes over the edge of the waterfall.

I know what I have to do. The rules have to be broken. In an instant I've grabbed the air. I frantically channel as much as I can hold, weaving an invisible net and swooping it up from the bottom of the falls. Seymour slams into it, and I fall to my knees. The net and my power hold, barely.

A shout pulls my eyes to the top of the falls. Marcus is clinging to a stone that juts out of the racing river, the lower half of his body already over the waterfall's edge.

"Let go!" I shout. "I'll catch you."

He looks at me like I'm crazy, but his grip slips anyway. He hits the net of air beside Seymour, and it feels like a punch to the head. It takes so much power, and there's no Emma or anyone else to draw on for help. Still, I stagger to my feet, holding my hands out as if willing the air to rise as I do. Slowly, inch by inch, I lift them. With a final breath I raise the net and drop Seymour and Marcus safely on the opposite side of the ravine.

Their distant faces show relief, and shock. It's the last thing I see before I collapse, eyes closed, onto the hard ground.

# 10

THE SOFT CRACKLE of fire wakes me. The air smells delicious, like roasted meat. I lie with my eyes open, looking up into the starry sky. My head throbs with each pulse. The stars go brighter, then dimmer, then brighter again. I rise slowly onto my elbows and look across the fire. Seymour and Marcus are watching me.

"Hey, look who it is," Seymour says. "Welcome back! You've been out a long time. You must be hungry. We've got roasted rabbit almost ready. Marcus caught it. I cooked it. Smells good, right?"

"Yeah. Thanks."

Seymour smiles as he moves toward the roasting meat. I see Marcus studying me across the flames. He looks concerned.

"What happened?" I ask.

"Oh, nothing special," Seymour says as he turns over the meat. "I slipped off the tree when that dragon flew over us. I was rushing down the river, went over a waterfall, and pretty much was going to die, but then something invisible caught me. It caught Marcus, too. Next thing we know we're sitting safe on the bank of the river, and you pass out. Marcus had to go back over the tree, put you on his shoulders, and haul you here. By then I had this merry fire going, and Marcus went off hunting. He won't tell me how he caught the rabbit, but it doesn't matter to me. After today we deserve a little feast. It beats the salty pork strips they gave us, right?"

"It does," I say, my eyes on Marcus. "Thanks for coming back for me."

Marcus stares at me, quiet for a moment. "Did you use your power?"

I see no reason to hide it. "Yes."

"How?" Seymour asks. "Can you teach us?"

"I don't think so," I say. "It came to me in the Blue Tower. Others there get the power, too, but I can control more of it. Or I could. The power seems weaker here, in Red. Or maybe I'm just rusty since Rahab won't let me use it. Watching you go over that waterfall got my blood pumping enough to do it again. I made a net to catch you."

"Told you!" Seymour glances to Marcus. "He's a freakin' magician."

Marcus ignores Seymour. He says to me, "Thank you."

"Yeah, good thing you kept us alive so that we can go get eaten by a dragon." Seymour lifts the roasted rabbit from the fire, holding it out proudly. "But as long as we're alive, let's eat, drink, and be merry. You ever hear that one? I think it was in a book or a song or something. I always liked it, though. Especially the eating part…"

Seymour keeps talking as he cuts the meat. He talks as

he serves it. Marcus and I do not talk much. We enjoy the rabbit. I lick my fingers and there's not a scrap left once we finish.

We each find a place to lay down near the fire. There are no pillows or blankets or furs. The night is dark and cold. Seymour eventually falls quiet and sleeps. Marcus does the same.

But not me.

I stare into the fire, watching the yellow and orange flames dance above the bed of coals. I think about Rahab summoning fire and controlling it above her hands, and about the fires hovering magically throughout the Red Tower. I hold out my hand. I focus on the fire. I summon the air and try to fuse the flames into it. It doesn't work. I use the air to make the fire blow this way and that. I try to lift a flame out of the coals, as if I could float it over my hand, but as soon as the flame separates from the larger fire, it goes out.

So, I cannot control fire. The girls can. What will happen if we combine our powers? If I can make it back to the tower, my Mom and I can find out.

The longer I gaze into the fire, the more I feel the weight of the darkness around me. The coals burn bright red. The color and the warmth draw me in, as if my mind can touch the blazing embers. A memory comes.

Water glides past. Wind blows. A thick oar is in my hands. My whole body aches. A boy sits in the front of the boat, shouting *Pull! Pull!*

My knees bend, my arms pull. Another boy sits in front

of me doing the same motion. Others row behind me.

For a moment I think I'm in the Blue Tower again, in another race. But in the distance, the water stretches to a city. Only a few lights show in the skyscrapers. Stars are visible in the dark, morning sky. The city skyline is familiar, like home. I know its name: Chicago. And this is Lake Michigan.

*Pull! Pull!*

The shouting continues. My body obeys but there's no heart in it. The other boats are ahead of us. Too far ahead to catch.

Our boat bumps to the dock in last place. Other boys are already standing on the dock. They're wearing matching uniforms, clinging to their bodies like gloves. A few of them have shirts off, muscles bulging from the workout, sweat dripping. They're laughing and looking past me, across the water. I turn and see the object of their attention—the girls' team, on the opposite dock.

I scramble out of the boat and join the other boys. Maybe they're hot from the rowing, but I slide on a jacket. The jacket makes me look bigger, I think. It's not the team's uniform. I don't have one of those. I didn't make the team last year.

The boys move toward the boathouse. Across the water, I see the girls going the same way. They're going to meet us. They're going to talk to us. Already my palms are sweating. My mouth feels full of cotton balls. I'd rather dive into the cold water than have to talk to them.

Except. Except I see her as we approach the

boathouse.

*Samantha Jones.*

She's near the front of the girls, walking like she owns the world. Her face has bottled up the sun. She laughs with her friends and it makes my teenage body quake.

Everyone moves toward a board where papers have been posted. As the crowd gathers, Samantha scans our group of boys. She's smiling. I swear she noticed me as her eyes passed. Maybe today I'll talk to her. I'll just say "Hi" and she'll say it back and then all will be right in the world.

*Stay cool, Paul.* I take a deep breath.

Everyone's crowding around the board. I'm probably supposed to look at the board, to care what it says. All I care about is Samantha. In this churning group of sweat and hormones and rowing uniforms, no one will notice if I inch closer to her. Maybe I can bump against her side. My hand might even accidentally graze her leg. *Hi*, I practice under my breath. *I'm Paul.*

She's at the front now. Only a few people are between us. They're girls, too, but they might as well be trees blocking my view. I squeeze between them. It's not hard. I'm smaller than everyone.

Samantha is almost within reach when a boy steps to her side. One of the bare-chested boys. He's a head taller than I am—a long, floppy haired blond head. He puts his arm over her shoulder. They're both looking at the board. I'm looking at his arm, a vile hook. I'm close enough to see the dark hairs in his armpit, to smell him. It's a king-of-the-jungle smell. Damp, earthy, powerful.

"Congrats Sam," he says. "Welcome to first team!"

She turns and looks up at him and the lines of her jaw and chin make Aphrodite scream bloody murder from Mt. Olympus. No mortal should have such a face, such eyes. Those large dark pools look at the boy and smile. It might have been a minute since I last breathed.

"Thanks, Johnny," she says. "I heard you're captain this year?"

"Yeah, we're gonna have a great season together." He unclenches his vile hook from around her shoulders. He turns and bumps into me as he passes. "Watch out little man," he grunts.

Another bare-chested boy gives him a high five as he joins their group. Samantha steps into a huddle of other girls. They're giggling and whispering about something. The only word I hear from their huddle is *Johnny*.

There's no longer anything separating me from the board. There's no excuse not to look at it. I shuffle forward with the other stragglers. The board has six pieces of paper. The top three say *Boys First Team, Boys Second, Boys Third*. Each page of paper is yellow and wrinkled, with names scrawled on it. I don't bother looking at the first or second team pages. My breath freezes while I scan the names on the *Boys Third* page. Steve Williams. Patrick Johnson. Name, name, name. I reach the bottom. Paul Fitzroy is not listed.

*Maybe Second Team?* It's a stretch, but I can't resist the flicker of hope. I scan more names. No.

*First Team?* Scan again. No, of course not.

I try to stand up tall and cling to any remaining dignity

when I turn away. It's a ten second walk to get around the boathouse and then I'll be free from these rowers. I tried last year. I tried again. This is the end of it. Who cares? I never thought I'd be a rower. Never really wanted to be.

I'm five steps away, composure in check, when Samantha sees me. Our eyes actually meet. We're only a few feet away. I'm suddenly as hot as Mercury before the sun. Then she smiles and it's like a solar flare melting every element of my being.

"Hey Paul," she says. "How'd you do?"

*She knows my name! She wants to know how I did!*

But I didn't make the team. I can't bear to say it. Composure disappears. The dam bursts. Tears blind my eyes and leave me only one viable option: flee, escape. I run from Samantha, the boathouse, and the rowers as far and as fast as I can.

# 11

"GET UP," Marcus says, shaking me. "Time to go."

The campfire has burned down to ashes. The sky is ash gray. Everything feels burnt up, except the memory from last night. It is planted in my mind like a tumor, making me feel as weak as I did on the dock by Lake Michigan. The boys were stronger. The girls were out of reach. Just like in the Red Tower.

Seymour holds out a handful of berries. "Here, I found them by the river. They'll give you some energy. Marcus searched for more rabbits but didn't see anything. We have enough salted pork to get us through another day or two, but then we'll need to get back to the tower. Marcus says we should make it to the ridge up there and back before it's dark again. He says we should leave now."

I nod, yawning, and reach for the berries.

Seymour laughs. "Boy, you look out of it. Not enough sleep? Remember, we've got to find a dragon's tooth. They don't just fall from the sky."

"Right. I'm fine." There's not much choice. We can't go back to the tower empty-handed, and we can't stay out here long with so little food.

I lift my pack and we start the trek up the slope to where we saw the dragon fly. Marcus filled our canteens from the river, so my pack is heavy. Seymour was right, the berries give me some energy, but I still feel burdened by the vision in the fire.

Marcus leads at first, but he is too fast for Seymour. The only way to stay together is to let Seymour take the lead. He chats happily as we hike, while Marcus is quiet behind me. At some point Seymour gets to a topic that actually grabs my interest.

"...like that dragon, yesterday," he says. "I figure it must be the same kind of dragon as Behemoth. Maybe it even *is* Behemoth. You know, the giant creature below the tower. And it—"

"How would it get out?" I ask.

"Who knows, man? Maybe there's a cave or tunnel or something. I still have no clue why there's a dragon here in the first place. I mean, you guys have memories of earth, right? Dragons were in fairytales. There were no real dragons. Komodo dragons, sure. But flying, fire-breathing creatures? Nope, don't exist. So whoever makes this place with five towers decides to create a dragon. Why? And what are the odds it would actually eat us? I mean, Behemoth talks, so maybe we can just strike up a conversation. I figure..."

"Seymour," I interrupt. "You think somebody *made* this place?"

He looks back at me, a wide smile on his face, probably

glad one of us finally responded to him. "Sure, why not? If God made Earth, then he must have made this place, too."

"Ever heard of the Big Bang?" I ask.

"Um, nope." Seymour laughs.

"Okay…" I glance back at Marcus. His blank stare says he's never heard of the Big Bang either. Maybe it's time to bring up the past—the pleasant parts, at least—in case one of us doesn't make it back and the others can help with remembering. "I studied science," I say. "I was a doctor in the 21$^{st}$ century. I did brain surgery. What about you guys?"

"Whoa, the 21$^{st}$ century?" Seymour keeps his eyes on the path ahead as he talks, his breathing heavy. "In my time people kind of doubted the world would make it that long. I lived in Germany. My last memory so far was in 1939. It wasn't good. But like I said, I was a chef. And a great one!"

"You were German?" I find this hard to believe. My few memories of Germany involve cars made with quiet precision, which is basically the opposite of Seymour.

"No, Austrian," he says, "but after school I moved to Germany. Better market for a chef. And, truth be told, I followed a young woman named Frau Manziarly. Boy, could she cook. I was smitten. Never caught her as far as I know. But along the way I learned to make the best weinerschnitzel. Oh, what I wouldn't give for a kitchen and the right ingredients!"

For some reason I can't remember much about Germany's history. Maybe it is one of those areas of memory still behind the clouds, waiting to be revealed. Some things seem better kept in the dark—like Samantha

Jones and not making the rowing team, like whatever cut off Seymour's memories in 1939. I ask him, "Why did people in your time doubt the world would make it?"

"There was a big war," he says. "I was only thirty years old. I cooked for a German leader in Berlin and he…well, I'm not sure I want to talk about it, okay?"

"I understand," I say, too embarrased to say a word about what I saw in the flames. I look back to Marcus, who has been so quiet that I almost forgot he was there. "How about you?" I ask. "When did you live?"

He eyes me steadily. "Second century, Rome."

"Rome! Wow!" Seymour says up ahead, between breaths. "That must have been amazing. What did you do? Ever see the Roman Colosseum?"

"I fought there," Marcus says bluntly.

"Really?" Seymour asks. "What was it like? Did you have to fight lions or bears? Did you…survive?"

Marcus doesn't answer. I glance back. His gaze is distant, off to the side.

"You okay?" I ask.

He looks at me and nods half-heartedly. "I'm fine. I don't want to talk about it."

We fall silent after that.

The mountainside grows steeper as we continue our climb. When we stop for a rest and a drink of water, the Red Tower looks like a jagged peak in the distance, across the valley. I wipe sweat from my forehead and see reddish dust on my hand. We must be covered in it.

"Want to camp here?" Seymour asks, as he takes a bite

of bacon. "I'm beat."

"No." Marcus shakes his head. "We have to keep going."

"Why? What's the rush?"

Marcus eyes Seymour reaching for another bite. "Not enough food."

"Or water," I add. I point to the tower across the valley. "It will take us a long time to get back."

"If we ever do…" Marcus says.

"Come on, guys!" Seymour smiles. "Lighten up. We've known all along we're probably just going to be eaten, right?" He drops another piece of salted pork into his mouth and rubs his large stomach. "Might as well enjoy our last moments. Maybe fatten up a little for the dragon. Speaking for myself, I'll make a fine treat. And then I'll pop back into the tower and start over. So what's there to worry about?"

"I'm not going to lose my memories," I say.

"Me neither." Marcus stands and stretches, then slides his sinewy arms through the straps of his bag. "Let's get moving."

"Hey, wait." Seymour rushes to gather his things, but Marcus has already started climbing up the mountainside again. "Fine, fine, I'm coming."

I wait and take the rear guard as Seymour hurries to catch up with Marcus. The climb grows more and more difficult, with no trace of a path left. We resort to scrambling over and around and between giant reddish boulders. A few times I have to slow down to help

Seymour, as he can't fit through the narrow crevices where Marcus leads. Marcus doesn't say a word. He ventures ahead but usually stays within sight.

I'm helping to lift Seymour up and over a large rock when Marcus rushes back to us.

"Quick, follow me," he says. "I found a lair."

# 12

MARCUS LEADS SEYMOUR and me up to the ridgeline. We crouch behind a boulder and peek around at the dark opening of a cave. It is a hundred feet away, at the peak of the ridge's steep slope.

"I saw the dragon fly out of there," Marcus whispers, his gaze still fixed on the cave. "The lair should be empty now."

"*Should* be?" Seymour asks. "What if there are babies in there? Or eggs?" His scared voice is so close that I can feel his breath on my ear. It smells like bacon.

"We will move fast," Marcus answers.

"Not me," Seymour says. "You know how parents protect their babies. Didn't you ever learn about mama bears and their cubs? Don't ever mess with bear cubs. Well, what if dragons are like that? We might get inside, find a tooth, and then the dragon will come and breathe fire into the cave and we'll get roasted and—"

"Shhh." Marcus turns back with a finger over his lips.

"What?" Seymour asks. "Did you hear something?"

"No, but I've heard enough from you." Marcus looks

to me. "Any chance you could use your power? Maybe grab a tooth and make it drift over to us?"

"If there was a tooth sitting out in the open," I say doubtfully, "but I'd have to see it to move it."

"So sneak a little closer," Seymour says. "Marcus is right. You're the one who has the best chance. We don't have any powers. Other than finding berries and cooking and…"

Marcus clasps Seymour's shoulder, firmly. "I said that's enough from you. Stay quiet." He turns to me again. "It wouldn't be fair to make you risk it by yourself. Any ideas?"

I look along the ridge to the lair's opening. It is set into the cliff at an angle that wouldn't allow anyone inside to see anything coming. It could be very deep. "One of us will need to be a lookout," I say, "so if the dragon is coming, there can be a warning. The other two should go to the lair, but maybe one stays at the mouth of the cave, and the third goes in. That way we can communicate."

"I like it," Marcus says.

"But what if *another* dragon is in there? Or there are hatched babies? They're called hatchlings, right?"

"I said that's enough," Marcus demands. He turns to me and a slight grin tugs at the edges of his lips. "Let's give Piggy the lead job."

I laugh, but shake my head again. "We can draw straws. It's the only fair way. Besides, if a dragon comes, we're probably all getting eaten."

Marcus doesn't hesitate. He leans down to the ground

and plucks up a handful of dead-looking grass. He plucks out three pieces and breaks them into different sizes. Then he holds them up and mixes them around in his hand, so Seymour and I can both see.

"Shortest straw takes the lead," he says. "Middle straw in the middle. Long straw is the lookout. Deal?"

"Deal," I say.

"Okay, fine," Seymour says, "but—"

Marcus holds up his hand. "You first, Piggy."

Seymour sighs and reaches out. He slowly runs his fingers over the three strands of grass, then pulls one. "Seems pretty long," he says, relieved.

I take my strand next. Once I pull it out, I hold it up to Seymour's. Mine is longer.

"Oh no," Seymour says, his pink cheeks gone white.

Marcus reaches over with the one remaining piece of grass and holds it up against ours. His is the longest of all.

"Oh no. Oh…" Seymour breathes out heavily, shakes his head, then starts rummaging in his bag. He pulls out a strip of bacon. "Well, like I said, eat, drink, and be merry, for today we die."

Marcus insists that we move into action. The dragon could come back any time. He finds a position just beside the ledge that leads into the cave. He can't see far inside from there, but he has an unimpeded view of the valley, which lies completely still. Not even a bird is in sight.

Seymour and I move as quietly as possible toward the mouth of the cave. The smell is overpowering, like a pack of wet dogs. The opening is a narrow crevice, twice my height, but so thin that I can almost reach both sides when I hold my arms out. This means the dragon can't fly into the lair, but I can't see very far inside. Maybe it gets bigger beyond the opening. I stand to the side to let Seymour pass.

To his credit, Seymour doesn't whine or hesitate as he moves past me, deeper into the cave. I look from him to the ledge outside, where Marcus is keeping watch, and back. Seymour turns a corner and I can no longer see him. But a few moments later, I hear him.

"Whooaaa." He sounds amazed.

I can't see anything, but it doesn't sound like he's found a dragon. "What is it?"

"Gold." His head appears around the corner. "Cipher, you gotta see this. It's a pile of gold and jewels, stacked taller than I am. Come on."

I glance to Marcus, who is staring out over the mountains. He probably can't hear Seymour from this distance, but I could hear him if he shouted. I turn to Seymour again, shaking my head. "We don't need gold! Just look for a tooth," I say. "Hurry!"

"Okay, fine." Seymour ducks out of sight again.

A minute passes without a sound. My foot is tapping impatiently. Surely I would hear him if something bad happened. Maybe he's just searching deeper in the cave. Or maybe he's filling his pockets and his bag with gold. Either way, it can't be good.

"Get out!" Marcus shouts. He's on the ledge, pointing to the distance. Our eyes meet. "It's coming. Get out, now!"

I shout the message into the cave: "Seymour! Get out! Dragon's coming!"

No response.

When I glance back to Marcus, he's nowhere to be seen. I don't know how much time I have, but I can't just leave Seymour in the cave alone.

I rush in and turn the corner. Before me is an immense cavern, with a pile of treasure just like Seymour said. A beam of light from a tiny crack in the ceiling shines down, making the gold glitter. Seymour stands beside it, stuffing gold into his bag.

"Seymour!" I shout.

He turns to me with a huge smile. He holds up a long, sharp tooth.

"Come on, leave it!" I say. "The dragon!"

His smile flees, but it's too late for us to run. A rush of wind makes me stagger forward. Claws scrape against rock. The walls shake. Then a head comes around the corner. Yellow eyes. Black irises. Just like the creature under the tower. *Behemoth.* Its mouth opens, showing teeth like swords. It lets out a deep growl as it coils back, as if ready to breathe fire.

But a sound outside makes it turn. The sound is faint but clear: Marcus shouting. He must be trying to help us, to divert the dragon's attention.

The dragon backs out of the tight crevice.

This time I don't wait for Seymour, but charge out of the cave and onto the ledge as the dragon takes off, soaring down the mountain. Below I see Marcus sprinting down the slope in huge bounds, hollering loudly as he goes. The dragon swoops right at him.

I summon the air. I form it like a long lasso and snap it around the dragon's neck. It is flying so fast that when the rope of air is pulled tight, it yanks me forward onto the rocky ground, flat on my chest. But I manage to hold on, and when I stagger to my knees, the dragon has stopped, sitting on its haunches on the mountainside, staring back at me. Marcus, just past it, looks up at me in shock.

Metal clinks by my side. It's Seymour.

"Is it...?" he begins to ask, but the dragon roars and silences him. It snaps back its neck and unleashes a blast of fire, fast as lightning, streaking toward Marcus. The fire pours over him and through him for several breaths.

When the fire stops, Marcus is still standing there. He falls to his knees and looks down at his hands, as if he can't believe that he hasn't been roasted.

The dragon has turned. It faces us. In a flash it breathes out another blast of fire, this time right at Seymour and me. I channel the air into a shield in front of us, holding it as tight as I can. The fire slams into the shield, bending it for a moment and then snapping it, like a lion charging through a spider web.

The blaze hits me with amazing force and heat. My vision blurs and shifts, like I've just dunked my head into the Blue Tower's Sieve.

I'm sitting at a bar. The surface is copper, almost the same color as the drink in my hand. Music steadily thumps, adding a rhythm to the den of conversation around me. Through a large window I can see the city of Toronto outside, blanketed in snow. Fires burn silently in sleek gas fireplaces. It's so warm in here.

A red-haired woman sits beside me. It's Samantha Jones, from the last memory, but now in her 30s. She wears a slim black suit and stylish glasses. She's only more stunning.

"And I really liked when you told us that part about the mind," she's saying, smiling a perfect smile at me. "Your mantra before any surgery. What exactly is it again?"

"Respect the mind," I say.

"Yes! It's perfect."

"It's not just for me," I say. "I couldn't do my work without nurses like you."

Again she smiles. It's the same smile she gave Johnny, the shirtless stud Johnny, on that dock in Chicago. She says that doctors like me inspired her to go into nursing. She says she really hopes she'll get a chance to work beside me. Half of my mind listens to her. The other half remembers my wife at home. *Toronto's not far*, I'd told her. *This is one of the biggest conferences of the year. They've offered me a keynote speech. I'll be back by Sunday morning.* She had not been happy about it. *Why do you need another keynote?* she'd asked. *You'll miss his game. Again.* That was true. I'd missed a lot of my son's games. But it was six-year-old soccer. No big deal.

"When did you first know you'd be a neurosurgeon?" Samantha asks. "I mean, really *know*?" Her hand is on my forearm now. She's just being friendly.

And I'm just being nice. She's trying to make it as a nurse. I tell her I'd wanted to be a doctor ever since high school, back when we knew each other. Then I tell a story about medical school, studying the brain, and realizing I had a special gift in understanding it.

Another copper drink comes for me, and a pinkish one for her. The glass in her hand has a bright red cherry in it. But it's not as red as her lips.

My drink is almost empty when Samantha says she wants to show me something in her room. It's a paper about a new surgical procedure. She has some questions about it. No big deal.

We ride the elevator together. She stands close to me. It's warmer that way. It's still snowing outside. And she's an old friend.

We reach her hotel room. She holds the door open for me.

# 13

GUILT WEIGHS ON ME like an anvil, pressed against my chest, pinning me to the rocky ground of the mountainside. Three bright suns shine down from the clear blue sky. I'm still alive. I don't feel burned, but the fire has left a different pain, maybe worse. A straight line cuts between the two memories, like a knife through my life. I'd tried out for the rowing team just to meet Samantha Jones. She'd been the girl of my high school dreams, forever out of reach. Decades later, Dr. Fitzoy had changed that.

So many questions remain, but one thing is clear: passion made me a fool, a cheat. Now the memory is another tumor that I can't remove. Not Cipher, not even the neurosurgeon, Dr. Paul Fitzroy.

All it takes is one little word or thought to make the neurons fire, and the memory comes back to mind as if no time had passed at all. Time does not heal wounds. I remember a patient once asking me if I could cut out part of his brain, to take a memory away. *No*, I'd said. *It's too dangerous, and there's no guarantee of success. Bad memories are like cockroaches. They know how to survive anything.*

But what if it's different here, in the towers?

I started with no memories at all in the Blue Tower. Perhaps there is some way to keep them from coming back, to erase them, or to heal them. Abram told me the Scouring could purify our memories. He said it was a process. In Blue my old pride felt cleansed. Now Red shows me…Samantha. Can that be scoured? Maybe even painful memories could be used for good. It's a hope worth clinging to.

Footsteps approach, knocking loose rocks that roll down the steep slope. I hurry to my feet and suddenly realize my clothes are…*gone*. My boots and bag are gone, too, and there's a circle of ashes around me. Apparently only my body gets to be invincible to dragon fire. I cover myself with my hands.

The thin figure climbing toward me is similarly bare. It's Marcus.

"Nice outfit," he says with a smirk.

"Thanks. You too. I think the fire…"

"Yeah, I know," he says, glancing down. "At least it only burned clothes."

"Did it show you anything?"

He nods.

We're quiet then. He doesn't want to talk about it. Neither do I.

"Where's Seymour?" I ask.

"I haven't seen any sign of him."

That's weird. He was right behind me. He must have been hit by the fire just like I was. I look to where he was standing, expecting to see a pile of ashes, but there's only reddish dirt and stones, no footprints leading away. Except...

"We should go back," Marcus says. "We won't make it long out here without food or clothes."

"Wait." I move to where Seymour had been standing. Pressed into the dirt is the dragon's tooth that he had been holding. I kneel down and pick it up with both hands. The tooth is faded yellow like a fossil, but still long and sharp as a cutlass.

"A tooth?" Marcus asks, looking over my shoulder. "How?"

"Seymour got it in the lair. There was a pile of gold, too. We might have made it out if he hadn't tried to take the gold. I don't know how the tooth is still here if Seymour isn't. It doesn't make sense..."

"Nothing we can do about it," Marcus says. "There's no use looking for him."

I consider objecting, but I know Marcus is probably right. He begins walking away. With the tooth in hand, I take a final glance at where Seymour had stood, and to the ridge. There's no living creature in sight.

I follow Marcus down the steep mountainside. Neither of us speaks. I now miss Seymour's chattering; it distracted me from my thoughts and memories. In the quiet, I focus on taking one step at a time. It doesn't take long for my bare feet to collect scrapes and bruises from the rocky ground. Marcus doesn't complain, so I don't either.

We return the same way we came. We cross the tree-trunk bridge and stop by the riverside for water. My feet hurt badly. I think about Samantha, and my wife. I wonder what Marcus is thinking about—the Roman Colosseum, a fight, a woman? I'm not brave enough to ask, because I'm not brave enough to tell him what I have done.

"You hungry?" I ask.

He turns back. "You have food?"

I point downstream to a small bush that Seymour had identified. It has a few blueberries scattered among its branches. We pick them and sit beside each other and eat. We stare up toward the ridge with the dragon lair, and the ranges of mountains behind it. The three suns hang low in the sky. In the opposite direction, beyond the distant Red Tower, the sky is going gray, sliding into darkness, like a dimmer switch pressed ever so slowly down.

"You know why we have three suns?" I ask.

"No," Marcus says. "Do you?"

"No clue."

Marcus sighs, closing his eyes. "I loved the old sun, the one on earth. I loved feeling its warm light on my face. I loved seeing it reflect off my sword."

"I loved watching it set," I say, "dropping like a ball into the ocean."

A few moments pass in quiet. We finish the berries.

Marcus stands. "Ready?"

I stay seated on the ground. My feet are killing me. Marcus's feet look as bloodied as mine. Even with our boots on it took us half a day to get from the Red Tower to here, and that was going downhill.

"No," I say. "It's going to be dark soon. I need rest. Can't we sleep here and go the rest of the way tomorrow?"

He studies me, then nods. "It'll be cold without a fire."

It is cold, but we sleep deeply. It helps.

The next morning we head out, with nothing to pack and nothing to carry except a dragon's tooth. With our feet hurting, we make slow progress limping and hobbling up the steep slope to the Red Tower.

The sky is dark by the time we reach the thin bridge. A huge flame flickers on the top. It lights our way forward. This time I do not crawl across the bridge. I walk.

When I reach the other side, I glance back, somehow hoping to see Seymour following us. He's not there. The tower's fires cast our two shadows over the entire length of the bridge, dancing like ghosts in the flickering light. We left with clothes and supplies and three people. Now two of us return with nothing but a tooth and more memories. Not a good deal.

Marcus and I pass between two torches on either side of the open iron doorway. Once we're inside, the door falls shut behind us. We're both covering ourselves, ready to be embarrassed, but there's no one waiting for us. I guess I had expected some kind of welcoming party. We have the dragon tooth. We win, right?

"What now?" I ask.

"I'll get us new clothes and boots," Marcus says. "Then we show Rahab the tooth."

# 14

"ALPHA! ALPHA! ALPHA!"

The chant grows louder as Marcus and I approach the Feasting Hall. He'd found us both fresh clothes and boots before anyone saw us. Everyone must be in the Feasting Hall. Now we hear them, chanting with a shout of celebration, of honor for a victor. But it's not for us, even though I carry the tooth wrapped in a bag slung over my shoulder.

"Alpha! Alpha! Alpha!"

When we reach the doorway to the Hall, the crowd is gathered before Rahab's throne. Her red dress glimmers like lava against the rust-colored rock of the throne. This time there's someone on the throne beside hers. It's Max—who everyone here knows as Axe—with his arms raised as the chant continues. He no longer wears a collar around his neck.

"He must have captured someone," Marcus says.

We approach the edge of the crowd. Marcus surprises me by starting to chant with the others, lifting his fist into the air with each shout, "Alpha! Alpha! Alpha!"

This goes on and on. I can't bring myself to join in. So what if Max caught someone in the Scouring? I caught plenty when I was in the Blue Tower. I scan the crowd for my Mom but don't see her. No sign of Seymour either. No Emma, Kiyo, or anyone I truly know. And now Marcus seems to care more about the Alpha than what we just went through. I feel very alone.

Finally Max—or Axe or Alpha—stands from his throne. The cheering continues as Rahab rises from the throne by his side. She holds up a golden crown that glows like fire in the light of the Feasting Hall.

A ripple of "ahhs" momentarily replaces the chant from the crowd.

"Your new Alpha!" Rahab announces, as she lowers the crown onto his head.

The chants come again, even louder. "Alpha! Alpha! Alpha!"

I put my fingers in my ears. My eyes close. The chant throbs around me like waves pounding against rock. A memory I'd seen in the Blue Tower surges up amidst the throbbing sound. A crowd had gathered around me when I was a surgeon. They had cheered for my work, for saving a life after a successful operation. I had loved it, basking in the praise. Axe must feel like that now.

The chanting begins to fade. I open my eyes and see flames extending high above Rahab's arms. "We have gone too long without an Alpha," she says. "We have gone too long without victory!"

The crowd cheers.

"Now we will restore Red's proper place," Rahab says. "We have taken from Black. We will take the lead again, and your Alpha will show the way. As is the Alpha's right, he will choose servants and take his rightful place in the highest quarters of the Red Tower. And you will give him the honor that he is due."

Rahab's flames extinguish as she sits. Axe now stands alone before the crowd, above us like a king. Boys and girls alike begin to bow, falling to their knees.

"Thank you, thank you," Axe says, a wide smile on his face. "Now let's celebrate! Bring out the cask!"

There's a rush of action. A large, round cask is hauled out and placed at the end of the table that stretches the entire length of the Hall. People begin to fill their cups. When Axe steps down from the throne and the dais, the crowd parts for him. He goes straight to the cask and holds up a huge mug under the running tap of liquid until it flows over and spills out onto the floor. He laughs and jumps on the table and drinks it down while the crowd cheers again, *Alpha! Alpha!*

Once the mug is drained, Axe starts to sing. Everyone around me joins in raucously. The words I manage to understand make me cringe. In Blue we sat in classes and used our minds. Here it's all passionate revelry. The crowd sways as the song comes to its chorus:

*Fire, fire, fire,*
*It all burns in fire.*

As the song ends, many around me begin to pair off, boy and girl. The singing and dancing continue, and I start to back away, alone.

An arm grabs mine.

Marcus. A girl is close by his side.

"Come on!" he shouts over the singing. "We have to show them what we brought back."

*The tooth.* I'd almost forgotten it among the chaos.

Marcus doesn't wait for an answer. He grabs the bag from my shoulder and pulls me with him as he starts to wade through the crowd. He heads straight toward Axe, still on top of the table. Without waiting for me, Marcus leaps up beside Axe and grabs his arm to get his attention. I watch in shock. I've never seen Marcus so excited about anything. And he's said we'd show the tooth to Rahab, not Axe. What's come over him?

Axe stops, glaring at Marcus. Others go still and quiet around him, following his lead. "You think you belong here?" Axe demands.

Marcus falls to a knee and lifts his hands, holding out the tooth like it's an offering. "I'm Marcus." He glances back to me. "That is Cipher. We have brought back this for you."

Axe looks down at the tooth, then at Marcus, then at the crowd. His eyes pass over me uncertainly. I count two breaths that pass in tense quiet.

"A dragon tooth!" Axe suddenly shouts, raising his arms in victory. "Our power grows! Well done, Marcus." He takes the tooth and then grabs Marcus' hand and raises it overhead. "Look and learn, friends. Marcus has earned a spot in the Scouring, with me. Welcome to group one!"

As the crowd cheers, Marcus smiles and motions for me to join him. "Cipher, too," Marcus says to Axe. "He was with me."

I step forward.

Axe looks down at me. A look of disappointment passes over his eyes. "He's small. Just him?" he asks.

"Yes," Marcus says. "We lost our third."

"So be it. Marcus and Cipher, to group one!" Axe drapes arm over Marcus' shoulder and starts to sing again. *"We fight till we die. Fire, fire, fire…"*

Everyone joins in. A few people slap my back in congratulations. At least Marcus remembered to mention me. But I have a bad feeling about the promotion. I manage to slip away from the partying crowd and move toward the door. As I am passing, I look up at the board that shows all the tasks.

There's something that wasn't there before. An arrow points from the right of task number 1, the Scouring, to a list of many names, with Axe at the top. There are fifteen names total. Two of them are crossed out: Lin and Rose.

I swallow. *My Mom?*

Three new names are at the bottom of the list: Ellen, Hank, and Emma.

*Hank? Emma? From Blue?*

"Notice anything?" Rahab asks beside me. I hadn't heard her coming.

"What does it mean?" I ask.

"Rose was captured," she says. "We lost two, gained three. Not bad, right?"

"Which tower took her?"

Rahab shrugs. "Axe said Black attacked. Could have been them."

Her casual tone makes my blood boil. I take a deep breath. *Don't use power. Don't use power.* "And the ones Axe captured, Emma and Hank," I say stiffly, "where are they?"

"They start at the bottom," she answers. "Don't bother looking for them. They're locked away for now."

"And their memories?"

Rahab's eyes burn into me. "Probably seared away. Behemoth decides. That's usually what it takes for them to become Red. Most do not come here as…contaminated as you."

I'm not sure what she means, but her words make me think of the memory of Samantha. My gaze drops to the floor. "I know I'm not pure."

"Ah, but you *will* be scoured," she says. "Don't let shame hold you back. Your passion must grow."

"Passion was my problem."

"No, no," Rahab says, lifting my face by the chin until our eyes are level. "Untamed passion, perhaps. But there are worse faults, like having no passion at all."

I feel exposed under her glare, like she knows exactly what I've seen. "I don't understand."

"You will, Dr. Fitzroy. Passion can be redeemed. Shame can be scoured. The fire burns at first, but it refines in time."

For the first time, she sounds like Abram. "How does it work here?" I ask.

"Begin by admitting, out loud, what you've done. We have the Pairing for a reason. Tell the girl who pairs with you. All of it."

Emma flashes into my mind. We shared memories like this in the Blue Tower. She is a healer. She knows me. If anyone can help me recover, it's her. If she's really here, would we be able to pair? Would she remember me? I can't imagine telling anyone else what I've seen.

"Where can I find Emma?" I ask.

"You can't," Rahab says.

"Why not?"

"She is not yours to find. She has already been claimed."

*Already claimed?* "What do you mean?"

"Enough questions," Rahab says impatiently. "Prove that you can serve the Alpha, the Red Tower, and me. Prove that you are ready to advance, and then we will talk more." She spins away and strides back toward her throne at the front of the Feasting Hall.

The huge room is even louder than before. Boys and girls singing, shouting, dancing. No one tries to stop me as I leave. Emma is here now. I have to try to find her, no matter what Rahab said. But the leader did give me a clue: *they start at the bottom.*

Down through the tower it is.

It doesn't take long to get lost in the twisting corridors of hewn red rock. My feet hurt badly from the barefoot hike with Marcus. They throb inside my boots.

By the time I stop and sit against a wall, I feel more

frustrated than ever. I came all the way to the Red Tower only for my Mom to be captured by Black, and for my new friend Seymour to have been burnt up by a dragon. His memories were probably wiped. Now Emma and Hank might be wiped, too.

Tears start to fill my eyes, blurring the torchlight on the wall before me. I hug my knees and stare into the flames.

Another vision comes.

I'm sitting in a soft brown leather chair, staring into a roaring fireplace. The mantle is a huge slab of stone. Above it there's a large, golden-framed portrait of a family of three. My face from before has a square jaw and penetrating brown eyes. The woman painted by my side, my wife, has gentle blue eyes and graceful beauty. Our son is between us. He has her eyes.

But they're both away tonight. It's just me in the house.

My hand reaches for a glass of amber liquid, with two cubes of ice. A half-empty bottle sits beside it. I drain the glass and pour more. The edges of the flame are fuzzy in my vision. I hold up a glowing screen and swipe through images of smiling friends.

A text pops up: *Still a good time?*

I respond: *Yes, door's open.*

The glass empties again. My body has melted, comfortably numb, into the leather chair. In the memory I know what I'm thinking, sitting in that chair—what I wanted, what I deserved because of what I had achieved. There's no thought at all of my wife and son in the golden-framed portrait.

A car door shuts outside. Then there's a steady, approaching click of heels on the brick path around to the back of the house. The clicking fills me, Cipher, with dread, but a different sort of feeling swells in Dr. Fitzroy.

The back door opens.

A smug grin crosses my face as I refill the glass. I try to look away, to leave the memory, but I can't. I try shouting at myself but there's no sound. I want to shake my own shoulders so hard that Dr. Fitzroy's heart rattles in his chest. I want to tell my adult self to look at the portrait. To stop this. To be loyal. But I can't change anything now. The vision and memory march forward ruthlessly.

The clicking heels enter the room. There's a smell of perfume—exotic spices. The woman approaches and leans over me, her familiar face close to mine, her long red hair spilling down. It's Samantha Jones.

# 15

"MORNIN' BOYS! Guess who got paired last night?" A scrawny kid stands on top of his bed wearing only his undergarments and a silver collar around his neck. He points his thumbs to his puffed up chest. "This guy!"

Somebody throws a pillow at him. He dodges it. A second pillow flies and hits him square in the head.

"So what!" another boy shouts, "You got lucky 'cause of the firewater."

The scrawny boy doesn't back down from his perch. "You wish, man. Zelle would never pair with you."

The banter goes on. The commotion rouses the rest of the boys in the room.

I sit up in bed and rub my eyes. Someone found me lost in the tunnels and brought me here. He called this place the Barracks. It had been too dark to get a good look then. Sleep came the moment my head hit the pillow, after the long day of trekking through the mountains, learning my Mom is gone, and seeing another, shameful piece of the past. It's another tumor I can't remove.

The three suns beam morning light through an opening

in the far wall, making the long room glow like an orange ember. The ceiling is low above two lines of plain white beds. There must be a hundred beds, but only about half are full, and only with boys. The room reminds me of the recovery room in the Blue Tower, after the Scouring. At least I haven't woken up paralyzed, or wiped clean.

The boys start to gather around a large fountain in the center of the Barracks. Water bubbles up in the center and fills the large stone basin to the brim, spilling out onto the floor and draining away. The boys use the fountain to wash off their hands and faces before pulling on their clothes and boots. I stay quiet as I wash up alongside the others. I wonder if my eyes are red and puffy from crying last night. No one says anything to me. There's no sign of Hank, my friend from Blue. Marcus just slaps me on the back and smiles as he passes.

"Hey guys," someone shouts, "look who's back!"

A small group has surrounded a boy near the door. It's Seymour, with his freckled face and round body. He waddles toward the fountain in the center. He looks just like he did yesterday before a dragon's fire had hit him.

"Piggy!" another boy shouts.

A chant begins. "Piggy, Piggy, Piggy!"

It reminds me of the Alpha chant the night before. Apparently the Red Tower loves to chant.

Seymour's cheeks go red, but he's not the shy type. "I guess it fits," he says with a nervous laugh. "My skin's kinda pink. But you all look like a bunch of muddy pig feet."

The boys break out laughing. "Piggy's back!" someone says happily.

As everyone scatters and returns to cleaning up, I approach Seymour. "Hey Seymour, welcome back."

"Seymour?" he asks. "You know me?"

"A little." I'm at a loss for what else to say. Are there rules about this? Am I allowed to tell him that he got burned by dragon fire? That on earth he was a chef in Germany before he died? It might be better to let him start discovering this on his own, again.

"You were here before," I say. "Do you remember anything?"

"Not a thing." He glances around the room. "I mean, I woke up and a woman named Rahab told me this was the Red Tower and then she took me to see this awful creature and then dropped me off here. But before that, no, I don't remember."

*Interesting.* Rahab takes everyone to see the dragon first, but she had Seymour escort me straight to the Feasting Hall instead of coming to the Barracks. Maybe that's the difference between the ones who are wiped and those who show up with memories intact. It gives me some hope that Hank will remember, since I still haven't seen him yet.

"Don't worry," I say. "The memories will come back."

"Thanks. I hope so. Where's everyone else going?"

It's surreal to get this question from Seymour. The little that I know about this place I learned from him. "All of us have different tasks. I just got promoted to the Scouring group. You'll probably start at the bottom of the list, like I did." I decide not to mention dragon's teeth, not yet anyway. "Maybe you'll be on pig duty."

"Oh." He suddenly laughs. "I guess that's why everyone was calling me Piggy. That's funny. At least I know what a pig is, or I hope so. It's an animal. Four legs and a snout, rolls in the mud and eats a lot, right?"

"Yes." I smile. He sounds just like his former self.

"Line up!" a boy shouts. He's standing by the door. "Come on now, line up! I'm the Barracks leader today. Everyone who knows your task, get to it once this door opens. For those who don't, you newbies, welcome to Red. You'll be with me today. Your tasks will be assigned later in the Feasting Hall. The first rule is: do whatever the girls tell you to do."

As the boys form a single-file line, I make my way to Marcus near the front. He should know what we're supposed to do in the Scouring group…other than fight in the Scouring.

"Hey Marcus," I say. "What should we do?"

"We must train for the Scouring," he says, quiet but intense. "I've been waiting for this fight."

*Train? Fight?* We didn't do much fighting in the Blue Tower. The first time I got an assignment for the Scouring I was in an underwater dining room eating squid soup. An envelope from Abram told me I would lead a group into the Scouring. We prepared in a classroom. Sarai lectured to us, and then we discussed our strategy as a team. We survived the first one—capturing Emma but losing Kiyo. I survived the second and third Scourings, too. The fourth time I let myself get caught by Red. I still don't really understand why the towers have to fight. No one in Red seems to care about *why*. The boys don't spend much time thinking, as far as I can tell.

The Barracks door opens. Boys begin filing out for their various tasks. A huge dark-skinned boy bellows out for the Scouring group to gather.

I follow Marcus to join them. There are five of us. They're all bigger and stronger than I am. No surprise. We make quick introductions. The three boys I haven't met before are Jafari, Khan, and Seth.

Marcus whispers to me that Jafari has been in the top group a long time, that he's like Axe's second-in-command. Marcus says this would be our chance, finally, to show our own skill. I nod along, but if I can't use my powers, I'd rather feed the pigs. Maybe even get another dragon's tooth.

Jafari leads us through the back of the Barracks to a training ground outside. It is perched on a terrace, with a stunning view of the mountains. The terrace is square-shaped, about fifty feet to each side. The surface beneath our feet feels like padded clay, red and soft. There's a balcony above, where six girls gather by the railing. They are high enough that we can't hear what they say. It is just enough to get that prickly feeling at my neck, knowing I'm being watched. Or maybe they're doing something to me through the silver collar around my throat.

"I'm using this," Jafari says, holding up a long staff. "Who wants the first go?"

*Not me.* He's twice my size, and a vein bulges on his bicep like a snake crawling under his dark skin. His hair hangs in dreadlocks to his shoulders.

"Not without a horse," says Khan. He has long black hair tied behind his back.

Jafari laughs and spins his staff. "No horses in the Scouring, my friend. You got lucky last time."

"I'll go first." Seth steps up, gripping his own staff. Neither staff has pads. Seth's long, freckled arms move fast, whirling the staff like a helicopter's blade. "Somebody needs to knock you down."

"Bring it." Jafari motions for Seth to come.

They begin circling each other. Blue never would have fought like this. *The mind,* Abram once said, *a far more powerful weapon.* I agree. But apparently the boys in Red don't have powers. So they train with weapons. But why try to hurt each other when we need to work together?

Still, Jafari and Seth look impressive as they trade blows, blocking most of them. Their staffs crack loudly against each other. Their shuffling steps kick up a cloud of red dust that cakes onto their now sweating bodies. The girls watch from the balcony above.

Seth is faster and smoother with the staff, but he's not strong enough. He blocks most of Jafari's swings, but Jafari wears him down. He slams down so hard that even as Seth blocks the blow, he falls back onto the ground.

Jafari swings at Seth's head, but stops it suddenly. The end thuds softly against Seth's ear. Jafari holds it there. "Nice try, sheepherder."

He backs away and Seth rises. "We could have used a little more of that last time in the Scouring," he says. "Save some for Black, okay?"

"Okay, whenever my girl lets me." The boys laugh together, but I don't know what it means. As if sensing my quiet, Jafari turns toward me. "Newbies, who's next?"

I swallow. I manage not to step back.

Marcus steps forward. "Me."

He goes to the rack of training weapons and takes a dull-edged sword and a small round shield. He spins the sword twice, and nods as if satisfied. When he turns to Jafari, Marcus is smiling. "Feels good to have a sword in my hand."

"Ah, the dragon hunter," Jafari says. "Let's see what you got."

Marcus surprises all of us, even Jafari, as he breaks into a sprint, sword pumping, arms swinging. Jafari takes a step back, raising his staff protectively.

But he's too slow. Marcus charges and leaps high into the air and strikes like lightning, his sword stabbing down at Jafari, piercing his neck just above the silver band.

Marcus lands on his feet. Jafari collapses.

Seth rushes to Jafari's side and tries to raise him. But the large boy is motionless, his dark body like a huge lump of coal on the reddish clay ground. Blood pools around him.

Seth looks up in shock. "He's not breathing."

"You…killed him," Khan says, with fury and awe in his voice as he slowly approaches Marcus. "Jafari was our strongest. Now he has to start over. You will pay for this."

Marcus doesn't answer. He doesn't back away, even though Seth and Khan are both coming at him, weapons drawn.

I don't have a weapon, but I come to Marcus's side. He's the closest thing I have to a friend here. I can use the air if it comes to it. We're outside, not technically *in* the Red Tower, or so I can argue to Rahab.

"Stay back," Marcus says, stepping in front of me.

"Stop! Stop!" Axe shouts, racing onto the training ground. "All of you, weapons down. Down! Now!"

Seth and Khan obey, dropping their weapons to the ground.

But not Marcus. He keeps his sword in hand. The dull metal is covered in blood.

Axe glares at him. "I said weapons down."

"Make me," Marcus says.

"You asked for it." Axe steps quickly to the weapon rack and pulls out a battleaxe with dulled blades on both sides. It looks too heavy to swing.

By the time Axe turns back, Marcus is already charging. Axe takes off in a sprint, directly at Marcus. Neither one slows. Just as they are set to collide, Marcus leaps like he did at Jafari. He brings the blade stabbing down.

But Axe reacts quickly, dodging right. Marcus misses and lands in a crouch. Axe spins and swings the battleaxe in a blur, so fast that Marcus has no chance to recover. The flat of the metal blade slams into Marcus's head.

Marcus collapses onto the red dirt. He's still conscious,

lying on his back and gazing blankly into the sky.

"You've got guts," Axe says, kicking away Marcus's sword. He looks to the balcony above, and he holds up a hand with his pointer finger raised. The girls lean over the balcony as if trying to get a closer look.

Marcus's hands suddenly go to the collar at his neck, gripping it tightly. His face floods with anger and fear.

"You're paired now," Axe says. "You'll obey your mate whether you like it or not. Welcome to the team."

Marcus rises slowly to his feet. He opens his mouth to say something, but his lips immediately press tight again. He goes rigid, his eyes wild and panicked.

"That'll be enough for today," Axe says. "Khan, you're my right hand now. Take Jafari's body to the fire. He'll be back. We need him." Axe turns to go, but pauses. "We're going to need these new boys, too. We don't have to like each other. But we have to fight together for Red."

# 16

MARCUS LEAVES after the training, probably to repent and face punishment for taking out Jafari. Maybe he'll have a little meeting with Rahab and one of her fireballs. Unless…she decides to praise his passion instead. She's still a mystery to me.

Axe goes back to his quarters, wherever they are, leaving only Seth, Khan, and me on the red clay surface where we fight with padded weapons and, apparently, sometimes kill each other, temporarily.

Khan tries to haul Jafari's large body onto his shoulder, but it weighs too much for him to carry alone. Seth comes to his side and starts to help. The two of them begin shuffling away from the training ground.

It'll take a long time with just the two of them. "Want help?" I ask.

"We won't stop ya," Seth mutters, adding under his breath, "*dragon boy.*"

Maybe they think I'm on Marcus' side. Maybe they're right. But I'm not the one who did this.

I manage to step behind Seth and take Jafari's feet

overhead. Khan leads the way, his muscles straining under the weight of Jafari's upper body. As we pass through the Barracks, the few boys in the room look at us with confused stares. We're the Scouring team. We're carrying Jafari's lifeless body.

Khan leads us out of the Barracks and through a dozen twists and turns in the Red Tower's tunnels, gradually making our way up. My legs ache and sweat pours. I don't know how they could have made it the whole way with just the two of them. I've completely lost track of our path when Khan finally brings us to a stop in front of a large, iron door.

A girl waits there, like she knew we'd be coming. She's tall, with short black hair and skin the same dark color as Jafari's. "Set him down," she commands.

Khan turns back to Seth and me. "Gently."

Together we lower the body onto the ground. All three of us lean over, hands on our knees.

The girl bends over Jafari, cupping the back of his head in her hands. They look very similar. She whispers faintly, "Brother, my brother. You will be back. You will remember. I will teach you again, little brother. We will pair and we will leave together. Our promise cannot be broken."

She leans her forehead against Jafari's and stays there, silent, for a long time. When she rises, tears streak down her cheeks.

"I'm sorry," Khan says.

"Don't be," she replies. "It's not the first time. It was

much worse on earth. Here he'll be back. Here he'll remember and get another chance. He'll learn eventually. I'll never give up on him."

"You were his sister?" I ask, amazed. Other than me finding my mother, this is the first time I've discovered anyone who knew each other on earth, much less family.

"I *am* his sister. I'm Jacana." The girl looks me up and down, now looking more fierce than sad. She looks like the type who wouldn't flinch when facing a tiger. "No time or space can change that. You should know. Rose told me you're her son."

"Yes." This catches me off guard. "You knew her?"

"Of course," Jacana says. "We were in the Scouring group together for a long time, before she got taken. We'll miss her."

"Do you know where she went?" I ask.

"Black captured her. They'll wipe her. She'll need you to help her remember."

"How can I find her?"

Jacana smiles, her straight white teeth like pearls. "You'll find a way, son of Rose." She looks down at Jafari's body, large and still on the red stone ground. "If there's one thing I've learned in this place, it's that we all have old ties here. The kind that never break. My brother and I have been separated and found, lost and reunited more times than I know, probably more than I can remember. Not that it makes losing him any easier. He'll come back needing to relearn all of it. And I'll reteach it, just like before."

She kisses her hand, then bends down and presses it to

Jafari's forehead. She stands and presses the same hand to the center of the iron door. Its dark, cold metal immediately begins to glow yellow, then orange, then red. A shape forms in the fiery hues, a single flame that flickers as if alive. It reflects brightly off the ruby ring on Jacana's finger. She turns her hand over the fire, and the door slowly swings open. There's a stone stairway and bright blue sky through the door.

"Do it right," Jacana says to Khan before walking away, red dress swaying.

"Almost there," Khan says to Seth and me. "Let's finish strong."

We haul the body up onto our shoulders again. Khan leads us through the open doorway. As soon as we're outside, a blast of cold wind hits us. We're hundreds of feet above the ground, with the Scouring far below us. There's no railing. The air is thin. The stairway coils up to the top of the Red Tower. Each stair reaches as high as my knees, and we'll have to climb more stairs than I can count.

Khan starts the ascent. As I try to keep up, my calves and thighs protest. I keep my eyes on the step in front of me.

*One step at a time. Don't look down. Keep climbing.*

A drop of sweat falls into my eye, making me slip. The sole of my boot lands partly over the edge, with no railing between the open air and me.

I stagger and fall back toward the wall. My lost balance makes Khan and Seth fall to their knees, trying to hold up Jafari's body on their own.

"Quitter," Seth spits. "Mighta killed us."

"Sorry. I slipped." My back presses against the wall, staying as far from the edge as I can. The wind whips at my hair, cooling the sweat on my face. "I'm tired. Can we take a break?"

Khan glares down at me like I'm pathetic. "We'll do it ourselves."

As he and Seth carry the body ahead, my head hangs in defeat. I have to be stronger. I'm group one just like they are. My body might be weak, but my mind is still strong. Maybe the strongest.

*Respect the mind.*

We're not *inside* the Red Tower. We're outside, climbing these stairs with a giant limp body. I don't need to ask for permission. I focus on the wind whipping around me and channel it into a tight, powerful stream, which I slide under Jafari's body like an invisible bed, and lift.

Khan and Seth snap around, astonished.

"I got it," I say.

On my feet again, I slip past them on the stairs and carry the body, floating invisibly a few feet in front of me, up the path. The effort drains me, but I refuse to show it. The body is weak, but the mind is strong. I am still Cipher of the Blue Tower. I do not have to conform to all of Red's ways.

When we finally reach the top of the tower, I lower Jafari's body on the ground and release the air. The top is a circle twenty feet across. A low wall rings the edge like a parapet, rising only as high as my knees. In the center of the circle there's a large fire blazing out of a recess in the ground. There's no wood or fuel that I can see, but around the fire lays an orderly circle of dragon teeth. This must be where they bring the ones we find. Maybe they somehow fuel the fire. The heat feels like a sauna, drying my sweat as soon as it emerges from my skin.

I sit on the ground, beside Khan and Seth, with my back against the parapet. Vast mountain ranges spread out into the distance. The three suns blaze just above them in the sky.

We sit in quiet for a while. Khan breaks the silence. "Thanks," he says softly, his eyes studying the horizon. "Go ahead, put it in the fire."

"The body?" I ask.

"Yes. That's the way we do it here. He'll come back."

I hesitate, studying Jafari's large form on the ground. For some reason I can't bring myself to summon the wind. I can't bear the thought of the body burning.

"If ya don't," Seth says. "We will."

He starts to stand, but I put my hand on his arm.

I lift the body into the fire. The flames blaze brighter for an instant, and then the body is gone and all is back to normal, flickering fire. It almost seems…uneventful.

"How do you do it?" Khan asks me.

"The power came in the Blue Tower," I say. "I'm not sure how. At first it was only when I got angry. Then I got better at controlling it."

"So Rahab won't let you use it?" he asks.

"Not inside the Red Tower," I say. "But I figured we

were outside…"

"Creative." Seth glances at me with a smirk scrunching the freckles on his face. "But ya better get used to life for a boy *inside* the tower."

"I'm trying," I say. "I don't exactly…fit in here. Blue felt more like home. Were you guys ever in other towers?"

Seth shrugs. "Wish I knew."

"Do you remember anything from before?" I ask.

"Oh yeah, lots," Seth says. "Khan and I were a lot alike, even if I'm much better looking."

Khan laughs but doesn't look at us. He still seems more interested in the view.

"How were you alike?" I ask. It's hard to believe. They have to be from far different places—Khan with his straight black hair and olive-colored skin, Seth with his red curls and freckles.

"We herded animals," Seth says.

"Not alike," Khan replies. "Very different."

"Eh, horses and sheep are not so different," Seth says. "They both eat grass, run around, and serve men."

Khan turns to Seth with one brow raised in amusement. "Starting this again?"

Seth winks at me. "Khan here thinks horses are better than sheep."

"This is obvious," Khan says. "A flock of sheep is hardly more than a field of grain. Let them grow, eat them, and use some wool. They have no brains, no souls. But horses, ah, they are our friends. We ride them across the plains. We charge with them into battle. A man with a horse is like a god. A man with a sheep is… as annoying as Seth."

Seth bursts out laughing. Khan turns away with a bemused smile, looking out over the mountains again as if the debate is won.

"Khan just thinks he's special because he groomed a warlord's horses. He even named himself after the guy." Seth nudges Khan's shoulder to get his attention. "Genghis, right?"

Khan grunts in agreement and stands, catching my eyes. "Sheepherder will answer your questions. I'm going to have a look in the fire." He walks around the blazing flames to the other side of the wall, where he's blocked from view by the fire.

"Guess he didn't want to talk?" I ask.

"Eh, he's easy to get worked up," Seth says. "All you have to do is mention horses and Genghis and he'll go stare into the fire."

"So he can see his past?" I ask.

"Aye. To each his own. I've seen enough of the past lately. I'd rather enjoy the mountain view. Reminds me of home."

*We can control when we see the past.* It was looking into water, in the Sieve, that showed memories in Blue. Fire for Red, water for Blue.

I ask Seth, "What's home for you?"

"The Scottish Highlands," he says with reverence. "There was no finer place on earth. It was close to the heavens. Windswept mountains and the deepest, clearest lakes you've ever seen. I had a little place there, a warm home made of stone, full of children and song. My sheep roamed the grassy hills. It was a good life."

*A good life?* This is the first time anyone has sounded so pleased with their past. "Why do you think you ended up here?"

"Aye, that's the question. I figure we got lucky. We're the chosen."

"Chosen for what?" I ask.

"To stay alive. To remember the past. It beats death, right?"

"I guess," I say, "but didn't we already die?"

Seth reaches over and presses his freckled hand to my chest. "Bu-bump, bu-bump. Aye, that's a beatin' heart. You ever met a dead man with one of those?"

I shake my head as my former doctor mind considers it. Sometimes a heart could stop, and a person could look dead. But then you pump it back to life with fists on the chest or, better yet, an electromagnetic pulse. It was my job not to give up on a body. There was something in the brain that held the secret to life. That's why I loved to study it. But I never figured out the secret. Some people's bodies died temporarily, only moments later they'd come back good as new. Other people's bodies lived while their minds died. As long as the heart pumps blood and neurons fire in the brain, you're certifiably alive.

So I admit to Seth, "We seem alive."

"Aye," Seth laughs. "Everyone here should quit whinin' about whatever they left behind. Remember it, sure. Learn from it. Scour it. But we should be dancin', singin'. We died. But now, my friend, we're alive!"

The suns are low on the horizon when Khan approaches us from around the other side of the burning flame. He looks golden between the fading sunlight and the pulsing firelight. His hand rests on the collar at his throat. "They're calling us," he says to Seth.

"Aye, felt that," Seth says. "Just had to finish teaching Cipher here why it's good to be Red, good to be alive."

Khan does not look so sure. "We have no choice."

He holds out his hand to Seth and helps him up. The two of them say a quick goodbye, telling me I'm free to stay here but should head to the Feasting Hall by sunset. Then they take off down the stairs, bounding like mountain goats. The girls who paired with them must have ordered them to come. I figure it's like what I had with Emma in Blue. She was my servant, just as the boys serve the girls here. They share feelings through the link. My hand goes to my neck and feels the metal band. It's cold to the touch despite my closeness to the fire.

I could look into the fire. I could see my past. *My Mom, wife, son…Samantha.* I have to know more. I can't resist it.

The flames pull my gaze into a vision.

It's a picnic. I stand beside a foldout table and pour a cup of lemonade. The glass pitcher is wet with condensation. Past the table there's an oak tree shading a grassy lawn where kids are running and playing.

"Aren't they adorable?" the woman beside me asks. She's my wife, Susan, smiling warmly under a white sunhat, as she watches the children play.

"So adorable!" answers another woman, who stands to my other side. It's Samantha, the woman who came to my home at night. She smells of the same perfume. She grins at my wife. "Your little Benjamin looks just like his dad."

*Benjamin.* That's my son's name.

I sip the lemonade. My throat is tight.

"You should see pictures of Paul's dad," Susan says. "Benjamin is his spitting image."

"He must been a handsome man," Samantha replies.

The two of them continue talking, casually, about kids and the weather, while we drink lemonade and sweat beads on my forehead. Behind us a large white steeple rises with a cross at the top. Its shadow falls directly over us.

One of the children trips and starts to cry. It's not Benjamin, but a little girl. Susan rushes over to her to help, gently soothing the child's bruised knee and ego.

With Susan occupied, Samantha leans closer to me, and whispers, "Friday night was fun. When can we do it again?"

"Please," I say softly, "not here."

Her smile does not falter. Her lips radiate like embers. They spark into fire and burn the outer edge of my vision until the whole memory is engulfed in flames and blows away like ashes in the wind.

# 17

THE THREE SUNS descend behind the mountains when the vision ends. I'm still on top of the Red Tower. Still alone. No one can see my flushed cheeks or tears. No one can know how it ripped me apart to see myself standing between Susan and Samantha, helplessly watching as my universe imploded around me.

The sky grows dark. It's time to go to the Feasting Hall. It's time to leave the past, as much as I can. I turn away from the fire and start the climb back down the tower. It's easier going down, without a body to carry.

By the time I make it to the doorway into the Hall, the boys and girls of the Red Tower are looking for their spots. As before, the black rocks on the long table have names carved into them. I head to the front, where the Scouring group sits.

A familiar voice brings me to a stop.

"Hey Cipher!" Seymour approaches me with a goofy smile. "This place is amazing, right? I spent all day learning how to take care of the tower's pigs. And I get to come here! Just look at all these girls. Did any pick you for

Pairing?"

I shake my head.

"Yeah, me neither." He lets out a nervous laugh. "Guess we're still free agents then. Seems like they only pick the tall ones, the strong ones, and the handsome ones."

I look at his pudgy face, then down at my feet. "Guess so. If we even want to be picked…"

"Hey, no use worrying about it!" he says. "But you gotta tell me, what kind of magic makes those flames float up there by the ceiling? And what's with that woman on the throne? Rahab, right? She's the one who took me to that awful dragon at the bottom. Don't get me wrong. She's beautiful, stunning. But kind of…terrifying, don't you think?"

"She's like wildfire," I say, "better viewed from a distance."

Seymour laughs. "So, when do we get to eat? It smells great in here."

I force myself to be patient with his barrage of words. He was the one who showed me how this worked when I first arrived. It's the least I can do to return the favor.

"We'll eat soon," I say. "We each get assigned seats. Come on, I'll show you."

I lead him toward the far end of the room, where there are empty spots along the benches lining the table. I explain as we go that food will be served and then we'll go to the board to see our tasks for the next day. I'm careful not to say more than the basic facts. It feels crazy not to tell him about his own memories, but it seems like he should uncover them some other way.

"Seymour, see?" I point to the rock bearing his name. It's the last one, the furthest from Rahab and Axe.

"Oh yeah, great, thanks! Want to join me?"

"Sorry, I can't."

We say goodbyes and I'm turning away when something makes me pause. The rock to the left of Seymour's shows the name Hank.

*Hank. Is it really him? Will he remember me?*

Moments later he approaches us. He looks just like he did in the Blue Tower. He's tall, with sandy brown hair and a thick frame that looks stable as an oak. A short boy is by his side, talking. The boy must have newcomer welcome duty, like Seymour did when I first arrived.

My breath freezes when Hank first catches my gaze. *Remember, please remember.*

He pauses, as if processing who I am, but then he smiles and runs toward me and wraps his large arms around me. He squeezes so tight I can't make a sound. I had almost forgotten how big he is.

"Cipher!" he says, letting me go. "You're here. You look…rough, but hey, you're here! Wait, do you remember me?"

"Of course, Hank. Respect the mind, right?"

"Respect the mind!" he says.

My throat tightens. I hardly expected to see him again, much less to have our memories intact. "I can't believe you're here," I say. "And you weren't wiped."

"Nope, I let them catch me in the Scouring. They didn't kill me."

"You *let* them?" I ask.

He shrugs. "I told Emma I'd help. She really wanted to find you."

*She came for me.* "Is she okay?"

Hank hesitates, looking worried. "I'm not sure. We were together in the Scouring when Red got us. You know this leader, Axe, he's the one you…in Blue…"

"I know. It's Max. He doesn't remember."

"I figured," Hank says. "It's probably better that way. He's stronger now, with a beard and all. It's like he fits better here in Red. In the Scouring he led an attack against us. It wasn't pretty, but Emma…she should be here."

"You haven't seen her?" I ask.

He shakes his head. "Haven't really seen anyone here until now."

"The girls get their own quarters," I say.

He glances around the room. "So I guess I have to learn some new rules. Everyone's dressed the same, so no levels?"

"Right, it's not like Blue. Instead of four levels, there's a long list of tasks that seem like a ranking. The first task is the Scouring. I already had the lowest one. I had to go out and bring back a dragon's tooth."

"A dragon's tooth?" Seymour interrupts. "There are dragons here?"

"At least one," I say. *He really remembers nothing.* I'm still not ready to break the news to him. "It's the creature you saw below the tower. It's called Behemoth."

"Well then, I'd rather feed the pigs!" Seymour laughs uneasily. "Hey, it looks like we should be sitting down. Everyone else is. I don't want to start out in trouble and have to go out and fight a dragon or something. Know what I mean?"

I turn to Hank and can't resist a smile. His solid presence is more comforting than ever. "Seymour's probably right," I say. "We should sit. I'm at the other end of the table. You're here beside Seymour. He just had his memory wiped, but loves to talk. Good thing you're patient. We'll catch up more after we eat, okay?"

Hank clasps my shoulder. "I look forward to it, my friend."

I turn away and walk the entire length of the table, checking the names on the rocks in front of the few empty seats. Still no sign of Emma. I make it almost to the end, just a few paces away from the dais with the two thrones, when I see the rock that says "Cipher."

Axe gives me a cold smile as I take my seat, three from the front. Marcus has the spot to my left. He says hi but barely seems to notice me. His eyes are on the girls across from us. They are stunning in red sequined dresses. They pay as much attention to me as to the rocks on the table.

Food comes. It's bacon and beans, served the same way as before. No one talks to me, so I just listen and observe as I eat.

The girls are talking too quietly for me to hear above the noise of the Feasting Hall. Marcus and the boy beside him are discussing the Black Tower. It is the same kind of myth and awe that I heard when I was in Blue. They talk about how strong the warriors are in Black, and how no powers can be used against them. I know why. I remember the girl from Black who managed to shut down my control of the air. Her name was Monica. I don't want to face her again.

After the bowls empty, Rahab stands. The Hall goes quiet.

"Welcome to our great Feasting Hall," Rahab says, voice booming magically as before. "We have three newcomers since our last Scouring. Two of them are with us here. Hank and Ellen, stand."

At the far end of the table, near Seymour, the two of them rise. I take a deep breath, forcing myself to stay composed. Where is Emma? Others in the Hall applaud dutifully. Hank and the other new girl sit again.

"This brings our numbers to 91," Rahab continues. "We remain near our lowest. There was a time when we filled two tables like this. Now we have grown weak, as Black and even Blue have grown strong. We must do better. Your task numbers are on the bottom of your stones. There are five days until the next Scouring. Let passion burn. Thrive like fire."

Rahab's words are identical to what she said before, except now we have 91 instead of 90. I wonder how long she has been saying the same thing.

Everyone begins checking under their rocks.

"Number 1," Marcus says.

I push the flame-shaped tip of my black stone, tilting it over until it falls backward on the table. A chalky number 1 stares back at me. The crowd begins to rise. Most of them scramble excitedly toward the board of tasks. A few shuffle slowly after them. They probably know their tasks. They probably don't like them.

"Scouring group!" Axe shouts, stepping down from his throne. "Gather around me!"

# 18

ELEVEN OF US huddle together like a football team at the front of the Feasting Hall. The others begin to discuss our strategy for the Scouring. Axe is the good-looking, bearded quarterback, sitting above us on the raised dais. The girls play flashy positions like running back and wide receiver. That makes the boys—Khan, Seth, Marcus, and me—the linemen. It's better than the bench.

"What about Yellow?" one of the girls asks.

Axe has already said he wants to capture from Blue. He says they are the easiest. He doesn't know that he only caught Hank and Emma because they came willingly for me.

"Anyone else?" Axe asks the group.

"Green." It's Jafari's sister, Jacana. His spot in the Scouring group hasn't been filled. "Green is right beside us," she says. "If we go straight to them, that's the opposite way from Black. We need to avoid Black."

"We can take Black." Marcus steps forward confidently. "I have battled lions in the Colosseum. I have survived the Black Tower."

*The Black Tower? Marcus?* He never said a word about this during our whole trek for a dragon's tooth.

A few of the girls laugh at what he said. Khan and Seth look angry, probably because of what Marcus did to Jafari.

"It's bold, and suicidal." Axe fixes an amused stare at Marcus. "You mean the Roman Colosseum, the ancient wonder?"

"It was not ancient when I fought there," Marcus replies.

"Very interesting," Axe says. "My workers built a copy of this Colosseum. I won many bets there. My daughters loved to watch the fights."

"Where was this?" Marcus asks.

"Macau, China," Axe says. "It was a tourist magnet. I owned many casinos."

"What are casinos?" Marcus asks.

The question makes me smile. Marcus has no reason to know what Axe means, but I do. Axe, or Max, must have lived in the same era I did. And he must have been rich if he had workers who built copies of ancient wonders. It's hard to imagine. He seems so…physical.

"We'll talk later," Axe says to Marcus. "First, we need to get you paired." He glances around the group of girls. "Any takers?"

A girl raises her hand. She has glitter on her long eyelashes and cheeks. She literally sparkles.

"I'm Zelle."

"You must be strong." Axe looks her up and down. "You were picked to take Rose's place."

*Rose, my Mom.* He says this so casually, like he doesn't even care that we lost her.

"The girls can tell you," Zelle says cheerfully, "I summon fire faster than anyone here. I'll take Marcus. He's been to Black. That's so…hot."

Marcus's cheeks go red. "Um, thanks."

"It's not so simple, Zelle," Axe says. "Anyone else want Marcus?"

"Me." Boleyn steps forward. She's the dazzling girl who escorted me into the Feasting Hall when I first arrived in the tower. "I'll make him pay for what he did to Jacana's brother."

"Very well. Moving on…" Axe flashes a mocking smile at me. "Anyone want to pair with our new runt from Blue?"

The way he says this reminds me of the memory of the rower Johnny with Samantha, of Luther in the Blue Tower, and of every stud everywhere who has treated me like crap. I think about summoning the air and throwing Axe out of the room. I'm the most powerful. I can be the Alpha. But all at once the girls turn and stare at me and I forget about Axe. I pull at the collar around my neck, feeling the heat creeping up my neck and into my cheeks. No girl speaks. It's like my memory all over again, looking up at the list of names who made the rowing team and my name is not there. Johnny gets Samantha, and I run home crying.

"He's stronger than you think." Seth breaks the awkward silence, and I instantly decide that he will forever be my friend.

"Rahab doesn't like him," Zelle announces without looking at me, like I'm not even standing there.

"I'll consider him," Boleyn says. "But I prefer Marcus."

"Me too," says another girl.

Axe laughs. "Well, you girls figure it out and pair before tomorrow's feast. Assuming you hold your places in my group after the Arena."

The girls exchange glances among themselves and tell Axe that they will. It sounds like their place in our group is not set in stone. Can the girl performing in the Arena somehow take their place? And how would they settle the dispute about the Pairing, anyway? Arm wrestle? Fire summoning contest? Maybe I should have said something better about myself, like Marcus did…

The group continues discussing which tower to attack in the Scouring. I learn that of the six girls, three of them are already paired: Melissa with Axe, Jacana with Khan, and a cute freckled girl named Amy with Seth. That leaves three girls who need to pair: Boleyn, Zelle, and Bea. They all want Marcus. Or maybe whatever boy takes Jafari's place and joins us. No one wants me.

The stairs down to the Arena bring back memories. Last time I was at the back, with Seymour and Marcus. My Mom had been performing, and I tried to use my power before Rahab shut me down. But my Mom picked me as the winner anyway. Our time together was too short.

We're halfway down the stairs when I turn to Marcus behind me. "You didn't tell me about Black. What was it like?"

"Not bad," he says.

"How was it different?" I ask.

"In every way."

So…he doesn't want to talk about it. I get that. He rarely wants to talk about anything. I try yes or no questions.

"Did you start in Black?" I ask.

"As far as I know."

"So you didn't have any memories when you showed up there?"

"None."

"Did you gain any powers there?"

He doesn't answer. His face is blank, but not hard to read. He's not going to talk about it.

We enter the Arena and Axe leads us to a designated area for the Scouring group. He tells us that it's the same rule as usual: no boys from our group can enter the Arena. It would be beneath us. This is training ground for the up and comers, a way for lower levels to impress a girl and get paired. I learn that tonight two girls will perform. First a girl from the Scouring group, like my Mom. She is allowed to choose a boy to replace Jafari. Then—the part that I missed after I got knocked out trying to reach my Mom—a girl who has not made the Scouring group gets a chance to impress the Alpha. If she's spectacular, he can pick her to take another girl's place in our group.

"That's how Rose got into the Scouring," Axe says. "Our last Alpha couldn't resist picking her. Too bad she couldn't save him in the Scouring. And this last time she couldn't save herself." He looks to his pair, Melissa. "Lesson learned?"

"Yes, stick with me," Melissa says, spinning the large ruby ring on her finger. "Would you be the Alpha without me?"

"Fair enough." Axe smiles. "Just don't get captured."

"That won't happen," she replies, glancing to me, "as long as we keep our Scouring team strong."

Rahab welcomes everyone and announces the rules. The competition will go just like it did before. The boys around the Arena look eager. The girls look disinterested, but a little nervous.

Zelle takes center stage first. She starts summoning little fireballs that could fit in her palm, and juggling them. She summons more and more, until she has at least a dozen fireballs whipping up and down in a blur.

Boys spring into action. At least twenty of them drop over the wall and into the Arena. One of them is Hank. He's a head taller than most of the boys, and fast. He ignores the weapons scattered around the sandy pit. He races toward the raised platform in the center. He closes to within ten steps before another boy trips him from behind with a staff.

Both of them go down on the sand. Other boys charge ahead, trampling over Hank like mad bulls. As I watch him rise slowly to his feet, then fall back to his knees, I wonder if it's always like this when you put the male species around a single female. The males compete until she knows who leads the pack.

When it's over, bodies litter the Arena. Most are still moving, but keeping their distance from a large boy who stands before Zelle with an axe slung over his shoulder. Rahab appears beside Zelle and whispers with her. Zelle walks away with the boy who won by reaching her first. That must be the normal way of things. It makes me appreciate even more that my Mom picked me even though I didn't win.

A group of boys—who must be assigned the cleanup task—clear away the remnants of the first fight, including the bodies that didn't rise. Hank manages to stagger out on his own. The crowd begins to chant for another performance.

A new girl moves to the center platform. She sings and summons fire. Her voice is magnificent, but her flames are very weak. They drift up only a few feet before fading away.

"Not spectacular," Axe decides, before the girl has even finished. "I'll keep looking."

# 19

THE NEXT DAY, Hank is nowhere to be seen. The rest of us wake in the Barracks and go about our daily tasks. I report to the training ground and receive a fine collection of bruises from Seth, Khan, and Marcus. At least they seem to take it easy on me. Khan and Marcus go at each other hard, but they end in a draw. No other boys show up, so Zelle must not have chosen the Arena winner for our group. Or maybe Rahab has someone else in mind. Either way, once we finish the training, I'm free to roam around the tower, looking for Emma and Hank.

I get lost and find my way back to the Barracks and the Feasting Hall a dozen times. It gives me a better sense of how the place is laid out. Unlike the Blue Tower with its hollow core and long path winding up, the Red Tower has stairs and twisting corridors everywhere. Many doors in the highest parts of the tower are locked. I figure they lead to the girls' quarters. There's no sign of my two friends.

The horns bellow and everyone reports to the Feasting Hall again. The meal and the task assignments go about the same as the day before. Everyone treats me like the runt.

Axe mentions something about his servants, which piques my interest. When I ask him who the servants are, he tells me that it's none of my business. He could be hiding Emma, keeping her locked away. It makes me want to blast him with the wind again, but that's not an option in the Red Tower. I need some other way to knock him off his throne.

After another trip down to the Arena, with more boys charging each other like bulls and another girl not meeting Axe's standards, we report back to the Barracks and sleep. I dream that I'm operating on a brain to remove a tumor. The patient survives. The tumor was not malignant.

In the morning, the boys form a line to head out for their tasks. Hank stands near the back. He must have come while we slept.

I rush to him before the Barracks door opens. "Hank, you're back!" I say, noticing that he has a black eye the size and color of a plum. "Everything okay?"

"Good as ever, my friend." He clasps my shoulder, appraising me. "How about you? You look rough."

"I'm fine," I say. "Just took some hits on the training ground. What happened to you after the Arena?"

He rubs the collar at his neck. "I woke up in a nice room by a fire. A sweet girl named Apple was there. She served me food, bandaged up a couple cuts. She told me I'd gotten trampled in the Arena."

"I saw that. It looked bad."

"Eh, I've had worse." He waves off the concern. "Anyway, Apple and I talked a lot. I told her all about the

Blue Tower, and how you led us in the Scouring. Last night she told me it was time for me to go. A boy came and brought me here to the Barracks with all of you chumps."

"Did you pair with Apple?" I ask.

"No. It's no big deal. She said she was still thinking about it."

"Well I'm glad you're back. Do you have a task today?"

"Number sixteen. Pig duty."

"At least it's safe," I say, suddenly wondering if I can join him. Feeding pigs sounds better than another round of bruises on the training ground. And I want to hear from Hank what happened in Blue after I left.

I tell Hank to wait a minute and find Khan at the front of the line of boys. He grunts at my request but agrees to let me have a rest day, just this once, since we still have four days until the Scouring. Maybe he can see my bruises need healing, or he thinks training me to fight is pointless.

When I return to Hank, he's with the two other boys who have pig duty: Seymour and Jafari. They are talking together, smiling, and making a very odd pair. Seymour is short, rotund, and has the pinkish hue of hot-washed skin. Jafari is tall, lean, and dark as a panther. But their shoulders and their smiles are both wide. Hank is taller than both but just as jovial. The three of them make a merry band.

Hank and Seymour introduce me to Jafari, which is awkward. Then Seymour starts prattling on about pigs in the way that only he can. He says we'll be feeding them, washing them, making sure they're happy. Then he starts speaking about the pigs by name. He says his favorite is

Chuck.

The line of boys begins to file out. The Barracks opens to a hallway, where most of the boys head up. We head down. Seymour leads the way, talking non-stop. Jafari and Hank talk in front of me.

"Hey, you." The voice comes from an open doorway as we pass. It's Jacana, Jafari's sister. She's pointing at him.

He stops and instinctively straightens, shoulders back. "Who are you?"

"Jacana," she says. "You had pig duty?"

He nods. "My first task."

"Consider it revised," she says. "I need help with something. You look like the right fit. What's your name?"

"Jafari. Or so I've been told."

"A good name. A fresh mind. We can work with that." Jacana looks to me. "What are you doing here?"

"Khan gave me the day off," I say. "So I'm helping them."

"With pigs…" she says, like it's an insult. "No wonder Rahab said you're off limits."

"What's that supposed to mean?" I ask.

"Girls have their ways." She winks at me, then grabs Jafari by the hand. "You boys enjoy the pigs."

She leads Jafari away. He's docile as a child by her side. *Docile, the same Jafari who fought Marcus!* It's amazing how getting wiped can change people. Maybe we do need a reset every once in a while.

"Where are they going?" Hank asks.

"No clue," I say. "These halls and corridors weave all

through the tower."

"We'll miss him!" Seymour says, motioning for us to start moving. "But the pigs await. We should be getting close. Can't be much further. The stones are getting darker. Maybe we'll take the next right. Then we'll smell them. Oh, you'll think it smells bad, but there's something rich and living and natural about the pigs. You'll learn to like it. Takes some getting used to, the manure especially. But they…"

Seymour talks more as we walk. He gets into pig anatomy and eating habits. I think about Jacana and Jafari. How is she going to help him remember? Just tell him everything he needs to know? She could pick and choose anything. She could shape his mind and his reality, like treating someone with amnesia. *Respect the mind.* If Emma has been wiped, I want to be the one to help her remember.

"Smell that?" Seymour says, taking a big sniff. "Almost there!"

He leads us around a few more turns and into a long, open room. The smell is sickly sweet, and so potent that I have to keep my shirt over my nose to avoid gagging. There's a path down the middle, and along the sides are dozens of pens. We walk the length and I count four or five pigs per pen. That means there are hundreds of the animals in the room. It smells like more.

At the far end, the room extends onto a muddy terrace open to the sky. There's no door or wall separating it from the rest of the room, so a steady breeze blows in and out, making the stench a little lighter near the fresh air.

"You guys mind if I clean?" Seymour says. "I did it yesterday and I think I'm getting the hang of it. All you'll need to do is feed them. You fill up the containers there." He points to a trough full of slop. "And dump them out in each pen. Remember, Chuck, the biggest black pig, he eats *a lot*."

"Got it." I look to Hank and he nods.

Seymour springs into action, as much as Seymour can spring into anything.

Hank and I move to the huge trough. The containers are hollow clay bowls. Hank and I each dip them into the slop, and with the scoop of mushy, mixed food inside, the bowl becomes very heavy. This is going to be a long day, but at least we can talk.

"When did you last see Emma?" I ask.

"In the Scouring." He pauses, heavy bowl in his hands. "She took a hard hit. We were both surrendering, but we got caught between the Black and Red teams. Never a good place to be."

I should have been there. I could have protected her. "Who did it?"

"Easy there," Hank says. "No need to kill anybody over it. Even if she got wiped, she'll get her memories back, just like we all do."

"Who did it?" I ask again.

"The Alpha."

"Max. I knew it. He wouldn't answer when I asked about her." My mind races through the possibilities. *Is she his servant? Has she been wiped?* The thought of Axe barking orders at Emma makes me sick to my stomach.

"What are you going to do about it?" Hank asks.

"I'm going to knock him off his throne."

"Same old Cipher." Hank smiles. "But in case you forgot, he's a lot bigger than you…and you can't use you powers here."

"You heard about that?"

"Sure did," he says. "The first night in the Feasting Hall everyone was talking about some boy from Blue who blew all the fires out. Apparently, the woman who leads this tower doesn't like you very much."

"It's not that simple," I say. But maybe Hank's right. Why else would Rahab tell the girls that I'm off limits? "She *has* let me stay in the Scouring group."

"Is that a good thing?" Hank asks.

"I don't know." I pour out a bowl of slop into a pen and watch the pigs battle for prime eating position. "I can't just fight Max," I say. "I need to think of some other way."

*What makes him tick?* I've learned more about the guy. He was in Blue, and on earth, he was in China. He said it was thousands of years after the Romans. Maybe he lived around the time I did. He'd proudly told Marcus that he'd owned casinos and won bets. Maybe I could use that.

"Anything I can do to help?" Hank asks.

I smile. "It helps a lot just knowing you're here. At least somebody has my back."

"You got that right," he says. "Now, could you fill up that bowl and help me feed some pigs?"

As we work, Hank gives me an update on the Blue Tower. Not much has changed. Kiyo, my first friend in this place, was doing well the last time Hank saw her. She made it to third class pretty fast, after she caught a boy from Black. She was not in the Scouring when Hank and Emma got captured. Blue's numbers have been hovering around 144. "You got the momentum going in Blue," Hank says. "I'm sure you'll do the same here. Hey, what's Red's motto?"

"Not sure." I remember what Rahab always says in the Feasting Hall. "It might be: *Let passion burn.*"

"Eh, doesn't have the same ring to it," Hank says.

"Maybe if I'm the Alpha I can start something new."

Hank laughs. "Only a matter of time."

<h1 style="text-align:center">20</h1>

THE BELLOWING HORNS wake me. The boys in the Barracks begin to rise and wash up and form a line before the door. We find our groups by task. There's a new boy to take Jafari's place for pig duty. He says his name is Nigel. He looks about as weak as I am. Jafari has been promoted to task number 7: Runner. He's learned Jacana is his sister. He's learned what Marcus did. It won't be pretty if they fight again.

Khan, Seth, Marcus, and I spend the day on the training ground. It's just the four of us because Axe doesn't show up, and Rahab still hasn't assigned a sixth boy to our group. As we train, I manage to stay on my feet for a while, but Khan takes me down with a staff to the side of the head. Seth makes quicker work of me, with an elbow to my right eye. I'll have a black shiner to match Hank's. After that, Marcus pulls me aside and shows me how to hold a sword. The blisters on my hands begin turning into calluses.

At sundown we go again to the Feasting Hall, and then the Arena. This time the performer is Apple, the girl who took care of Hank after he got trampled. She has a clear voice and a single, razor-thin flame that stretches to the ceiling. Only six boys go after her. It's the fewest I've seen, but before anyone has even reached her, Axe says, "I want her with us."

And just like that Apple joins the Scouring group, taking Bea's place. Apple hardly seems impressive enough for the change, but this is completely up to the Alpha's discretion. Unless he is only doing what Rahab says. Whatever is behind it, no one reveals anything to me. The girls remain a total mystery. I pick up only bits and pieces from the boys' bantering. No girl has hinted anything to me about Pairing. They just watch me get pummeled on the training ground. *You're off limits*, Jacana said. Or I'm just the runt.

The horns blast to dismiss us from the Arena.

We sleep.

The horns wake us. My body protests at getting out of bed, with bruised muscles, a bruised ego, and an eye nearly swollen shut. But there's no choice. It's the training ground again, and again. We train, we feast, we sleep.

Each day after training, with my tiny window of free time, I head out of the Barracks on a mission to find Axe's quarters and, I hope, Emma. Axe of course won't tell me where to go. My attempts to follow him fail, because the boys are required to return to the Barracks immediately after the Arena each night. I ask around but no one seems to know, or want to tell me, how to find Axe. One boy says to me, *Just keep going up*. I try that but find myself circling round and round the same reddish pathways carved into stone. The low ceilings make the tower feel like a maze of tunnels with flames burning on torches every twenty feet.

Marcus is the only one who gives me useful information about Axe. He tells me the Alpha wanted to talk to him because of his memories of the Roman Colosseum. Marcus said he didn't know many details, but apparently Axe had been a very wealthy man in China. He had four daughters who loved to watch fights in the replica Colosseum. One of his daughters had fallen for one of the fighters. Axe had placed a large bet against the fighter his daughter loved. He had won the bet, but she'd found out about it. Marcus said that whatever happened, it must have ended badly, because Axe became very upset and refused to talk more of the story. This all confirmed an idea formulating in my mind: to avoid a fight against Axe by drawing him into a bet.

But time is running short. We have only two days before the Scouring.

I head out exploring again after we finish training. When I circle around to the Feasting Hall for the seventh time, with its dozens of doors leading out, a girl is there in a red dress. I ask her for directions to the Alpha. She points to one of the hallways leading out. "You turn right there, then go up there, then right again there, and then you're there, or something like that."

I follow her directions and get lost again. I'm not even sure how to get back, so I start heading down instead of up. When I finally get back to the Barracks, it is empty. The boys are out doing their tasks. I sit on the bed and wait and think. Jafari shows up in the doorway a while later.

"Cipher," he calls out. "You seen Khan?"

"No, sorry," I say. "We finished training already. He could be anywhere."

"If you see him, tell him the Alpha wants to see him." Jafari leaves as quickly as he entered.

*The Alpha wants to see him.*

I jump off the bed and rush after Jafari. He's turning a corner when I leave the Barracks. I follow him as fast as I can but there's no way I can keep up. He's too fast. No one else is around. This seems like my best chance. I feel desperate.

Before I even consider what I'm doing, I summon the wind. Only a little at first, giving me a boost in speed from behind. Rahab does not appear.

I turn the corner after Jafari just quick enough to see his next turn. I keep the wind blowing at my back, whipping over my head, and at my back again, in a small, contained loop. It's enough to keep me within the same distance from Jafari. It's enough to remind me how much I've missed this power.

After a long pursuit, I make another turn only to find a dead-end tunnel with Jafari nowhere to be seen. Veins of faint gold line the walls, and specks of red rubies glitter in the torchlight. I'd passed this alcove before but thought nothing of it.

The entrance must be here.

I release the wind and enter the alcove to inspect the

far wall. There's a small flame, the size of my fingernail, in the center of the wall. The color blends with the red stone almost flawlessly. It's only visible up close.

I press my finger against the small outline of a flame. It is warm to the touch. Then I put my whole hand over it. My eyes close. It is so quiet. Envisioning the flame, I begin to weave air into it.

A touch on my shoulder startles me. The power slips away. I turn around and find Rahab standing directly in front of me, arms crossed. I stagger back but bump against the wall.

She must have appeared out of thin air.

"Thought I wouldn't notice?" she asks, staring down at me like she could shoot fireballs out of her eyes.

I swallow, heat rushing to my cheeks. "Notice what?"

"Don't play stupid with me."

"I need to find Axe."

"You see him every day in the Feasting Hall and the Arena."

"Are these his quarters?" I ask. "Where his servants are?"

"You want to find her that badly?" Rahab sees right through me. But for once she doesn't seem angry about what she sees. "You're willing to risk getting reset for her?"

I hadn't thought of it that way, but… "Yes."

Her hand moves forward, between us. A small flame surges from her pinkie finger, and another from her thumb, like two candles being lit. The two flames join a few inches above her palm and coil together into a bright blaze. The heat from the fire warms my face.

"Your instincts are…advanced," she says. "It usually takes those from Blue the longest to learn that two are stronger than one. How did you meet this girl?"

"Abram told me to capture her in my first Scouring."

"I see." She looks past me, at the sealed door, as if this information has revealed something so important that she's momentarily forgotten I'm standing in front of her, guilty of summoning the wind in her tower.

Maybe Rahab, powerful as she is, doesn't know everything. When I heard Abram talking with Daniel, the leader of the Green Tower, it was clear they spoke rarely. She might not know that Abram thinks I'm some sort of chosen one. She knows about my power over the wind and my scar, but what if she doesn't know…

"Abram told me other things," I say. "He said that Blue had never had a student as strong as I am. He said that I'm the first to bring the towers to 720 total and to make equilibrium possible."

"Yes, I know." Rahab does not look impressed. "Do you have any idea *why* you have more power than others?"

"I…no." I'd asked myself this many times in the Blue Tower, but now I almost take it for granted.

"It's nothing to be proud of," Rahab says. "Your capacity for power, like everyone else's, is precisely equal to the gap between your highest potential and your lowest failings. So, tell me Cipher, what *could* you have done on earth…and what *did* you do?"

I cannot answer. I am transfixed by this concept, this

question. I had thought I was special. But now I see that I am no different than I was—the same Dr. Fitzroy who thought that he was better than everyone else, that they needed me and my talents. The truth is…I'm powerful because…I'm the biggest disappointment to ever enter the five towers.

"Now you see," Rahab whispers. "To whom much is given, much is required."

My head hangs. "I've made many mistakes."

Her hand clasps my shoulder, hot to the touch. "Don't be so cold," she says, "be thankful you are here. You don't deserve it, but you still have great potential. Sometimes those who have made the worst mistakes become capable of the greatest deeds. Do not underestimate the Scouring. It can close any gap and open the doors to the White Tower and make all this worth it. You understand?"

I look up and meet her fiery eyes. "Yes."

"Good. First, however, you must be paired."

I glance back at the hidden entrance to Axe's quarters. Knowing the source of my power does not change my goal. "Can I pair with Emma?" I ask. "We are strong together. We've captured many in the Scouring. We'll fight for Red."

Rahab grins in amusement as she shakes her head. "Emma is the Alpha's servant. Someone else will pair with you."

"Who?"

"She will summon you."

"But—"

Rahab holds out her hand, cutting me off. "You are lucky I have decided, one last time, to forgive your violation of my rules. You will accept this Pairing, and you will serve the Red Tower. Save your power for the Scouring."

"I can use it there?"

"Yes," she says. "It is outside my domain. But the Alpha will not take kindly to you overshadowing him."

I stand up straighter. I'm not being demoted or wiped, and maybe this is how I can challenge Axe. If only I could have Emma and Hank with me. "How do you choose who goes into the Scouring?"

"It can be done many ways," Rahab says, dodging my question. "Eleven have been chosen. The Alpha, the six most powerful girls, and four boys."

"So we still need another boy."

"You have someone in mind?"

"Hank," I say. "From Blue."

"Tell me why."

"He's as strong as any boy here. He would be a great asset to our team."

"Very thoughtful," Rahab muses. "You at least try to sound loyal to Red. But the Alpha is responsible for leading our team into the Scouring. He decides how to use our— how did you put it—*assets*."

"Is there any other way? Maybe I didn't live up to my potential on earth, but I want to try here."

She looks surprised, but not upset. "There is one possibility. It has been many Scourings since such a thing has been tried. The consequences can be…serious."

"I'll risk whatever it takes."

"Very well. If you could convince the Alpha to share his leadership, I will not intervene. See, I am not like Abram, always meddling. He likes things cold, clinical, and controlled. Suitable for a neurosurgeon, you might say. Here you must pursue your passions to understand them, just as everyone else does. Tell me Paul Fitzroy, what is the effect of boys' competition over a girl?"

Her question leads me straight to the memory of Johnny and Samantha on the dock of Lake Michigan. I was no threat to Johnny, but it still felt like a competition. I became willing to do anything to get Samantha.

"The effect is passion," I say.

She smiles. "No boy is immune, not even the Alpha."

"You think he would agree to compete with me?"

She steps back, hand on her chin. "Over a girl, perhaps. Why, the Red Tower might benefit if you both lead teams and try to capture more than each other. If you convince the Alpha of the terms, I may even choose Hank to fill the final spot for the Scouring."

"Thank you," I say. "But…why are you helping me?"

"We leaders always seek the light, in our own ways. But don't ever let me catch you using your power in my tower again. My tolerance, even for you, has limits." She nods to the door behind me, which has opened without a sound. "Good luck in there."

She spins away and walks off without another word.

The open doorway leads to stairs going up. When I

enter, the door drops silently shut behind me. Red torchlight guides the way to the top of the stairs, where another door waits. This one is made of iron with rubies forming an intricate flame pattern in the center. It matches the door to the dragon at the bottom of the tower.

I press my ear to the door. The voices are muffled and faint, but I can tell they are close. It sounds like two girls on the other side of the door. I can't detect what they are saying, but one sounds just like Emma.

My heart thumps in my chest as I knock.

A narrow slit slides open at head-level, and two bright blue eyes appear.

# 21

"EMMA!" I SHOUT from outside the door.

Her eyes look surprised through the narrow slit. The opening quickly slides shut. Then the door begins to swing open, revealing a huge room. In the center there's a table with a feast spread over it. A fireplace crackles to the left, and on the wall to the right there's a rack of weapons, mostly axes, and an opening to another room.

Emma and another girl flank me as I enter. They both wear drab brown robes and silver collars around their necks, just like mine. They're the only girls I've seen in the Red Tower with collars. As I pass the table of food, I realize that the far end of the room has only open air where there would normally be a wall. There's no glass or window, just a gap from floor to ceiling with an expansive view of the other towers and the Scouring far below.

"Who are you?" asks the girl to my right. "And why are you here?" She has plain brown hair to match her drab brown robe. Her round face and green eyes remind me of Seymour.

I turn to Emma, on my other side. She's looking at me

151

like she's never seen me.

"Emma, it's me. Cipher."

She stares at me blankly.

*No, no, no.*

I clasp her shoulders and look into her eyes with desperation. "Emma, *Emma...* Do you remember anything?" I ask. "Do you remember the Yellow Tower? The Blue Tower? *Me?*"

"Why are you here?" she asks.

"I saw your name on the board... I came as soon as I could."

"My name?" she asks. "The board?"

"What are you doing?" This time it's Jafari's voice, loud and low as he enters the room through a door at the side. He hurries to me, fists clenched. "Did you follow me?"

I shrug innocently but don't answer.

He looms over me like giant. "*How* did you get in?" he demands. "The door only opens from inside."

"Rahab let me in," I say, my voice cracking only a little.

"You lie."

"I swear. I told her I wanted to find Axe's quarters. She opened the door."

Jafari shakes his head like he still doesn't believe it, but he steps past me. "Whatever, none of my business. I'm just a runner. You're the Alpha's problem." He leaves through the door and sprints down the stairs without another glance back.

"What business do you have with the Alpha?" Emma asks.

"It's about the Scouring," I say somberly.

Emma and the other girl exchange a look, then both nod.

"Come," Emma says. "The Alpha is this way."

We enter a smaller, round room. Like the larger antechamber, it has an expansive view over the towers and the Scouring. But instead of a completely open wall, there are five perfect squares revealing the view. Half of the room is a raised platform with a chair like a throne at the back. Axe sits there, leaning back with one leg draped over the throne's arm. He's still Max, the same boy from Blue. Even if he is the Alpha.

"So the wind-boy has come." He drops a red grape into his mouth. He takes his time chewing. "What do you want?"

Emma stands close by my side, and behind her, between the door and me, the other girl is now idly wielding a fireball above her palms. There's no retreating now. Axe will test me. He senses weakness.

"It's about the Scouring." I keep my voice easy. "Last time Red brought three back, and lost two, right?"

"The two we lost were weak." He sounds defensive.

"I thought one of them was the Alpha."

"A weak Alpha," he says. "Why do you think Red's numbers were dwindling?"

"Because Black is so strong."

"We're stronger, as long as we have a strong Alpha."

"How did Black take two of us last time?"

"They attacked with twelve at once," he says. "A full

force. We were fighting Blue. We'd caught a few, but when Black came, two didn't stay close enough."

"The old Alpha and Rose?"

"Like I said, they were weak. I had already captured three. We couldn't afford to lose more. Besides," he motions to Emma, "our new catch is quite something, don't you think?"

I look at Emma. She still registers zero recognition of me. It's devastating to see the face I know so well, but for her to see nothing.

"Can't keep your eyes off her!" Axe laughs.

When I turn back to him it's easy to keep my face blank, because I feel numb. "How did you capture her?"

"You know Blue," he says. "They always think they can outmaneuver us, think they're so smart. Maybe they are, but you'll learn here that sometimes strength and passion are all you need. No need to overthink things. This girl was near the front of the fight. I made a mad dash at her. She and a boy went down easily. All it took was a couple hits. They were easy as potato sacks to haul out of there." He lifts his arm, flexes his bare bicep, and sighs. "It was a good workout."

My pulse is rising, anger swelling. "You hit her?"

"Of course. Good thing I did, too. Otherwise she would have run away when Black's ambush came. But don't get yourself worked up. She got a clean slate when she began to serve me."

I glance at her, and the collar. Could this mean it wasn't a full reset? There's still so much I don't know. "The other boy who was caught from Blue wasn't wiped," I say to Axe. "Neither was I."

"Yeah, everyone knows that, wind boy. You're the first one to just waltz into the Red Tower without a fight. And now you're bringing back dragon teeth." He leans forward in his throne. "What's your secret? Going to *ride* a dragon next? Try to fight for my spot as Alpha?"

I smile, considering what to say. He's revealed a weakness. "I'll tell you," I say, "if you let me borrow your servant for a while."

He laughs. "You've got guts, kid. But I don't play games like that. You want something from me, you fight for it. You're in Red now, not Blue. Don't forget it."

"Fine. Then I have a challenge for you."

"Oh?" He stands and strides toward me. "You wanna go now?"

I hold my ground. "You think anybody will care if you fight me here, on your turf?"

He stops in front of me, with a snarl under his scraggly beard. "I'll beat you anywhere, any time."

*Got him.*

"Let's make it a bet," I say. "Neutral territory. In the next Scouring, you get six on your side, I get six on mine. Three pairs each. Whoever brings back the most captives wins."

He looks surprised. "You're serious?"

"Always."

"Why should I risk it?" he says. "I'm already the Alpha."

"And you can stay the Alpha either way. I just want your new servant."

He pauses, glancing at Emma. "What are you offering in return?"

"If I lose, then I'll be your servant."

He grins and reaches out his hand. "You're on."

We shake. He squeezes hard, making the bones in my hand groan for mercy. The expression on my face must be amusing, because Axe looks as pleased as I feel about our deal. Soon enough, one of us will be disappointed.

# 22

JAFARI IS WAITING for me when I return to the Barracks from the meeting with Axe. He tells me I've been summoned, just as Rahab warned. He leads me away through the winding red tunnels, mostly going up. We stop in front of an unmarked door in a long unmarked tunnel. Jafari knocks and the door opens.

A girl stands inside. She wears a red dress and has mousy brown hair and eyes. I recognize her as Apple, the one who took care of Hank, performed in the Arena, and got picked to join the Scouring group.

"Welcome Cipher," she says, with her hands folded in front of her. "Come in. Runner, you may go."

Jafari bows low, then races off. I follow Apple inside.

The room is small and simple. The walls are reddish, rough rock. Two chairs sit in front of a fire burning merrily in the hearth. It looks like my Mom's old room. It could even be the same room, except that the window looks over the mountains instead of the Scouring.

"Have a seat," Apple says. "You know why you're here."

She must be the one Rahab told me about. She's in the Scouring group, and she's not paired yet. I sit in the chair closest to the door. "You want to pair with me?" I ask.

"*Want* is not the right word, but it'll do." As she sits across from me, her brown hair bounces lightly on her shoulders. "I have chosen you."

"You didn't get many choices." I mean it as a joke but she doesn't smile. "So what now? Touch my collar?"

She blinks in surprise. "You know how it works?"

"I had a servant in the Blue Tower. She had to wear a silver link that looked just like this. It seems like these work the same way. You'll know what I'm feeling, and I'll have to do what you command. Right?"

"I think so. This will be my first Pairing since…"

"Since what?" I ask.

She looks down at her folded hands. "I was wiped."

"Oh, sorry."

"Don't be. It happens to all of us."

*Not me. Not yet.* But I don't say that. "Why did you choose me?" I ask.

"Your friend, Hank, told me about you, and what you did for Blue. The other girls look at you and see a weak body. They think your powers with the wind are no help to you here. Or they are intimidated. They've seen how you stand up to Rahab. Most boys in Red don't bring any powers with them. You might be the first, but…like I said, I don't remember much."

"Did you have any competition over me?"

Apple slowly she lifts one hand, palm up. Her eyes

concentrate. A flame the size of a peanut appears above her hand.

"This is the most I can make," she says softly.

"But I saw you in the Arena," I say. "You were controlling more than this."

"No." The flame above her hand extends up, thinning out like fine, glistening twine. "I can stretch the fire far, but that weakens the power. It wouldn't stop much in the Scouring. It wouldn't have stopped you when you were in Blue."

She lets the flame go out. The room goes dimmer.

She's right. I remember girls from Red in the Scouring, flinging fireballs the size of pumpkins. My wind overpowered them. But I also remember fighting in the Scouring when I didn't see any fire coming from Red. I still don't understand why. "How much difference is there between the girls' powers?" I ask.

"A lot."

"Why?"

She twiddles a ring on her right index finger. "I should not say."

"Did Rahab tell you not to?"

"Not exactly."

"Rahab told me our capacity for power equals the gap between our potential and what we did with it. Is that how it works?"

She spins the ring around and around. Her cheeks are red as if she's embarrassed. "We are not supposed to speak with boys about our ways."

I reach out and take her hand, then guide it to the metal band around my neck. "I've had a servant with a link. I know what it's like to be the master. You may be able to make me obey, but you'll also *feel* what I feel. Trust me, I'm not just going to be any boy to you. The more I know, the better we can work together. And if you have something sensitive to tell me, you should do it now before you have to *feel* my reaction. That can be very…uncomfortable."

She pulls her hand away and resumes the ring twiddling in her lap. Her cheeks are still flushed. My hopes sink, but then she says, "You will tell no one what I tell you."

"I promise. And you can enforce it."

"Okay," she sighs. "Here's what I know. Rahab says our power over flames depends on three factors. You are right about the first part. Our capacity—our upper limit— is set by the gap, as you put it."

"So, maybe you lived up to your potential?"

"I doubt it. I have no idea what my capacity for power is, because I know so little about my life before. That's the second factor. Our power over fire grows with passion, which grows with memories. The more we remember, the more power we wield."

"We can fix that, right?"

"The Pairing might help. I've tried looking into flames on my own and haven't seen much. But if I do learn more, that still leaves the last factor. It's the hardest to understand. It's for the whole Red Tower and depends on many things, like how united we are, how many dragon teeth we find, and how much passion we bring to our tasks.

Above all, the stronger our Pairings, the more fire the girls can wield. The six rings given to the girls of the Scouring group collectively determine this final factor."

"Fascinating," I say. This could explain why sometimes Red slings fire all over the Scouring, but other times resorts to nothing but axes. "Why doesn't Rahab explain this to everyone? Why keep it hidden from the boys?"

"It is not Rahab's role to explain this. The Alpha knows. Perhaps he says nothing because he is ashamed of our weakness now." Apple pauses, meeting my eyes. "You should know something."

"What?"

"I'm the weakest girl in the Scouring group."

"Really?" The word slips out before I can stop it. "How do you know?"

"The girls always know. I can't explain it. The rings give us the ability to tell who's strongest with the fire just by looking at each other. It's as easy as seeing which boy is the tallest in a room."

I have no reason to doubt her. She's the weakest. It explains her feeling embarrassed. But it doesn't make sense. Why would Axe pick her? *Unless…* He picked her when he knew I still needed a pair, and that none of the girls in the Scouring group wanted to pair with me. Rahab knew about this, too. She said a girl would summon me. Now Apple has done just that. It's sabotage.

"I understand if you don't want to pair with me," Apple says, still studying her hands and spinning the ring around her finger. "Like you said, we have little choice."

This can't be right. We do have a choice. I still have this body and heart and mind. And Axe has no right to his position—his "captures" were my friends sneaking into Red. He cannot beat me with tricks. Apple has some power. It will be enough.

"Look at me," I say.

She raises her head. There are tears in her gentle brown eyes.

"We will figure this out together," I say. "Between my power and yours, we are going to be the strongest pair. Okay?"

She smiles. "Hank said you were a natural leader, even if you pretended you didn't want to be."

*Hank.* He seems to believe in me more than I believe in myself. "So are you ready?" I ask.

"Yes. Can you scoot closer?"

I slide my chair beside hers. She reaches around the silver collar and places both hands on the back of it, at the nape of my neck. She leans her forehead against mine. Energy moves from her to me, and back. She smells sweet, like baked apples. I can't help but smile at the thought. *Apples.* Sweet, innocent, and always good. Maybe she is not the strongest with the fire, but she will be my pair.

Her arms suddenly stiffen. She tilts over and almost collapses to the floor. I manage to catch her fall and lay her gently on her back. She's still conscious, eyes open wide.

"What happened?" I say. "You okay?"

She looks to the side, glaring sternly into the fire. "I remember."

# 23

APPLE AND I sit beside each other in quiet for a long time. The three suns fall lower in the sky, beyond the mountains outside. We gaze into the fire together. It's easy to forget how many colors live in the flames. There's red, yellow, and orange. There's even blue where it burns hottest, near the coals. Despite how long I stare, this time no vision comes. The collar feels cool at my neck.

"I was in an orchard, an apple orchard," Apple says, breaking the silence, but with her eyes still on the fire. "The apples were red and round and large on the trees. They shined in the morning sun. I had a basket in my arm. I could feel the warm breeze out of the east as it grazed against my skin and as I picked them from the trees. I chose the best one to eat as I worked. It was larger than my fist. I savored each bite, so juicy and sweet, before stowing the half-eaten apple in a pocket of my white apron. I could see nothing but rows of trees, but I knew, somehow I knew, that my home was not far away, with my parents and my brothers, and that there was a village somewhere beyond that."

Apple winces at the memory. Her voice is barely audible above the crackling fire.

"The first change I noticed was the smell," she continues. "It came faintly on the wind. But it was unmistakable: *smoke*. There should not be this smell of smoke in the morning. But the smell passed, and I went back to picking my apples. My basket was almost full. It grew so very heavy, and I would fill it many more times this day. I walked back toward my home to unload this basket. And as I went a new smell came. It was smoke again, but metal, too. The sharp, intense smell of metal, like freshly oiled steel. Never had I smelled such metal. I quickened my pace but froze when I heard the scream. My mother's scream. She was shouting, *No, no, no!*

"I snuck forward. I saw them from a distance. Soldiers. I cannot remember their faces, only their dark uniforms and their black boots. There was more shouting, then gunshots. They dragged the bodies to the ground outside our home. One of my brothers ran, but he fell, too. And all of it washed over me like a fire as I looked down at my basket of apples. They were so red, blood red."

Apple's chin falls to her chest. She takes deep breaths.

"You don't have to continue…" I say softly.

But she does.

"There was a small shed. It was close to me, so I hid inside. Thin columns of sunlight shined through the slits in the shed's wooden walls. There were baskets and pruning shears and sprays for the trees. We had begun storing our apples there. To protect our harvest, like always, we had small containers on the ground in each corner, where we kept rat poison. I gathered it up, every last drop. I used the shears, delicately, to poke little holes in the apples in my basket. I poured the poison into every one. My hand didn't even shake as I did it. I was more careful than I had ever been in my life. When I was done, I huddled in the corner, hugging my knees, staying as quiet as I could. A hard voice outside said something I did not understand, but the language was familiar, Russian, I thought, and it sounded like orders being given. Then boots clopped away, but some steps drew closer. A shadow passed and blocked the sunlight coming through the slits. I closed my eyes, wishing to be anywhere else.

"The door suddenly kicked opened, and a single soldier was there, gun raised. He saw me immediately. I will never forget the look in his eyes, like a rat chancing upon a fresh apple. I hated that look. I hated him. There was nowhere to run. Instead I rose slowly and lifted an apple and held it out to him. The soldier hesitated, but then he stepped past me, took an apple from the basket, and bit into it fiercely. He chewed, swallowed, and took another bite. He ate down to the core, watching me the whole time with a hungry look in his eyes. After he tossed the apple to the ground, he grabbed me and dragged me outside. No one was left. I screamed for help but no one came. The ravenous look in his eyes began to change, going pale and weak. He raised his gun at me and shouted something. I only smiled as he fell on the ground, twitching once or twice before going as still as a dead rat. I hid in the orchard until dark."

Apple turns to me for the first time since she began her story. The intensity of her eyes makes me swallow. Her lips are pressed into a tight white line. "They took everyone I loved," she says. "I hated men after that."

"I'm so sorry." I don't know what else to say. Her words make me feel defensive, even though I hadn't done anything wrong, not to her. Maybe I wasn't honest to my wife, or to Samantha, but it was nothing like what those soldiers did. Apple glares at me like I did it. She's a completely different person than before this memory. She should know I'm on her side.

"It doesn't have to be like that here," I say. "I will protect you."

"I protect myself," she snaps. "I know what you're feeling. You think you're innocent. But there's something boiling inside you. You see, Cipher, no men are innocent. Now, tell me what you remember."

I shake my head, trying to protest. Her command comes through the link, squeezing like a vice, constricting my thoughts and forcing my mouth open, my tongue to speak.

The whole story comes tumbling out.

I tell her how my dad left my mom and me, how much that hurt growing up. I tell her about finding my mom here in the Red Tower and losing her. Then come the harder parts: Dr. Paul Fitzroy, the arrogant neurosurgeon, the absent father, the cheater. I tell her about Samantha. She was the pretty girl in high school, the one out of my reach. So when I clawed my way to success and riches, she was the one I wanted and got. She was a conquest, a trophy. And nothing would have stopped me.

When I finish, my mouth is dry. My soul aches.

"See, I am right," Apple says. "No man is innocent."

She issues another command through the link. It is an order to stand and step away from her. I have no choice but to do what she wills. I move to the door, staring at her in shock. I thought I knew her. I expected some understanding. I was wrong. But she's wrong, too, in shoving me out.

"We weren't meant to be alone," I say, meeting her eyes.

"We'll see, Dr. Fitzroy. We're stuck together for now." She turns away and stares into the fire as she orders me to leave, without saying a word.

# 24

HANK GETS THE sixth Scouring spot. When we arrive in the Feasting Hall, the rock with his name sits beside mine at the front of the long table. It surprises everyone but me. Apple watches all this across the table. She doesn't let me speak a word to her. She doesn't smile the entire evening.

Pairing goes better for Hank. The next morning, the final day before the Scouring, he tells me about it on the training ground. He says his pair, Zelle, is nice and hasn't commanded him to do anything yet. I tell him he's lucky, but that's all Apple will let me say about it. She's with the other girls on the balcony above, watching us. I want to hide somewhere. Hank waves at Zelle with a smile.

During the training Hank manages to knock Seth down twice, and Khan once. They knock him down more than that, but it's better than I can do. No one knocks Marcus down. He hardly bothers trying with me. Normally I'm mincemeat for him. Today I'm even worse. My time with Apple makes my feet sluggish on the red clay. I want to shout up to her: *I've changed, I'm not like Dr. Fitzroy or the soldiers you saw.* True or not, Apple won't let me shout. She'll just let me fight and collect my daily bruises.

After the training, Hank and I stay outside. The other boys leave. The girls walk away from the balcony, and no commands come from Apple. It is a rare moment of quiet. The cool breeze blowing from the mountains makes me feel more alive.

"Nice work today," I say to Hank. "I knew you were strong, but didn't know you could use a weapon."

"Not really. Plenty of room to improve." Hank shrugs his broad shoulders. "It's different from digging with a hoe."

"Is that what you used to do?" I ask, remembering what he told me when we were both in the Blue Tower. He was an American like me, but centuries earlier.

"I did my fair share of digging," he says. "Hey, when you paired with Apple, did you see more memories?"

"Hers but not mine," I say.

"Oh." He looks surprised. "I saw both."

*Interesting.* It had been odd when no vision came while I stared into the fire. Perhaps Apple wouldn't let me see? But Zelle would let Hank?

"What did you learn?" I ask him.

He gazes out over the mountains. "I was on the run."

"From what?"

"I told you before about my traveling, city to city, teaching and preaching. Remember?"

"Yes. You always put your horse first."

Hank laughs. "An itinerant preacher without a horse

was a dead preacher in those days." His smile fades. "But I didn't remember why I was traveling so much, living such a hard life. Now I do." He shakes his head, eyes closed.

I've never seen Hank so serious. "Want to talk about it?" I ask.

"Sure, if you don't mind," he says. "I figure that's the whole point of remembering. We tell it again to expose the memory. That weakens its hold over us. Promise you'll still be my friend, no matter what I say?"

"Of course, Hank." I try not to sound as interested as I suddenly am.

"I had the most wonderful neighbor," he begins. "We lived in the foothills of North Carolina—that was in America, where you lived, but centuries earlier, before the revolution. Our town had about sixty people, a single church with a tall white steeple, and good soil. We grew what we needed. I raised a little tobacco and was pretty good with leather, repairing shoes and saddles. But I was one of the wilder ones. I fermented the peaches and the apples, made the cider for the cold winter nights. Some didn't appreciate it. But I wasn't married and didn't have any kids, so it wasn't much harm, or so I thought."

"What happened?"

"Well, my neighbor, he was a better man than I was. We'd grown up together. We'd fished and set traps for rabbits in the forest. When he found himself a good young wife, I was the best man in his wedding. I helped him build a nice three-room house just down the road from mine, and he and his wife began to fill it up in no time. They had two daughters, cutest little girls you can imagine, with big brown puppy dog eyes. They'd stop by my place with their mother and I'd give them each a piece of taffy. Their mother was something special. I'll tell you, for a single man like me in the foothills, there wasn't anything finer than a visit from her. She was radiant and sweet as the peaches I grew. Problem was, maybe she liked to visit me, too, when her husband, my friend, was traveling. He had to go a long way sometimes. At first he'd leave for a week, but then he got into politics, being the good man he was, and he'd have to travel to the state capital for a month. You can imagine how hard that was for his young wife. She started visiting more often. It started small, like those little taffy gifts. But then it became more. We'd do anything to stay warm on those cold winter nights, you see? And a little brandy with a friend by the fire, now that was warm, too warm…"

*Cold winter nights. Like Samantha and me in Toronto.* "I understand."

"This is all bad enough, I know," Hank continues. "But nobody knew until a stranger came to visit our little town. It wasn't anything unusual, just a man passing through and trading some things. I exchanged a few bottles of my strong cider for a nice hide of leather. Others made their own deals. Later that night he must have gotten into the drink, and a fight broke out. Somebody drew a gun and things ended, well, the way things ended when a gun and drinking get involved. The next morning they went on the search for the murderer. Whoever had done it was long gone. They came to me and asked, *Where were ya last night?*"

"My, oh my," Hank sighs, running his hands through his hair, "that wretched question sealed my fate. I had nothing to do with the man getting shot, and that's the truth, but I couldn't tell them where I was that night. I just couldn't. And that's because I was in the arms of my best friend's wife."

His head drops. He sniffles and rubs at his eyes. When he looks up, he surprises me with a smile. "I messed up real bad, you see. Honor and my conscience left me no option but to leave. The whole town—except for her—figured I was the murderer. So I picked up right away and rode off. I brought nothing with me but a pair of boots, the clothes on my back, a horse, and the good Lord's book. I skipped around for a while, until I met a Methodist preacher. I didn't tell him what I'd done, of course, and he took a liking to me. He told me whatever my sins were, they would be forgiven and that I could work for the Lord. Well that was sweet music to my ears. So I got to work. Not that I could make up for what I did. I know that now. And now you know."

I clasp his shoulder. "And you're still my friend, Hank."

"Thanks, Cipher," he says. "It feels good to tell it. Real good."

# 25

"WE SHOULD EAT here more often." Seth stands by the open window, looking out over the Scouring as night falls. A cool breeze blows into the warm room, ruffling his orange hair. All six boys in the Scouring group are here: Axe, Khan, Seth, Marcus, Hank, and me.

"Bah," Khan says. "We'd be too soft."

The other boys laugh. Khan has a point. The room is decadent, unlike anything else in the Red Tower, or the Blue Tower for that matter. The twelve chairs around the large round table have lush red cushions, and the ceiling and walls are framed in wood and lined with gold. The ceiling has a fresco painting of the Red Tower, with a dragon soaring above it and a woman with flames dancing above her hands. A twelve-armed candelabra burns brightly at the center of the table. The plates are porcelain white. The cutlery and chalices are gold.

The door to this dining room was always locked before. Apparently we dine here instead of the Feasting Hall on the eve of the Scouring. It's a high honor, getting to plan for battle here. For tonight, Axe and I have agreed: first we will pick teams. Three pairs each. Then each of us can plan whatever strategy he wants.

The six girls, our pairs, arrive not long after we do.

"Welcome!" Axe greets.

As soon as Apple walks in, at the back of the group, she issues an order through the link, commanding me to smile. I obey, and as I meet her eyes I understand. She wants—she demands—that we reveal nothing of what happened between us. What we must convey to the others is that everything is awesome. We are a pair. Synced and happy and ready to fling fireballs. I'm actually glad to obey this time.

Everyone finds their assigned seats, designated by the same rocks used in the Feasting Hall. Apparently the rocks follow us, or we follow the rocks. The pairs sit together. Melissa with Axe, Jacana with Khan, Amy with Seth, Boleyn with Marcus, Zelle with Hank, and Apple with me. At the round table we are equals, except that Axe's chair, the Alpha position, has a higher back with ornate carvings of flames along the top.

A team of boys enters the room with food. This must be their task. The feast they set before us, for the first time in the Red Tower, is not just pork and beans. There's roasted meat, fish, bread, vegetables, and fruit. It's like they brought something from every tower. Which seems impossible.

Axe raises his golden chalice. "To victory."

We toast with him and begin to eat. The group chats happily in small groups, as if unconcerned about what will happen tomorrow. I try to finalize my plan. It's not complicated. Axe and I will pick three pairs each. He gets to pick first. The big question is whether he will pick Boleyn and Marcus. If he does, then I should probably take Seth. Khan is stronger, but Seth and Amy together seem more powerful than Khan and Jacana. Besides, I like Seth more. It's risky not to pick Hank first, but surely Axe would take Seth or Khan over him. He barely knows Hank, and from what I can gather, Zelle is treated about like Apple—as if she's weak.

The plates are nearly empty when Axe bangs his chalice on the table. Every eye turns to him.

"We'll be doing things differently this time," he says. "Pairings will stay the same, but we are going to divide for the Scouring."

"Divide?" Boleyn asks. "What do you mean?"

"I will lead three pairs," Axe says, "and Cipher will lead the other three."

Boleyn's face is inscrutable, except for a slight lifting of her brow. "Has Rahab agreed to this?"

"She has not objected." Axe sips casually from his chalice. "Each group of six will still try to capture as many in the Scouring as possible, like always."

"Even if we *could* do this," Zelle says, tension thick in her voice. "Why would we want to? We'll be weaker if we split up."

"Especially whoever ends up with the wind boy," Jacana says. "I refuse to be on his team."

Axe looks to me across the table. I was not expecting

this. Maybe I won't get to choose my team after all, if some of them refuse to join me. Does that mean I need to give some inspiring speech? A pep talk? If that's what it takes to win Emma back, then so be it.

"I've captured many in the Scouring," I say. "Outside this tower, I will use my power and—"

*Silence.*

It's a command from Apple.

I stare at her wildly, desperately. She knows exactly how I feel, and she's not budging.

"Cipher's right," Hank says, looking at me with confusion. I nod meaningfully to Apple, and he seems to understand. "He has more power than you'd believe. He can stop all of your flames. He can drag people out of the Scouring without lifting a finger. Trust me, you *want* to be on his side."

"I like this plan," Marcus says. "You've all heard Rahab. We need to do better. There's no harm in trying something new."

"No harm? Really?" Boleyn glares at Marcus, then at me. "What if we're captured? Wiped? Some of us didn't just waltz into the Red Tower, pick up a dragon's tooth, and join group one. Some of us have been here for ages. We've worked, grown, gotten wiped, recovered again, and become stronger again. I'm not going to risk that for some ill-advised experiment."

"Enough debate," Axe says. "The decision has been made. It's time to pick sides."

"I'm not debating," Jacana snaps. "If you don't give me

one good reason why I should do this, I'm refusing."

"I'm the Alpha. I don't have to explain myself." Axe rises to his feet. "You know the rules. Anyone who doesn't obey me gets wiped. Even you, Jacana."

A slender flame begins to bounce across Jacana's fingertips. She is quiet, watching the flame, thinking. "Fine," she mutters, turning to me. "But if this doesn't work, you're going to burn."

I want to say it will work, but Apple still won't let my lips budge.

"Alright, alright." Axe grins as he looks around the table. "I take Amy and Seth."

*Amy and Seth?* Why didn't he pick Marcus and Boleyn? We all know they're the strongest. Is it because Boleyn doesn't want to join me? Whatever the reason, it's worth the risk. Marcus is an unstoppable force.

Now if only Apple will let me speak. When I look to her, I try to send as many good emotions as I can through the link. I'm sorry about my past and about hers. I'm hopeful about what we can do together. I'm desperate to help our team unite. I make every ounce of my expression scream to her: *Please?*

Her hard stare softens, slightly. Her brown eyes blink. She looks down at her hands and…relents. The command is gone. The room is quiet.

I point to the pair I pick. "Marcus and Boleyn."

"Very well," Axe says. "Jacana and Khan, with me."

I breathe a sigh of relief. I get Hank and Zelle.

"Now that wasn't so hard, was it?" Axe steps back

from his chair. "My team, let's go. We'll see the rest of you chumps in the Scouring."

The other two boys and the three girls on Axe's team rise and follow him out. The flames of the candelabra flicker as the door closes. Five faces turn to me.

"What now?" Boleyn asks. "You have a strategy?"

"Yes," I say, smiling toward Hank. He showed me this, whether he knows it or not. "If we're going to fight together, then we have to know each other." I glance around the group, then at the candelabra flames. "It's time to talk about the past."

# 26

I TELL MY STORY first. I was a brain doctor in 21$^{st}$ century America. I struggled as a child without a father and with my mom not around. Apple listens carefully, watching and judging, so I add that I was not a loyal or honest man, especially not with my wife. I became no better than my own father, maybe worse. The others get the point. Apple doesn't make me say the details I choose to leave out. She knows them. She must understand. It could hurt our team, because we might not like each other very much if we shared all the dark secrets of our past, summoned up by the various memory devices of the five towers.

As I finish, no one looks at me like a villain. There's even sympathy in some of their faces. I breathe easier. It feels good, like a boiling pot venting some of its steam. Hank is right. There's power to this process—the telling and re-telling of our own stories. It somehow removes the past's grip, finger by clutching finger, slowly freeing us.

Apple goes next. The four others listen with rapt attention.

"I lived in an apple orchard in Europe," she says.

"That's why I picked my name. I don't know my real name yet, or when exactly I lived, but it was a time of great conflict, or war. It was a hard time. I lost my whole family. It made me furious. I wanted revenge, and I got it." She looks to me, then around at the group. "I will stop there, but I confess this, and warn you all: what I have seen has made it difficult to like men or…want them to exist at all."

The group falls quiet. We avoid eye contact. At least Apple was honest.

"Marcus," I say. "How about you?"

He tells his story more meekly than I had heard it before. Maybe it's because of the link around his neck, or maybe because of Apple's warning. He explains that he was a Roman gladiator who spent his time battling in the Colosseum. He survived fights against lions and bears. He lost an eye. Scars covered his body like ornaments. His fame grew so much that he fought against the emperor's own champion, and he won.

"I spilled a lot of blood," he says at the end.

None of us ask questions, not yet. We all know how hard it is to remember, and to talk about it.

The next up is Boleyn.

"This can be short," she says. "What I remember is that a mirror before me reflects twin flames of candles, flickering on either side of my face, casting a glow of red. My silk dress is dark and shimmers with every movement, making me think of blood. It is like the dress I wear now." Boleyn looks to me, her expression cryptic. "The story from there burns with passion, perhaps like yours."

"That's it?" Apple asks, glancing from Boleyn to me. "How is it like *his* story?"

Boleyn does not answer.

"Tell them." Marcus leans back in his chair with his arms crossed. He has paired with Boleyn. He must know more about her.

"You say nothing of your forbidden love, and you expect me to share more about mine?" Boleyn asks Marcus. "Do you want me to *make* you speak?"

"No need," Marcus says. "I'll tell them." He pauses as if collecting his thoughts. "This might sound hard to believe, but I fell in love with the daughter of the Roman Emperor. And she loved me, too. It was impossible for the Emperor to approve this. She helped me sneak in and out of the palace. Until we got caught. I dropped instantly from the Emperor's champion to his lowest slave. In my last memory I'm standing in the Colosseum, wearing a worn tunic and chains around my ankles. No armor. No weapon. There's sand under my feet. Thousands cheer. The noise is deafening. My love sits by her father's side, forced to watch as a gate opens and lions emerge. At least ten of them. I haven't seen how it ended, but you can guess as well as I can."

My head shakes in disbelief. *They fed Marcus to the lions. Because of love.* No wonder he's been so quiet and distant. It sounds like he didn't even do anything wrong.

"You left out one part," Boleyn says, eyeing Marcus.

"What?" he asks.

"That you feel so guilty and numb and bitter. You think

you never should have fallen for the Emperor's daughter. You think you never should have loved!" Boleyn slaps the table fiercely. "That's where you're wrong. Love wasn't the problem. The world was, with its rulers and laws and violence."

"That's what *you* like to believe," Marcus replies, his voice hard as iron. "Order exists for a reason. I broke it, and I rightly suffered the consequences."

"*Rightly! For love?* You see?" Boleyn looks around the group, her face full of emotion. "This is what's inside him. Truly, he's being honest. I suppose we'll all be a little more honest now, shall we?"

No one answers.

"Very well," Boleyn continues, "listen to this whole bloody mess and tell me how I'll ever get over it. Remember the mirror I told you about? Well, a man comes into the reflection. He puts his hands on my shoulders and looks into my eyes. Only he's not just any man. He is the king, and he is married to the queen I serve. He asks me to call him Henry. He tells me I look ravishing. We do not hold back. How could I? Can you imagine how a commoner's status might rise? I played the fiddle of passion like a master. The king appeared in the mirror again and again. I bore two of his children. He told me he loved me. Maybe I even loved him. Maybe I thought he would marry me. He divorced the queen and…and…" Boleyn bites her lip. Her hard, sarcastic tone has gone soft.

"I know what happened!" Hank says, sitting on the edge of his seat and leaning forward. "He was King Henry

VIII. You became the Queen of England! You are Anne Boleyn!"

"So we all wish," Boleyn says, with bitter sarcasm. "There were two candles flickering in the mirror."

"You were *Mary*," Zelle offers in wonder. *"Mary Boleyn?"*

"Yes. King Henry married my sister, Anne, instead of me. Anne became queen, but not for long. Anne was as treacherous as Henry, but he had all the power. She did not bear him a son. The last thing I remember is the day he had her killed. My sister. The wife of my lover." Boleyn glares at Marcus. "There, I've told them, and you again. Are you pleased?"

"Delighted," Marcus says in a deadpan voice. "We rightly suffered."

Our group falls quiet. Boleyn's story seems too twisted for real life. The King of England…it's hard to wrap my head around. She remembers so much. She has so much passion. No wonder she wields such power.

Hank breaks the silence. "Our pasts are similar," he says. "All of us. We took something that was good and we let it consume us. We couldn't control it."

"You may be right," Boleyn agrees. "Like Rahab says, let passion burn… What's your story, Hank?"

Hank tells the group his tale, covering nearly everything he'd told me the day before on the training ground, about his cider and his friend's wife. He does not smile. He leaves out only a few details. Again no one asks questions.

Zelle is the last to speak. "I lived around the same time

as Cipher," she says, "but across the Atlantic, in the greatest city in the world."

"Rome?" Marcus asks.

"Paris," Zelle responds. "Rome was a tourist attraction by my time. Your Colosseum was in shambles."

Marcus grins for the first time all night. "Serves it right."

"I'm like all of you," Zelle says to us. "I had issues with passion, but not with another person." She pauses and takes a long drink from her chalice.

"Go on," Hank says. "Tell them."

Zelle nods. "You heard how Hank made cider? That homemade stuff caused problems. In modern Paris we had a far better drink. It was red and luscious and alive. It was respected, even dignified. So of course I desired it. I worked long, long days. I managed businesses around the world. I earned a fortune. And I spent it on the finest food and wine. Mostly wine. I knew the best French vintners, personally. I ordered case after case. My townhome on the Seine had a cellar. I went there every night I was home. If I was traveling, I went to the bar. Wherever I was, I would open a bottle and forget about the business. I would forget that I was alone. At first it was a glass. Then a whole bottle. Then two. The mornings were awful. Fuzzy, spinning, sickly, hollow. Cigarettes were breakfast and lunch. But by the time the sun started to fall, I would feel the urge rising from my depths. I wanted it all over again. Sometimes my stomach couldn't even hold enough. I'd throw up just to keep going. I have no idea how it all ended. It doesn't seem to matter. I was in a red whirlpool sucking me down, down, down. I had no way out."

She takes a deep breath and looks to Hank. Whatever passes between them makes Hank smile tenderly. "You did good," he says.

Zelle places her hand over his. "We've learned from each other. The mistakes begin small. We love the first taste. Then we want another taste, and another. I have been in here long enough to be wiped more times than I can count, and every time I have to learn it again: it is the little decisions, the first *no's* or *yes's*, that set our course fatefully toward the fire…"

Her words drift off. Hank finishes for her: "Where passion burned."

# 27

WE LINE UP in two columns behind the gate that will open to the Scouring. The boys wield weapons and collars. The girls wear dresses and rings. Rahab stands beside the twelve of us. Apple and I lead one column. Axe and Melissa lead the other. Behind me are Marcus and Boleyn, then Hank and Zelle. A Roman gladiator, an English King's mistress, an American from the frontier, and a cosmopolitan Parisian. It almost makes me laugh. Just put a neurosurgeon in charge and it'll all work out.

"Remember," Rahab says. "Do whatever it takes to capture. But do not, under any circumstances, get in each other's way." She stares at Axe, then at me. "If either of you even attempts to stop the other group from capturing someone, you will be wiped."

"My team's going right," Axe says, turning to me. Strapped to his back, unsurprisingly, is an axe. "You better keep your distance. No stealing our leftovers."

I grip my staff and meet his stare. "We'll go left."

"Very well," Rahab says. "The terms of your wager will be honored." She steps to the side. "To victory!"

The iron gate begins to lift. It moves achingly slow, chain clinking as it draws up the massive barrier. We can see through the gaps in the gate. The team from Green emerges from their door to the right. Then Yellow, Blue, and Black around the wall.

*We'll go left…* I'd said it in defiance, but now I wish I hadn't. That's the way to the Black Tower. The last color I want to battle. Unless my Mom happens to be with them. It's possible. Kiyo came to the Scouring soon after she was captured. But could we stand against Black? It's risky. My whole team's at stake. Emma's freedom's at stake. The Red Tower is at stake.

Axe leads his group along the wall to the right. This gives us a new option. We don't have to go straight to Black. Going *left* now includes going to the middle.

I catch Hank's eyes. "To Blue?"

He smiles and taps the butt of his spear to the ground. "We know where they're weak. But respect the mind."

It's our rallying cry from Blue. *Respect the mind.* That's not going to work here. Rahab says, *Let passion burn.* It fits our pasts. Apple said that each girl's power over the flames comes partly from her memories of passion. Boleyn, Zelle, and Apple have that. So maybe we *are* supposed to let passion burn, as the fuel to their fire. If only we can harness it.

I try the words with our group, softly. "Let passion burn."

The others nod. Even Apple seems pleased. "Let passion burn," she echoes, along with the rest of the group.

It's not a shout or a battle cry. It's more like a dirge for our pasts and all that led to this battle. "Let passion burn. Let passion *burn*."

We charge toward the middle of the Scouring. No one gets in our way. The Black phalanx of twelve moves toward us, but slowly. We're the first to reach the milk-white stones forming the small circle in the center. I lead us to the left of the circle, keeping well to the side of it. The last thing we need is to be transported into a memory. We round the circle and sprint at Blue. Black does not change its path. They keep moving toward the center, as if uninterested in us. Maybe they're targeting Green or Yellow.

The first sounds of fighting come from Axe's team. They are far away now, still at the wall and colliding against Green.

Blue's twelve are close.

I reach for the air. The sensation is sweeter than ever. The air flows like electricity through my mind. But…the thread is snatched away. The collar feels hot around my neck.

Apple has taken control. She never hinted at this. She's smiling.

I'm furious. This is *my* power.

"Take him first!" shouts a blue-robed boy, pointing at me. He has long, curly hair and four stripes at the sleeves. It's Pierre, Fourth Class. He's the one who joined me in the Hunting in Green's forest. We were like rivals. He never liked me.

Now he's at the center of Blue's team. There are twelve of them, and six of us. They've stretched out to form a concave line, like an open net welcoming our Red team in.

*Water and air surrounding fire. Is this a mistake?*

Pierre moves forward. The Blue line collapses around us. Apple weaves together my power and hers to form a wall to our left. It is neither fire nor air. It is like thick, purple energy, blocking half of the Blue team.

Hank and Marcus charge to the right. Hank reaches Blue first and barrels into them with a swipe of his spear. Three are knocked to the ground. Marcus takes one down with the sword.

*It's not fair*, I think. *They don't have weapons.* But they have the mind. It makes it all the more frustrating that Apple controls my power. I stand with my staff raised before the three Red girls, ready to defend.

Boleyn loops fire around a boy from Blue. Zelle hurls a melon-sized fireball, but a rush of wind douses it. The wind blows harder. Marcus's sword flies out of his hand and blows a hundred feet, to the Scouring wall. Apple pulls on more of my power and stretches the wall farther, all the way from the white circle in the center to the Blue gate. It cuts off eight from Blue's team, leaving four on our side. Boleyn and Zelle wrap belts of fire around them. They can't run.

Hank and Marcus herd the four captives back toward Red. We move quickly, but I realize Apple has stopped moving.

"I can't hold it any longer," she says to me.

"Let me. Please."

She nods and the power passes through the link. She's right. The wall is immense. Holding this much fire and wind together—while the Blue team blasts air at it—requires complete concentration. I can hardly see what's around us. I focus on the weaves, threading them back together wherever Blue pulls them apart.

Apple takes my hand and pulls me after the others.

The four captives struggle along with us, slowing us down. As we make our way around the white circle again, the loudest sounds of fighting come from between the Green and Yellow gates.

I continue weaving, moving the wall with us to block any attacks from Blue.

We're halfway back to the Red Tower when something slams into my side, sending me sprawling on the hard stones. I manage to lift up. The force comes again. I reach for the air. But it's gone. Black smoke smothers the invisible threads.

*Black.*

I trace the power to its source. A girl dressed head-to-toe in black has locked eyes on me. She's only twenty feet away, standing at the front of her team. Her eyes are the only part of her I can see. She almost looks familiar. It could be Monica, the same powerful girl who fought against me during the last Scouring with Blue.

"There!" I shout, pointing at her.

Marcus seems to understand. He was in Black before. He charges at her fearlessly, just like he charged at Jafari.

But this time he has no sword. He leaps and crashes his elbow down on the girl's shoulder. She falls. The others from Black surround Marcus.

I grab the air and throw back the force that holds me down. Crouching, I pull on Apple's power and mine, as much as I can hold. A ring of air forms around Marcus. He grabs it like it's a lifesaver. In a breath I lift and drag Marcus away, over and above the Black figures surrounding him and back to us.

He lands smoothly by my side. He smiles as he looks down at me, holding out a hand to help me stand. "Not bad, wind boy."

"Thanks," I say, glancing to the girl in black, who's still down. "You too."

He flashes a rare smile. "It's what I do."

I form the wall again. We move toward the Red Tower. Other teams move around us. Marcus and Hank guard our sides. The girls keep the four Blue captives held tight in fiery chains.

To the left, Axe and his group are coming. They have two captives from Green. Their pace is as slow as ours with captives. Too slow. The Black team rallies into formation in front of us. I don't see the girl from before, but she could be hidden behind the square of shields. We have to get through them, or go wide around them.

Black was just waiting. They knew we couldn't capture anyone unless we got back to our gate, and unless we got past them.

They don't charge us. They hold their ground, huge

rectangular shields and spears raised. We can't wait, because Blue is pressing from behind.

Boleyn blasts a fireball at the boys from Black, followed by one from Zelle.

Their shields hold. They don't budge.

Ahead, Khan and Seth from Axe's group break into a sprint. They're trying to go around the left edge of the Black team. It's smart. We can divide their attention.

I motion to my group. "Right side!"

We veer to the right. As we try to round the edge, the Black team splits. Most of them go toward Axe's group. Four of them come at us. They strike as fast as snakes. A spear catches Hank in the shoulder. He goes down, but I use the air to keep him moving. Boleyn and Zelle send a wave of flames along the ground. It ignites the Black team's pants. They fall, rolling to put out the flames.

We are close now. We're only steps away from the gate. From victory. We have four captives. To the left, the other Red team is running beside us. There are five of them, along with two captives from Green. Someone is missing.

Melissa rushes to me and grabs my arm. "They got Axe. Help!"

Behind us, Axe is on his back, with a spear held to his throat by a boy in Black. He's surrounded. The look on his face reminds me of when I threw him with the air in the Blue Tower so long ago. He was the one who mocked Kiyo. He was the one who kept Emma from me.

"Cipher!" Melissa pulls at me. "You have to do something…"

She trails off as she meets my eyes. She knows I'm going to leave him. She looks furious.

"Red!" I shout. "Get inside now!"

# 28

AS THE GATE LOWERS, shutting off the Scouring outside, Melissa is in my face. She's inches away, screaming, "You left him! You traitor! You—"

The slap hits me before I can react, knocking my head to the side. My cheek feels hot.

Melissa raises her arm again, for another swing, but this time Hank grabs her. His large arms engulf her, gentle but firm. She writhes in his grip, still screaming and shouting at me.

I take a deep breath. We're back in the tower. No more using the wind, if Apple would even let me.

The group is silent. It's a bigger group than when we started. There's eleven from the Red Tower—everyone except Axe. Plus six others—four from Blue in their familiar robes, and two from Green in brown leather. All of them are staring at me, surprised, confused, waiting to see what I'll do.

"Red won," I say, ignoring Melissa. "That's what matters."

"You abandoned him," Melissa says, calmer now.

Anger twists her expression, but she has gone still in Hank's arms. "You don't deserve to be Alpha."

"We had to protect what we gained," I say.

She growls back, "You coward."

"Want us to open the gate so you can go after him?"

She takes a deep breath, scowling. But then she shakes her head slightly.

"Let her go," I say to Hank, and he does.

She straightens her dress and stands up straight. I wonder how long she was paired with Axe. And what happens when a paired boy is captured? Does she still feel what he feels? Black must sever the Pairing somehow. Maybe it hurts. However bad it is, Melissa isn't willing to risk her own place in the Red Tower, or her memories, to try to save Axe.

"Welcome back." Rahab's voice echoes down the stairwell that leads to the Scouring and us. She appears moments later, taking the stairs two at a time in her long red dress. She quickly surveys the group, then looks to me. "So you caught six?"

I nod. "Yes, and we lost one."

"Not bad," Rahab says. "Not bad at all."

"*Not bad?*" Melissa snaps. "We lost the Alpha!"

Rahab smiles at her, as if amused. "So it is a net gain of five. A good first showing for our new Alpha."

Melissa shakes her head defiantly, brown hair swaying. "No, it can't be *him*."

"You know the rules," Rahab says.

"I don't care about the rules." Melissa steps boldly to

Rahab. "Burn you. Burn the Red Tower and the new Alpha. I'll never follow him."

"Melissa, Melissa." Rahab sighs. "Must we do this again?"

Melissa raises her hand like she did with me, readying to swing. Just as she springs into motion, Rahab erupts into fire.

The light and heat are intolerable. I cower back, shutting my eyes.

In a moment it's gone.

Where the fire burned, Rahab stands alone. Melissa is nowhere in sight. There's not even a pile of ashes. The others whisper in shock.

"Khan," Rahab says calmly, as if she didn't just incinerate someone. "You lead this group and the captives where they need to go."

"Of course," he says, bowing crisply.

Rahab moves toward me. I step back without thinking.

"Some of us require many attempts, many fresh starts," she says. "We give as many as are needed." She lifts her hand to my cheek, to the same spot where Melissa had slapped me. It still burns. "But others of us rise quickly."

The group is silent, my heart is thumping, as Rahab's hand slides down my cheek to my neck, to the collar. She presses—on the inside, at the back center—and the seamless metal flashes heat and suddenly unclasps. Rahab holds it casually at her side. The bright silver ring gleams red with the reflection of her dress and the torches on the wall.

"Your new Alpha," Rahab announces.

"The Alpha," Hank says softly, falling to a knee.

The others stand still, like they're not ready for this. For a new Alpha. For me.

"Follow me, Alpha." Rahab turns to leave. She doesn't say anything to the group. No speech or coronation.

I glance to Hank. He smiles and motions for me to go. I catch Apple's eyes as I pass, and my hands go to my neck, to where the collar has been for so many days.

"Do you know what I feel now?" I ask her.

She shakes her head, looking more surprised than angry. "I can only guess."

So that's it. No more Pairing with Apple. I wish it had gone better between us, but it could have gone worse. We made a decent team when it mattered. "Thanks for trusting me back there," I say.

"I don't hate you, Cipher. But you can still be better." Apple looks away, to where Rahab has gone up the stairs. "You should go."

With a final glance at the group, I hurry after Rahab, bounding up the stairs until I catch her. The others will probably report back to their normal places—the Barracks for the boys, the individual rooms for the girls. Rahab doesn't speak as she leads me up through the tower. It reminds me of following Abram so long ago, when I'd first arrived in the Blue Tower. I've come a long way. *But you can still be better.* The Pairing made Apple the only person here who knew exactly what I felt. She didn't talk much about that. Maybe that was a form of kindness.

Rahab does not stop until we arrive at the Alpha's chambers. She stands outside the door and looks me up and down. I can't tell if she's surprised, or disappointed. She seemed to like Axe. "You know your role?" she asks.

"To lead our group into the Scouring?"

"That's a start."

"What else?"

"Our tower has 96 members now." She crosses her arms, like someone who is about to demand something hard from me. "We're well short of equilibrium."

"You mean 144?" I ask.

"Yes, as Abram told you. What you did for Blue, you must now do for Red. It should be your sole, consuming focus. Always be thinking and striving. Capture any one at any time and in any way you can."

"Any time?" I remember my voyage for the Hunting in the Blue Tower. Maybe this is like that. "You mean even outside the Scouring?"

"Not every Alpha is capable of this," she says. "Maybe you are. Use whatever it takes."

A hope rises in me. "Even my power?"

"Yes, and tunnels and pairs and dragon teeth," she answers. "Figure it out with that big brain of yours. You may have started Blue, but you're Red now. As the Alpha, you are no longer limited by this tower's rules. But your fate is tied to the tower's. If you succeed and our numbers rise, the fire will show you the memories that you need to advance."

"And if our numbers go down?" I ask.

"You will visit Behemoth. You will start over."

I swallow. *Behemoth, the dragon under the tower.* "Why is Behemoth here?"

She leans closer and smiles, as if taunting me. "He is simply a creation, as you and I are. Just think, how powerful must one be to *create* something so powerful?"

The question makes me think of Abram talking about the Genius in the Blue Tower, and Emma about the Healer in Yellow. *Facets of the same jewel,* Abram said. "Okay…so who created Behemoth?" I ask.

"It is not for me to tell you *who*," she says. "But there is a force that's underneath all of us. It animates us. It sparks love and life, spirit and fire."

"What force is it?"

"Passion, Cipher." She puts her finger underneath my chin and applies just enough pressure to pull my face within inches of hers. Her breath smells like hot spices, cinnamon and clove. "Didn't Apple teach you anything?"

"To be afraid of myself?" I say. "And…of her?"

"That's a good start." Rahab's eyes blaze. "Passion must be controlled, but without it we attempt nothing. Abram knows this as well as I do. Genius alone produces no virtue. It produces a machine without a heart." She presses her hand to my chest. "You are no machine, Cipher. But you must not be an animal, either."

Rahab steps back and glances to the closed door. "I've seen what you risked to find Emma. I suspect you would like to see her? Maybe even pair with her?"

"Yes, I'd like that." *Emma.* She will be my pair. It can't

be a coincidence that Abram assigned her as my first target. And I caught her. She was my servant. But she was so…extraordinary. I wanted to serve her. I still do. I want to help her find the rest of her memory and heal it. She's a healer. I was a doctor. If any pair can raise a phoenix from these ashes, it's us.

Rahab holds out her hand. A ring with a single, huge ruby rests on her palm. It's the same one Melissa wore. "Take it," Rahab says. "Your pair will wear this. It works like the collar."

"You mean she'll control me?" I ask.

"No one controls the Alpha. But, with this ring, she will know what you feel. She can show you things in the fire that you cannot see alone."

"That…never happened with Apple."

"I feared this," Rahab sighs. "Her story is especially hard. She struggles with Pairing. We have yet to find a good match. Do you think that she should be wiped?"

The question stuns me. Would Rahab really leave that choice to me? I could never wish that for someone. Apple shouldn't have to re-remember her hard past, over and over. "No," I say. "I don't want anyone to be wiped."

"Very well, we will let Apple's memories remain for now. She has much more to see. Would you like her to stay in the Scouring group?"

I consider it. She may not be as powerful as other girls, but we worked well together. "That's okay with me," I say.

"So it will be. She must choose a pair, as you will."

"Does that mean Emma will take Melissa's place?"

"Yes, if you choose her," Rahab says. "Remember, passion is like fire. It provides warmth and light in a hearth. But it remains dangerous. Here in Red you must look straight into the fire. You have to understand your past passions, and how they burned, before you can be scoured of the consequences."

"The Scouring," I say, thinking aloud. "How does it work, with the white circle and this equilibrium that you and Abram want? Are they connected?"

"Everything is connected," Rahab answers. "You can't rise above this process or earn your way to the White Tower. No one can. But rest assured, the Scouring cannot be stopped. Even if you must start again, and again, wiped clean like Melissa and so many others, you will be scoured."

# 29

RAHAB LEAVES ME alone before the door to the Alpha's chambers. Emma is within reach, but her mind is blank. I have to put my own mind in order before I can be much help to her. I'm the Alpha now, the one in command. But I'm the same boy who appeared in a dark lake underneath the Blue Tower. I'm the same Dr. Fitzroy. Apple had every reason to hate me after she learned my past. Hank had no reason to be my friend, except maybe that my failings were similar to his. We both failed to control our passions.

*Passion.*

Another facet of the same jewel. Rahab says we should pursue our passions, that we are made to feel them, to love. She says I came here cold. It's true. I began in Blue with a cold, clinical mind. But that has changed. Passion drove me to do everything I could to reach my Mom, and now Emma. Is that what Rahab wants from me? It would explain why she hasn't wiped me yet. Maybe this is all Rahab's plan. Let me rise to Alpha and gain complete control over a beautiful, blank-slate Emma. She doesn't even remember who she was before this place. She doesn't remember that she linked with me in Blue, that I captured her from Yellow, or that she lived in Victorian England, ran away from home, had a child, and suffered hard consequences. I could tell Emma anything. I could paint a new picture for her. I could tell her that she loved me. That I loved her. That's what I said to Samantha. That's how I conquered the girl of my high school dreams. That's how Dr. Fitzroy became a lying cheat.

And so, that's exactly what I must *not* do. If Dr. Fitzroy is the positive end of the magnet, here I must be the negative. Emma is too wonderful to be conquered. She is too good for lies. I must tell her the truth. All of it.

I knock on the door. Wood slides away, revealing a set of eyes through a slit. Not Emma's eyes. "Who is it?" the girl asks.

"Cipher."

There's no reaction.

"The new Alpha," I say.

The slit closes and the door opens. The inside looks exactly like it did when Axe was here, including the two servants by the door. One is Emma. I don't know the other.

"What are your names?" I ask.

"We are here to serve the Alpha," they both say.

"Okay. What are your names?"

The girls exchange a look. "We are here to serve," Emma says. "If you want us to have names, just ask. We will obey."

I shake my head. This is going to be complicated. Axe didn't even give them names. As Alpha he had the right to these two servants. He must have treated them like pets, or worse. At least pets have names.

Where to start? With the towers? With names?

I ask the girls to close the door and make a fire and bring some food. They spring into action, as if delighted to have these tasks, and I walk into the other room, the throne room. It's empty, with only the large chair sitting on a raised platform. To the left there are the openings in the red stone and the view over the Scouring. The vast space is quiet and empty, as if no fight just took place there.

Back in the anteroom, the girls have built up a roaring fire in the hearth. They are beginning to lay out a feast. There's a fresh loaf of dark brown bread, butter, and what looks like a leg of lamb roasting over the fire. Except there are no lambs as far as I've seen around the Red Tower.

"Where'd you get this food?" I ask.

"From the Alpha's supplies," Emma says. "Is it not to your liking?"

"No, I mean, yes, it's fine. Is that lamb?"

"Of course," the other girl says. "The Alpha's favorite."

They seem to be as confused as I am. "Do you know my name?"

"Alpha," they both say.

I almost laugh, but it's too surreal. They could have been wiped again to start fresh with me. Or maybe they're wiped every day. The thought sends shivers down my spine. "Please, don't call me that. Just call me Cipher."

"Cipher," they both say.

"You do know that I'm not the same boy who was the Alpha before, right?" I ask. "You remember him?"

They stare at me blankly. This is not going well.

"Axe?" I say.

"You want an axe?" Emma asks.

I sigh and step to the table. The food smells delicious. I grab a piece of bread and walk to the floor-to-ceiling opening on the far side of the room. Cool air blows up the steep rocky slope from the Scouring far below. I think while I eat, breathing the fresh air and gazing over the empty space. Maybe the lambs come from more distant parts of the Red Tower's land, or maybe Rahab somehow gets it from the other towers. The Black Tower is to my left. It looks close across the edge of the Scouring, but a steep mountain ridge separates us, blocking the view of Black's lands. The Blue Tower, as usual, is obscured by clouds. Yellow glimmers in the sunlight shining from behind me and the Red Tower. Between Yellow and Red is Green. The giant tree is not as tall as the other towers but it's certainly more…alive. Do people there live in the tree? Or do they all spread out in the dense forest beyond? I still know so little about these other towers.

I turn back to the table and sit and peek into the chalice. *Fresh milk!* I've had it only once here, in the feast with Axe and the others before the Scouring. Do I get as much as I want now? And where does it come from? I drain the chalice and wipe my milk mustache.

Emma comes with a pitcher to refill. As she leans over

the table, the metal collar at her neck catches my eye. She wore it when I last came to this room, but it must not be linked to me. I can't feel what she's feeling. Unless…she doesn't feel anything.

"Please, sit." I point to the empty chair beside mine.

Emma sits and stares at her hands clasped at the table.

"Look at me, please."

Her large blue eyes meet mine.

"That necklace, can you take it off?"

She suddenly looks afraid. She shakes her head.

"I know your name," I say.

She shakes her head, fear still in her eyes.

"Your name is Emma."

"As the Alpha wishes," she replies.

This isn't working. It seems the Alpha's servants are somehow programmed to remain blank, like unthinking robots. I want Emma back, not a robot.

"Do you remember anything?" I ask her.

"You are the Alpha."

"And the Alpha before me?"

She stares at me with innocent confusion.

"His name was Axe," I say.

"As you wish."

I scoot my chair closer to her. "Stay still, okay?"

She nods, studying me cautiously.

I reach slowly to her neck, to the collar. My fingers feel along the silver band, all the way around on the inside. There's no clasp or groove, not even at the back center. I press my thumb hard to that spot anyway, just as Rahab did. I summon the wind and direct a tendril of it into that spot. When nothing happens, I concentrate more and more power—enough to blow someone across the Scouring—into Emma's collar.

An invisible seal snaps. The collar falls off and clatters against the ground.

Emma gulps, eyes open in shock, like she just swallowed a gigantic bug with a thousand legs crawling down her throat. She wretches but nothing comes out. She's breathing heavily, eyes darting around, processing. Then her eyes land on mine. She sees me, she knows me, and she says my name like she used to: "Cipher."

# 30

"DO YOU REMEMBER NOW?" I ask.

Emma's hands clench the arms of her chair so hard that her veins bulge. But her breathing grows steadier, calmer. Then, slowly, her look of shock fades into a small, shy smile. Her grip relaxes. "Yes, it is coming back..."

"You came from the Blue Tower."

"Yes, Blue," she says. "Before that I was in Yellow. You captured me. I became your servant. But..." Her smile widens as she rubs her neck where the collar had been moments before. "You ordered me to treat *you* as the servant. You gave me the only bed. We sailed to Yellow. Our powers..." she pauses, as if struggling to explain what happened between us.

"I drew on your power to heal," I say. "You drew on my power over the wind. We melded the yellow and blue weaves together. We were very powerful."

"Yes, yes!" she says excitedly, her fingers tapping on the table. "I joined Blue. We captured many others. But, now I remember, you left Blue. You left me at the Scouring. You went to Red...to find your mother."

"I'm sorry. I had to go."

She leans forward. "What happened?"

"I found her. We talked about our past. It helped, a lot. It filled in many gaps. But we did not have much time together. Black captured her soon after that. It was the same Scouring when you and Hank came here."

"We wanted to find you. I…missed you."

"I missed you, too. Maybe I should have brought you when I came. I'm so glad you're here now." I put my hand over hers. Her skin is rougher, calloused, likely from her work as Axe's servant. "I'm so sorry about everything that happened. I tried to get to you sooner. I tried…" I look down, unable to bear her steady gaze. I'm not worthy of what she risked for me. It's my fault Axe captured her. It's my fault she has to relive these memories like this. "How can I make it up to you?"

"It's okay." She squeezes my hand. "But please, tell me who I was…before."

"Wait, you don't remember *that*?" Maybe the more recent memories, in the five towers, came back first. "You were—you *are*—Emma Chamberlain. You were the daughter of a British lord. In the 1800s."

"Chamberlain…yes…" Her hands grip the arms of the chair again, like she's holding on while accelerating down a dark tunnel of memories.

"Do you remember now?" I ask. "You had a husband, and a son."

She nods as tears come to her eyes. "I *had* them, but then…" Her voice breaks. She looks away. "I'm going to need some time."

"Yes, of course. You are safe here."

"Thank you, Cipher." She speaks delicately, with controlled refinement, but it's clear her mind is a million miles away, probably in an English countryside.

Emma needs time, and probably space, too. I rise from the table and see the other servant by the fire. I had almost forgotten about her. She's putting more wood into the flames. She deserves the same freedom.

I pull two chairs away from the table where Emma sits and tell the other girl to sit. She does as I say. I look into her blank eyes. They are green, speckled with brown, and wholly devoid of memory or sentiment. She's the one who looks a lot like Seymour. Her hair is the same color brown. Her cheeks look like they never lost their baby fat. Maybe she's Seymour's sister, or mother, or daughter, or something. If they really are related, Seymour should get her back.

I reach around her collar and do the same thing as with Emma, pressing on the inside and channeling hurricane-force wind into a single point at the back.

It works. The collar falls forward, into the girl's lap.

She stares at it in disbelief. She lifts it with a pudgy hand and flings it across the room. It lands directly into the fire. A perfect throw.

The girl looks to me, scowling. "Who are you?"

*The one who set you free*, I want to say, but she might have reason to be upset. Getting her memories back might not be pleasant at all.

"I'm Cipher, the Alpha," I say gently. "Who are you?"

"My name is Hayley. How did I get here?"

"You were the Alpha's servant."

"You mean, *your* servant?" she snaps.

"No, not me. The Alpha before me. Axe. I took his place. I've set you free."

Hayley shakes her head, confused. It's as if this information is too much for her to process. She stands and starts moving toward the door. I don't stop her, but as she approaches it, the door opens. Rahab is there.

Emma, Hayley, and I watch in silence as the tower's leader, wearing her usual red dress, strides to the fireplace. She reaches directly into the flames. She pulls out the silver collar, as casually as if she's picking up a seashell out of the ocean. She approaches me at the table. She holds out the collar accusingly. Her hand is not burned.

"It is one thing to free your servants," she says. "But it is quite another thing to waste a link. We have only 360."

This doesn't make sense. The collar clearly wasn't burning. It's as fireproof as Rahab. We also have a long way to go before the Red Tower would need 360 collars. "If there's that many collars here," I say, "then it seems like we're not running out any time soon."

"Not *here*, Alpha. That's how many the Five Towers have."

Abram said I was the first to bring the towers to 720. And there are 360 collars. "So, in total, there's enough for half of us?"

Rahab's fists, one still clenching the collar, plant in their usual place on her hips. "Obviously."

"Why?" I ask.

"You know how the collars work." Rahab glances to Emma by the table, then looks toward the door, where Hayley stands motionless as a boulder. "This one has been a servant a long time. She'll have to be wiped."

Hayley's face goes pale as she backs away.

"That's not fair," I say. "She just got her memories back."

"Fair?" Rahab's gaze swivels to me. "You would speak of fairness? You, who knows enough of your past to know you could be burning for eternity, but who knows not even by what love you were saved and came here, would tell *me* what is *fair?* I betrayed a whole city to be saved. It burned—with all its women and children—while I escaped. Is that *fair?* None of us can speak of fairness, Alpha. I expected more of you."

She spins off without another word. She takes Hayley's arm and they leave together, shutting the door behind them.

The fire crackles. The wind blows cool air into the room. Emma and I sit in quiet. We are back together, and her memories are returning. But it's hard to be happy. Not after what Rahab said. Do even the leaders suffer from their memories here? The guilt of the past hangs over us, only to be forgotten and remembered again. Hayley will be wiped. I will probably be wiped, too, someday. It's only a matter of time. It's the constant churn of this place— memories gained, pains felt, powers grow, only to have memories lost, and memories gained again. There's no way out.

Emma puts her hand over mine. "Don't blame yourself."

"I don't," I say, more defensive than I intended.

She smiles. "Come, let's sit by the fire. This wind is making me cold."

We move together to face the large fireplace. We sit on a fur on the floor. No servants have added more logs. There are no servants to come. So the flames burn low, the coals pulsing red and orange.

I look away. I don't want a memory. Not yet.

"Emma," I say, reaching into my pocket. "I have something for you."

"What is it?"

I hold out the ruby ring. "This is for the Pairing."

"It's beautiful!" Emma gasps, taking the ring. "What's the Pairing?"

"The Red Tower allows the girls to each pick a boy. The boys wear collars like the one you wore. All of them except for me, the Alpha. Each boy has to do whatever the paired girl commands. And each girl feels whatever the paired boy feels."

"Like the collars in Blue..." Emma says. "But not for servants. Why does Red do this?"

"Rahab says it allows us to see more from our past. But there's more to it. I think the pairs are supposed to teach us about controlling our passions. Kind of like how you helped me heal from the memories I saw in Blue. Ever since I learned you were here, I…wanted to pair with you."

"Thank you, Cipher. I accept." Her smile makes me feel warmer than I've felt in a long time. She slides the ring onto her slender finger. It's a perfect fit.

She looks at me, eyes open in surprise. "You…"

"What?" I ask.

"You feel…you…"

*She knows what I feel.* What do I feel? Love? Desire? Embarrassment?

Yes, all of these emotions. I'm an open book, like Emma was in Blue. It's only fair. I force myself to smile at her. "Hard to explain, right?"

She laughs. "You are a complicated boy."

"Guilty," I say with a shrug. "You're not so simple yourself. Go on and give it a try, if you'd like. Look into the fire."

She nods, turning to the burning embers.

As she stares, I gather more wood and add it to the fire. She never looks away. It's like she's in a trance. But by the time I sit by her side again, she's back, with tears on her cheeks. The memories must move faster than time here.

She takes her time as she tells me what she saw. It had been the memory of how she met the man she'd run away with. She'd seen it before, but this time was different. It was from *his* perspective. He was a servant in her family's manor house. They'd both known they could not be together there. So he'd convinced her to run away and tell all sorts of lies to cover their tracks. He'd been racked by guilt the whole time. They'd found a small, rustic cottage in some remote countryside. It was pleasant enough for a summer. But then came the winter, and the baby. He had gotten sick. That led to the vision I'd seen with her in the Sieve in the Blue Tower—of her returning home, begging forgiveness from her father, and being welcomed back with open arms.

We sit in quiet a while, before she says, "Your turn."

I'm ready now. Emma is with me. We are paired.

As I stare into the fire, the memory comes.

Paul Fitzroy drives a black car. It's dark outside. Beads of rain gather on the windshield until the wipers fling them away.

But this time I'm not inside my former self. I see myself from the outside. From Samantha's perspective. She sits beside me. She stares at my hands—Paul's hands—on the steering wheel. Her mind is reeling. Her feelings rage. She loves me. She hates me. The things she wants to do to me…

The car stops outside an apartment building. We are in a city. Downtown.

"Same time Saturday night?" Paul asks. "The house will be ours."

Samantha looks up to the top of the building. It is her building. She wants to get away from Paul. She never wants to see him again. But she can't bear to get out of this car. Not in the rain. She knows she'll have to stand on the wet sidewalk as he drives away, with a mess of pink and white petals under wet heels, freshly fallen from spring blooms that suffer the same dismal fate every year. Just like her.

She turns slowly to him—to me. Paul's face is smiling, but his eyes look tired. He doesn't want to talk about this. She doesn't want to talk about this. Maybe they could pretend everything is fine. Maybe they could make it one more day, one more week, until the next Saturday night when the house is empty.

But no. She thinks of those wet petals on the sidewalk. She can't let herself get trampled like those petals. She can't get out of this car only to start the same thing again. She knows exactly what will happen, because it's happened a dozen times before. First she steps into the lobby alone. She makes it to the elevator before she starts crying. Tears streak down her cheeks by the time she makes it to her apartment door. She's weeping as she unlocks it. The apartment is spotlessly clean and infinitely lonely. Paul pays for the place. It's their *little secret*. She can't tell her friends about him. She can't plan a life around him.

She has to say something. "Paul."

"Samantha." He smiles, like it's a joke. This whole thing is always like a joke to him—to me.

"We need to talk," she says.

The words have immediate effect. He takes a deep breath. His face goes tense. There's awkward quiet in the car. The rain falls steadily outside, splashing onto the hood and the windshield. She knew this would happen. *We need to talk.* They're the last words a man wants to hear.

"About what?" he asks.

"You know," she says.

"Is something wrong?"

This time she laughs. It's the kind of laugh that makes him lean further away. "Is something *wrong*?" she suddenly shouts. She takes a deep breath. She has to control herself. "*Everything* is wrong, Paul. How long do you expect me to go along with this? I can't keep waiting. You need to make a decision."

"I know." He sounds like he knows he has already lost. His eyes are down, watching as his hand moves from the gearshift to her knee. It takes four breaths, maybe five, before he manages to meet her eyes. "This is hard for you, for both of us. You know how I feel about you."

"So make your decision," she says firmly, not trusting him. He's done this before, playing sincere. Her gaze shifts to his hand on her knee. At least it's his right hand, the one without the pale line of skin on his ring finger, where the sun doesn't normally shine.

"I will," he says. "This Saturday, okay?"

*That's five days.* Can she survive five days? When she meets his eyes, she relents. He has the most sensitive brown eyes. "Okay. But that's it."

He smiles. "That's it, Sam. I promise."

She nods and gets out of the car as fast as she can. They say goodbye and the door closes and the black car races away. This time she doesn't make it to the elevator. She's staring at the petals on the pavement when the tears come, falling with the rain.

# 31

"WHAT'S GOTTEN INTO YOU?" Hank leans on a staff as we take a break on the training ground. He took it easy on me, I know, but for once I managed to stay on my feet as we sparred. The other boys from the Scouring group gather around us. It's Seth, Khan, Marcus, and Jafari, who was assigned to take Axe's place. We're all covered in sweat, bruises, and red clay dust. The six girls—our pairs— look on from the balcony above. Even if they can't hear us, they know what we're feeling.

"The Alpha doesn't even have to train, ya know?" Seth says with a grin.

"Axe got lazy," I say, still breathing heavily. "And you guys know I could use it. Besides, I needed to let off some steam."

"A memory?" Hank asks, leaning closer and dropping his voice.

I nod, but don't know what else to say. *A memory.* It sounds so innocent. It's not. I saw the truth in my own face, through Samantha's eyes. I had achieved more than I could have dreamed for as a lonely kid without a father.

But now, in this young body and through the surreal visions of the towers, I see that I cared only about myself. Otherwise I would have told Sam then, on that rainy spring night, or fifty times before—even before it all started—that it had to stop. If only I could undo it now. It took me a while to tell Emma. It helped to let it vent. She hasn't given up on me. Neither have these boys.

"Don't let a memory cause ya problems," Seth says. "Ya know the best thing to do about it?"

"What?" I ask.

He slams his staff to the ground, hard enough to send a cloud of dust flying. "Beat it out of ya system. Want another go?"

I raise my dulled sword and shield. Seth smiles as he spins his staff. The four other guys spread out around us.

A minute later I'm on my back, heart pounding, legs aching. Seth is standing over me with his staff raised in cheerful victory. He's right. The blur of the weapons slamming into each other, the shuffle of our feet, the blow to my gut—it all made me forget about the memory. For a moment.

"Ya okay?" Seth holds out a hand and helps me up.

"I'm good." I brush dust off my clothes, but leave my dulled sword on the ground. We have two days until the next Scouring, and I want to go after Black. I know the chances are slim that my Mom will be with them, but it's happened before. When I was in Blue, Kiyo went straight from a third-class member of Blue to a fighter in the Scouring for Black. And even if my Mom isn't there, Black has the most members. Capturing from them would bring the towers closer to equilibrium. It would also be revenge.

I glance at Seth's staff. "Do you think if we all used staffs," I say, "instead of swords and axes, we could get through the shields of a Black phalanx?"

Seth shrugs and looks to Marcus. "Ask him. He's been Black."

Marcus shakes his head as he answers, "Staffs might give us better than a zero percent chance. Slightly better."

"So what *are* they weak against?" I ask.

"They're not weak," he answers. "Their two girls shut down every other power, and the boys fight with fierce discipline. Plus, they get ten fully armed boys to our six. Sometimes they'll put a newcomer out with a phalanx, but we'd have no way of knowing who it is."

"That could be a weakness," I say. "Why do they do that?"

"I'm not sure," Marcus says. "I was wiped when I came here. The only things I know about Black were shown in the fire..."

"Like what?" I prod gently. "We have to learn from each other if we're going to fight together."

"It was just a flash of a memory," Marcus says. "I was in the Scouring, with Black. And I...stepped on the white circle, the one in the middle. The Black team knows that's the best place to capture someone, but also does whatever it can to avoid touching the circle."

"Why?" I ask.

"The circle shows each person a memory, an important

one," Marcus says. "It's some kind of key to the White Tower. Everyone in Black guards against it. I think Black reveals very little of the past. I've learned far more in my little time here, in Red. Not that I like it."

This explanation sends my thoughts spinning. The white circle is a key? When I fought in the Scouring for Blue, I stepped on the circle several times. My memory there was the same—a hospital where I was the doctor and my son was the patient, surrounded by my wife and others. I've never been able to finish the memory. Fighters in the Scouring knocked me out of it. I need to try again.

"So what did ya learn about your past here?" Seth asks Marcus.

"I was a Roman gladiator," Marcus answers flatly.

"And you fell in love with the Emperor's daughter," I add.

"Yes, Livia." Marcus runs a hand through his black hair. "I see her over and over again. She's the one who appeared when I stepped onto the white circle. She haunts every flame I see in this burning tower. Her curves and lips and olive skin made Venus jealous…"

Our group falls quiet for a moment, but then Khan bursts out laughing. "An emperor's daughter, eh? I knew we had something in common!"

Marcus almost grins. "Don't tell me you fell for one, too?"

"The most beautiful woman I'd ever seen was the daughter of my emperor, Genghis Khan. He had hundreds of daughters, so I figured he would consent to our marriage. But she was his *first* daughter. He wouldn't give her to me. So we ran away together."

"How'd that turn out for ya?" Seth asks.

Khan shrugs, a smile lingering on his face. "Don't remember. Don't really want to know. My new pair isn't making me look. So I'm not asking."

"Who's your new pair?" I ask.

"Apple," Khan says. "That girl you were with. She's not bad. A lot quieter than Jacana."

*Not bad.* That's an improvement. It makes me smile. "Who's with Jacana now?"

"Me, of course." Jafari thumps his chest. He and his sister will be a wild force together in the Scouring.

"I'm glad," I say. "So, I was asking, how do we take down Black?"

"If you really want to go after them," Marcus replies, "I think the best chance is shoving their girls into the white circle. Then they'd be distracted by memories, and you and our girls could use powers."

The boys look to me, but I glance up at the girls on the balcony. Marcus is right. If the girls from Black weren't in the way, we could weave our powers together. Maybe even Blue, Red, and Yellow at the same time. It could be as strong as my last Scouring with Blue, when I linked with Emma and Kiyo to hold Blue, Yellow, and Black. So. Much. Power. Maybe enough to capture everyone in the Scouring. Four teams of twelve. And if we captured all 48 in one trip, that would put Red's numbers at 144. Equilibrium. It's a stretch, but worth a try. My work as

Alpha would be done.

"Marcus, that's brilliant," I say.

"Or crazy," he says. "You really think you're that good with the wind?"

"It won't be just me. I have a plan."

# 32

THAT NIGHT I enter the Feasting Hall for the first time as the Alpha. The Red Tower welcomes me with a roaring cheer. They must have heard how many we captured in the Scouring. Their chant follows the deep drumbeat, "Alpha, Alpha, Alpha!"

I take the throne beside Rahab. It's not a comfortable seat. But as I look over the long feasting table, with the girls on the left and the boys on the right, I realize that I've accepted this tower. I'm no longer fighting against it. I'm fighting with it. My initial coolness is gone. Something about having Emma back and being the leader again has brought me around to Rahab's view. I still like Blue, but it *is* cold. Genius needs Passion—otherwise I'm the doctor who's always better than others, seeing them as tools. But Passion needs something else to control it—otherwise I'm with Samantha, fueling fires that should never be lit.

The evening's feast ends. There's a performance in the Arena. Our Scouring group stays the same. I wouldn't want it to change.

We continue training and planning until I stand with

my team of twelve before the gate of Scouring again. This time there is no division. The twelve of us know each other. I lead with Emma, followed by Hank and Zelle, Marcus and Boleyn, Seth and Amy, Jafari and Jacana, and Khan and Apple. The girls wear dresses, as usual. The boys wear identical metal helmets with two ram horns coming out of the sides. I'd found them among the Alpha's supplies. Khan told me Axe had never wanted to use them. Axe was a fool. They may be uncomfortable, but they serve as a uniform, uniting the boys as the collars link us to the girls. The helmets will also make it harder for other teams to recognize me, if they try to single me out.

We are ready when the gate rises. "Let passion burn!" I shout.

"Let passion burn!" the group responds, starting to chant.

We continue chanting as we charge into the Scouring. We draw everyone's attention. The other teams watch us go straight to the white circle in the center. We form a circle around it, careful not to let a toe or a heel step onto the milky stone. We face out. We watch. We wait.

None of us uses an ounce of power. We want to make Black come to us, but for their two girls not to have a target. Not yet. If they cloud us with their smoke, it will stop us from using our powers.

I stand on the opposite side of the circle from Black, with Emma close beside me. We face Yellow and Green. Their groups are hardly moving, staying close to their gates. I still know so little about how these two towers work.

Emma told me a little about Yellow. They are healers. But what else? And how does Green hold its own? When I went to their forest with the Blue Tower, the Green fighters hid until they had us surrounded, then sprang a trap. Maybe they wait until they sense another tower is vulnerable. It makes sense. They hide in the forest. They sneak attack.

A clank of metal makes me glance back over my shoulder. Black is coming toward us in a solid square of shields and spears. They're at an angle to reach Marcus first. The plan is working.

*Hold, hold*, I mutter under my breath. Our team has to hold until Black charges us. As soon as they do, I'll send a blast of wind at their backs to knock them into the white circle. Then the Black team will be distracted by memories. We'll fence in the girls with a wall of air and fire, and I can drag the boys out with the wind, one by one. The rest of the Scouring should be easy pickings after that.

"Now!" Marcus shouts.

I spin and summon the wind like a gunslinger. Marcus and the others from Red are diving out of the way. The team from Black is directly in front of me, their shields like an iron wall on the other side of the white circle. Emma's power floods through the link, and I fuse it with the air to send a white-hot howling blast, like a solar flare, into the backs of the Black team. At the same time the other girls from Red summon two walls of flames to lock them in and channel the wind. The Black team has nowhere to go but the white circle.

The front line of Black hits the circle first. They fall to their knees, their expressions going blank. Now the two girls are visible, dressed head to toe in Black. I pull more power. The gale force wind knocks one of the girls into the white circle, where she falls forward and folds over with her head bowed. That leaves only one.

But she stands perfectly still, her pose relaxed, her black clothes motionless despite the wind, her toes an inch from the white circle. Her shadowed eyes under the hood glare out at me.

*Monica.* The same girl who stopped me before. Again she looks familiar.

She holds out her hand, reaching over the white stones, and beckons for me to come. I pull more power, as much I've ever held, but still it has no effect on her. The black smoke smothers me before I can even see it coming, completely severing my link to the power. I hear a voice, Monica's voice, in my mind.

*Come to me*, she says. *I have what you seek.*
*What do I seek?*

Before an answer comes, something slams into my back and knocks me forward. All I see is a blur of green before I'm on my knees in the white circle. I'm instantly in the same vision as before, in the hospital hallway. Monica still stands where she was, but now she's at the end of the hallway. Her eyes are the same, but she's wearing pale blue scrubs like a nurse, instead of a black robe and hood. She has long red hair pulled back. She has a face I know, because…she is Samantha.

*No, not possible*, I tell myself. *It's an illusion.*

Samantha beckons for me just as Monica had. Then she enters a room at the side of the hallway. I rise slowly to my feet.

"We saw this before," Emma says from beside me. She must have been knocked into this, too. Maybe the link forces her to see whatever I see. She's also dressed like a nurse, as she was the first time we were in this vision.

I force myself to breathe, stay calm. "It's a hospital," I say. "Where people are healed."

"It looks…very clean," Emma says.

I move forward down the hallway, Emma following, toward the room that Samantha entered. I open the door and see the same scene as before. Five people are inside. Dr. Fitzroy stands there in his white coat, *my* white coat, saying at the foot of the hospital bed, "*I failed, I failed…*" A young boy lays motionless on the bed with a shaved head and his eyes closed. A woman in a black suit—my wife— kneels by the bed, crying. But this time I know one of the nurses in the room. It's Samantha.

She turns to me. My breath freezes. *She's in the vision. She shouldn't see me.*

"I told you, Paul," she says. "I have what you seek."

The dots connect like fuses. It feels like a bomb exploding inside me. It's true. Samantha is Monica. Monica is Samantha. She is here, in the Black Tower.

*The Scouring is finished.*

The words boom into the hospital room, just as they did in Blue. It is all the same. The booming words, my body frozen in place.

*The fire will try your work*, the voice says. *If your work survives, you shall receive your reward. If your work is burned, you must be purified.*

And then the fire surges, engulfing me, my wife, my son, Emma, Samantha, the hospital, and everything else.

# 33

MY MIND STIRS before my body. I lay on my back, on something soft. A fire crackles nearby, its warmth washing over me. The smell of burning wood and spices fills the air. My hands, my feet, even my eyelids refuse to budge. I stay calm. This is not the first time it's happened—the white circle in the Scouring, the obliterating fire, and the voice. Last time, in the Blue Tower, I woke up in a room of cots with Emma beside me. I had captured her. She was beside me in the vision. Surely she's still with me now. Did I capture anyone from the other towers? I'd knocked everyone in Black into the white circle. The more I remember, the more my gut wrenches with guilt, confusion, excitement. *Samantha is here. Why does she call herself Monica?*

Eventually, my eyelids slowly lift. The first thing I see is Rahab, sitting beside me on the floor.

"Ah, good," she says. "Our Alpha returns to life. Your body will regain motion soon. Consider it a blessing. You need time to think whenever the white blaze consumes you. That was *some* plan out there. Taking the battle against

Black all the way to the White Tower gate, eh? It showed guts. I liked it. And it turned out well, though it could have gone very badly."

"Emma?" I manage to croak, through unwilling lips.

"She's right beside you," Rahab says. "Hello Emma. Keep working on those eyelids. You'll get them open."

"What…happened?" I ask, unable to turn and see Emma.

"You two captured eleven from Black before the Scouring ended." Rahab sounds as pleased as I've ever heard her. "They've all met Behemoth, and they've been wiped. This brings our tower's numbers to 106."

"Who was lost?" My fingers and toes are beginning to wiggle.

"Hank," she answers. "There was an assault by Green while you and Black fought in memories. They took him."

"No…not Hank." *Green?*

"Don't look so worried," Rahab says. "He was captured trying to save you. Quite impressive, really. He had little he needed to see here. He was ready."

"Oh." This reminds me of something Abram told me in Blue. We can see some memories only in certain towers. Does this mean I'll have to go to Green, too? And Yellow? And Black? "Am I ready like Hank was?" I ask.

"No," Rahab says, "but you are close. The hardest things remain to be seen."

Enough mobility has returned for me to shake my head and sit up on my elbows. Emma lays beside me, eyes open, staring at the ceiling. Her skin is pale.

Rahab sits to my other side. Her auburn hair looks redder in the firelight. It reminds me of Samantha. *The hardest things remain.* My mother is in Black. Samantha, too. Maybe that's where I should go. It's not like when I was in Blue, when I thought I needed to save my Mom from the Red Tower. Now I know better. We need *each other* to fully understand our pasts.

"When can I leave Red?" I ask.

Rahab smiles at me, and it is not a kind smile. "If you leave before you have seen what you need to see, you will be wiped. Such a shame that would be, to have to start over with nothing. You'd have to do Red all over again."

Not good. "Is that what happened to my Mom?"

"There are layers of memories—those from earth, and those from here," Rahab says. "Sometimes it is better to remember the remembering than to relive the memory itself. It gives you more distance from the past. The Scouring requires being wiped and learning again and unfolding these layers. You *do* want to leave the five towers, I assume?"

I don't need to answer. The only other option is to be stuck here in this young body forever, always facing the risk of getting wiped. Rahab knows that. I sit up slowly and meet her bright eyes, which reflect the flickering fire. "Is there any way I could go to Black *without* leaving Red and getting wiped?"

"I wondered when you would ask." Rahab studies me calmly.

"Please tell me," I say. "I'll bring back captives if I

can."

"You still think very highly of yourself," she says. "Your mother may not want to come back with you. She has her own stories to learn, and Black may have more to reveal. As it likely will for you, someday."

"But doesn't Black reveal little of the past?" That's what Marcus told me.

"The Black Tower shows what must be shown."

The answer frustrates me. Maybe my Mom and Samantha don't need me. But *I* need them. I want to share our stories, to say sorry. I can't just wait for them to show up in the Scouring. And if I capture them there Rahab might wipe them.

"If I do bring back captives," I say, "will you promise to leave their memories intact?"

"Ah, you feel passion," Rahab muses. She glances to Emma, who is now sitting up as I am. "And what of you, Emma? Would you go with him?"

"I will follow Cipher," Emma says.

"Even into the dark?" Rahab asks.

"Anywhere."

Emma's answer makes me flush with embarrassment. While I'm thinking only of people from my past, of my own scouring, she puts me first. I don't deserve her devotion.

"Very well." Rahab rises slowly. "I will show you something about the Black Tower."

Emma and I manage to stand and shuffle slowly after Rahab to the far wall with the opening. The wind feels much colder away from the fire. The flat, empty stone ground of the Scouring is far below. The Black Tower stands like a thick iron pole along the wall of the Scouring to our left. But there's a mountain ridge separating us, with sheer cliffs rising hundreds of feet and descending directly down to the Scouring's wall.

"You see that you cannot merely walk to it," Rahab says. "The ridge is impassible. Others have tried, and they have ended up blank, back in our tower. But…" She turns to me, her gaze intense. "There is a way. A very dark way."

"What is it?" I ask.

"It is dangerous, but not for the reasons you might think," Rahab says. "You have to go through the tunnels, underneath the towers."

"*Tunnels?*" Emma asks.

I should have thought of it before. Maybe that is how the leaders of the towers meet with each other, and how food from one tower's land can reach another tower.

"How do we reach them?" I ask.

"Behemoth guards the way," Rahab says.

I'd hoped to never see that creature again. "Why?"

"It is the only way. The two of you must pass through his cavern to enter the tunnels. He might let you pass if you've brought our tower to 144."

"That could take a long time," I say.

"Not at your current pace," Rahab replies.

I look to Emma, and she nods. We can do this if we must. "So if we get the numbers," I say, "and Behemoth lets us into these tunnels, what then?"

Rahab's expression is solemn. "As you can see, the distance is not far from here to the Black Tower, but it will take you to the depths, to the edge of the very pit."

"What does that mean?" I ask.

"You will see," Rahab says. "But I must warn you, there is a place far worse than the five towers. You may glimpse it in the depths." Rahab surprises me by shuddering, her skin suddenly looking pale and cold.

"What is this place?"

"I will not speak of it."

"But…how could we glimpse it in the tunnels?"

"The tunnels pass by the pit, where darkness grows and pulls and tries to never let go. Some have been lost."

"They died? Or were taken to this worse place?"

Rahab seems uncertain. "There is only one way out."

*The White Tower.* That's where I want to go, but not without my Mom. "I have to try the tunnels," I say. "I want my mother back."

A faint smile forms at the corner of Rahab's mouth. "Passion can lead you to very bad or very great things."

"Which is this?"

"I'm not sure." She looks down. "Even we, the leaders, have memories. And so even we avoid the tunnels if possible. As much as I want to see Joshua, it is not worth what I must pass through to reach him."

Her explanation leaves me speechless. The leaders *do* have memories. They even have fears.

"Who is Joshua?" Emma asks softly.

"An old friend," Rahab says. "And the leader of the

Black Tower."

"You're *friends?*" I ask, failing to hide my disbelief. "How is that possible? You lead your towers against each other."

Rahab smiles. "The competition has its purpose. The Scouring has its purpose. Just as Passion, Genius, and the other facets each have purpose. They all work upon you, whether you like it or not. There, now I have told you what I can. I will not stand in your way. Lead on, Alpha."

# 34

IT DOES NOT take long for the Red Tower to discover that I'm nothing like our former Alpha, Axe aka Max. I sit on the throne beside Rahab in the Feasting Hall, but I don't serve firewater or stand on the table to dance and sing. Things are quieter, more thoughtful. I don't need to shout to show that I'm in charge. Everyone knows it. No one in Red remembers anyone capturing someone from Black, much less eleven at the same time. People whisper about me in the Feasting Hall, in the Barracks, and in the Arena as the boys compete. Furtive eyes catch mine, then duck back into conversation. People avoid me in the hallways. I go to the training ground and continue to improve, slowly. It's the only thing that takes my mind off the next Scouring, the tunnels, my Mom, and Samantha. Emma sits with me, talks with me. She heals my bruises from the training ground. But she can't heal the holes inside me, just as I can't heal hers.

In the next Scouring, we lose no one and capture six. All of them from Yellow. All of them wiped. There was no sign of Monica, but we kept our distance from Black. Their ability to shut down my power makes me wary.

In the Scouring after that, I hunt for Blue and see no familiar faces. We bring back three from Blue and two from Green. We tried to avoid Black again, but they attacked. Their girls neutralized ours, making it a pure physical struggle. The Red boys proved their worth. Jafari leapt over the wall of shields and took out the three captives by himself. Marcus, Seth, and Khan scattered the rest.

In the third Scouring since Monica stopped me, I lead our team to capture the entire team of twelve from Blue. It's hard to drag them all back, because the other towers know that's when we're weak. Black and Green rush at us. We lose Seth's pair, Amy, to Black. We would have lost more if not for Jacana and Boleyn guarding our retreat. Twelve gained should be worth one lost, but it doesn't feel that way. We agree to be more measured next time.

One of the new captives from Blue is Tom, who was the former American President Thomas Jefferson. We went on the Hunting together. We fought together for Blue in the Scouring. But despite my pleading, Rahab sends him to Behemoth to be wiped. I don't know enough about him to help reconstruct his memories. It seems too risky. The fire will have to show him in time.

Everyone has been wiped since Hank and Emma came to Red willingly, looking for me. I miss Hank. I couldn't bear to lose Emma again. We stay glued to each other's side every trip into the Scouring.

Days and weeks pass. The three suns rise and fall.

Then one day, without warning, two of the suns do not appear. There's only one, as there was when I first saw it during my voyage to the Yellow Tower with Emma. I wonder if the suns are something entirely different, like symbols that I don't understand. There's still so much I don't understand, but there's one thing I've learned well: how to capture in the Scouring.

It takes six more Scourings before we reach 144. Rahab announces it cheerfully in the Feasting Hall. She praises me as the leader and representative of our efforts. She says everyone may now see more of the past. She says the Scouring is doing its work, even for those who do not set foot into the battle. After the feast begins, I ask Rahab, sitting beside me on the throne, if Behemoth will finally let us enter the tunnels.

"It is now safe to ask," she answers, smiling.

The next morning Emma and I descend through the Red Tower together. We reach the door where Rahab first took me after arriving in Red. It is made of iron, with the shape of a flame formed out of rubies in the center—exactly like the door to the Alpha's quarters.

"Touch the symbol with your fire," I say to Emma, and she does.

The door opens, letting a dank stench spill out.

"Ugh." Emma holds her arm over her nose. "That's terrible."

"You don't like the smell of wet dog?" I ask, and she laughs uneasily. The joke would hide my fear, except that Emma knows what I feel through the Pairing. It probably has her on edge.

When we step through the door, it slams shut behind us. This time there's no Rahab on the other side. There's no handle or way out. The room is pitch black. A low rumble sounds like breathing near us.

"It's okay," I whisper, more to myself than to Emma.

"What should we do?" she asks.

"I don't know." A faint breeze of air brushes against my skin. There must be another doorway to reach the tunnels. "Let's look for an opening."

I take Emma's hand, and we move as quietly as possible, staying close to the wall. The deep breathing continues as we inch forward. My heart thumps quickly. We still can't see anything. Eventually we come back to the same door we had entered, with the flame symbol. It's still closed.

"It's a circle," Emma whispers. "What now?"

A faint light appears. I look back into the room. A huge yellow eye has opened. It stares right at us. The dragon's body doesn't move, except for a slight parting of its lips, revealing teeth as long as my arms.

"Do you want out?" the dragon growls.

I grab for the air but cannot find it.

"Not allowed here," it rumbles, sounding like an avalanche of stone.

I force myself to stay calm. "Rahab said you are Behemoth. She told us you would let us pass into the tunnels."

The dragon snorts and a dozen flames suddenly spring

into life around the perimeter of the room. The cavern is a dome. The beast has reddish black skin like magma. It stretches, straightening its short legs and raising its wings high into the cavern, almost touching the walls around us. It's the dragon we saw in the mountains. It's the dragon that breathed fire and burned Seymour to nothing and first showed me Samantha. It's the dragon with serpentine eyes fixed on me.

"Do you fear me?" Each word grinds out slowly from the creature. "You have much to learn. Even the wildest forces were made to be tamed."

With its neck arched up, there's a sudden intake of air, like a vacuum sucking up all the oxygen in the vast room. Then comes a deep growl and a blast of fire, spewing out of its mouth and up through a chute in the ceiling. The blazing fire lights the cavern completely and makes the room unbearably hot. Emma and I instinctively crouch back toward the door, but the fire relents.

"So be it, you may enter." Behemoth moves to the side, claws scraping against rock, and reveals an opening that leads down.

"We want to reach the Black Tower," I say.

The huge slitted eyes blink. "Go left."

I look to Emma. Her pale face is strikingly serene.

"I don't like this," I whisper. "What do we do when we come back? Tap its belly?"

"We will find a way," she says, turning to face the beast. "You are chaos, not destruction."

"Wise one," Behemoth growls. "Passion holds chaos at

its core. All was chaos before order."

"You don't have to be afraid," Emma says to me, grabbing my hand and pulling me forward. I spare a last glance at the dragon as we step into the tunnel. It eyes me like breakfast but does not move to stop us.

I try to breathe deeply, to calm myself, but it doesn't stop the shaking. Something about what Emma said, and Behemoth's answer, has unsettled me. It grows darker and darker as we descend. I can barely see my own feet.

"Can you light the way?" I ask.

"Sorry, my power's not working," she says. "We can feel our way." She sounds so confident, so unlike how I feel.

"Have you been here before?" I ask.

"Not that I remember, but it shouldn't be far. The Black Tower is close, to the left. Come on."

We soon reach an opening. Emma continues to lead, following the wall on the left. Her grip on my hand becomes my only orientation. There is an echo and a movement of wind that makes me think we've entered a vast room, maybe even bigger than the room with Behemoth.

Something snags at my foot, almost tripping me. There's a hollow thud and clinking sound, like whatever I tripped over was knocked away. After a few more steps I'm suddenly stumbling over countless clinking objects. Emma causes the same sound as she moves just in front of me.

"What is this?" I ask, trying to step carefully.

"I think the tunnel opened up," Emma says from

ahead, her voice echoing. "Maybe it's the pit Rahab mentioned."

She has stopped, from the sound of it. I move forward step by awkward step over the rolling, clinking objects. I still can't see anything. Then I bump into something. Emma.

"Sorry." I manage to hold her arm and stabilize both of us. The ground is no longer firm underneath. It is completely covered by these shifting, rolling, hollow things.

"Can you feel the air?" she whispers.

It is moving, swirling in a gentle breeze. This room must be huge. "Try again to summon a fire," I say. "We need light."

"No, something's not right." She sounds afraid, but mesmerized. "We have to keep going. Faster."

We hold hands as we stumble forward over the objects, always within reach of the wall on our left. We move faster and faster, fear tightening around us. We would run if we could, but we continually trip over the objects on the floor.

There's a shift in the air, as if maybe there will be another tunnel. We have to find the way out. The darkness makes it impossible. It would help to at least *feel* my way ahead, with the air. I focus and summon a thread of it. But the moment the air moves under my command, chaos erupts around us. The wind gusts and knocks me back against the wall. I collapse onto the clattering pile.

*This was to be*, says a booming voice, *but for you.*

# 35

A VISION OVERTAKES ME.

Samantha, an older, gray-haired Samantha, stands in a kitchen with marble countertops and pristine, white tile floors. The windows reveal a rolling green landscape. There is a red barn and a silo. Picket fences separate the fields in the distance. It is bucolic perfection. And Samantha is happy, deeply happy. I feel exactly what she feels, as if she wore a link around her neck. I have no option but to watch and listen, to experience the world as she does. Or as she might have. *This was to be, but for you…*

She looks from the beautiful view out the window to seven young children who sit at the kitchen counter. They are eating breakfast—scrambled eggs. Their red and blonde hair has a lustrous sheen in the morning light. Their bright faces stare at Samantha as they chew.

"Nana," one of kids says. "Where do eggs come from?"

Samantha comes to the counter and leans on her elbows, glancing from child to child. "Good question, Anne! Eggs come from chickens. We can show you today, if you'd like."

"Yes, yes!" The other kids join in. They are very excited about these chickens.

"Can we go now?" one of them asks.

"Finish your breakfast," Samantha says. "Your parents really ought to get you out of the city more often."

"But I like the city," a young boy says. "It has pigeons."

"Did you know pigeons can carry messages?" Samantha asks.

This strikes all the kids with wonder. Samantha tells them about how pigeons carry little notes tied to their legs. She says they always seem to know how to get back to the same place, like an internal homing device. She tells them how she hopes they'll learn to feel the same way about coming to see Nana in the country.

A man and woman enter the room. Three of the seven kids rush to them. There are hugs and kisses.

"Mommy! Daddy!" the oldest says. "We get to see chickens today!"

"And eggs!" another adds.

The couple smiles. The woman looks just like Samantha. The man is handsome, in a tweed coat and loafers. He looks to Samantha. "It's been a while since I've seen a chicken. Can we join?"

"Of course," Samantha says. "But breakfast first!"

The kitchen bustles with life as the children and their parents eat. Another couple enters. This time it's the husband who looks just like Samantha. These are Samantha's children and her grandchildren. The plates are mostly empty. Dishes are stacked in the sink as the sunlight streams in.

An older man opens the back door and steps inside. He wears a felt hat and a trim green coat. His boots are covered in mud.

"Don't you dare take another step," Samantha says, moving to him. She kisses him and smiles. "Ready to lead an adventure?"

"My, my," he says, lifting off his hat and bowing his head slightly. "You're beautiful as the sunrise."

"Oh hush." Samantha's cheeks warm as she touches his hand and feels the gentle and joyful glow of decades of knowing his love. "The children are listening."

The older man looks out over the group. There are eleven others now—the two younger couples and their seven children. "What's the adventure?" the man asks.

"To see the chickens," she says.

"Ah, and maybe find a green rooster feather?" the man smiles. "What are we waiting for?"

The kids rush to the door, squealing with excitement. Samantha helps them as they slip on their boots and coats and follow the man out the door. She turns back into the kitchen, where the two couples remain.

Her daughter frowns. "They're going to come back so muddy."

"Dirt does a kid good," Samantha says.

"It's cleaner than a city street," her son adds. "Thanks again for taking care of them. We've needed a break."

"Oh it's our pleasure," Samantha says. "You four finish up and get going. We'll take good care of the kids. You need time with each other. Just you. God knows Henry and I needed it. Would you believe we've been married forty years now?"

"We know, mom," her daughter says with an indulgent smile.

"And you know how we met, working in the hospital?"

"We know, mom," her daughter answers again. "He was a young pastor, you were a nurse and…"

"He had the tenderest heart," Samantha says. "Good thing I worked late that night to see him, because otherwise there was this young doctor who had been flirting with me. He was married. That would *not* have ended well." She looks to her son and her son-in-law. "You young men work too hard. Remember, there's different kinds of success. Like having a next generation and one after that to come out to your place and see the chickens, okay?"

"We know, mom," her son says. He rises and gives her a hug. "You've told us enough times now." He glances to his sister. "That's number four hundred fifteen, right?"

She laughs. "I'd lost count."

"That's okay," he says. "The more she says it, the better behaved we'll be, right?"

"Right," Samantha says, hands on her hips but smiling. "Now get going, you four. Don't you worry about the dishes. I'll take care of it."

# 36

WHEN THE VISION ENDS, everything is dark. Odd shapes are beneath me, like short and thick sticks, poking at painful angles. I try to sit up but slip and fall. The objects clink and clatter over each other. I reach down through them but there's no bottom. The things must be stacked high. They feel like bones, but there are so many…

"Cipher, here," Emma says, very close to me but completely hidden in the dark. Her hand finds mine. We help each other stand.

"We have to get out of here," I say.

"I know." Her breaths are quick and shallow. "You feel…like me. Let's hurry."

We manage not to trip as we find the wall and inch along it again. I don't dare summon my power, fearing another vision. This one was so beautiful and so good, but the voice said it didn't happen, because of me. It makes it painful, because if the Samantha in the vision is right, I'm the one who stole that future from her. How could I have known? Why would this place show it to me? There's something very wrong about it.

It is not far before we find a doorway. We enter and, finally, come to the end of the things on the ground. The solid rock is comforting under our feet. A speck of light the size of a pinhead shines in the distance. We begin to run.

The path rises steeply upward. My legs begin to feel the effort. As the light grows, we slow. We can see each other.

I stop to catch my breath and look back. It's too dark in the tunnel to see whatever it was we left. The sound of the clattering objects still reverberates in my mind.

"Don't stop yet." Emma pulls me forward. "Let's get outside first."

We press on to the opening. It emerges high on a ledge of a steep, rocky slope. Rows of terraced green hills lay before us, with a few figures scattered about in the distance. They seem to be working, heads down, oblivious of the strangers who appeared through the tunnel. The hills are bordered on the left by cliffs rising to a steep ridge. We must have gone underneath it, crossing from Red to Black. To our right, the hills flatten and lead to a shaft of seamless iron that jabs into the sky. The Black Tower. It is closer than I expected, and more intimidating. Beyond the tower the land flattens and stretches to the ocean, which extends to the horizon.

Emma sits on the ground, hugging her knees.

I sit beside her and think. The angle of our perch keeps us out of sight from the workers below. It's not an ideal spot for a conversation, but we have to talk. Emma knows what I'm feeling. I don't know what she saw.

"Back there," I say. "The vision I saw was…"

"Different," Emma finishes for me. "Mine was as well."

"How?"

"I wasn't in it," she says, pausing, as if trying to find the right words. "It showed a few people I knew, and others I didn't. Many children. There was so much life. They were so…happy."

"It was like that for me, too."

"Was it the woman you told me about?" Emma asks. "Samantha?"

I nod. "She was older. She had children, and grandchildren."

"And they were happy?"

"Yes."

"Were you in the vision?" Emma asks.

"No. Were you in yours?"

Emma shakes her head. Her eyes are moist as she gazes out over the hills. We are quiet for a while.

*The vision didn't have me in it. I wasn't even there.* Samantha had a husband. She'd met him in the hospital. They'd had children. They'd had a life together.

"Why were we shown this?" I ask.

"Maybe it's not enough to know what we *did*," Emma says. "Maybe we have to see what we *destroyed*. Those things, covering the ground…they were bones, weren't they?"

"It felt like it," I say quietly. *But how? Bones?*

Emma takes a deep breath. "When I was in the Yellow

Tower, I learned that some things can't be healed. I'm not talking about diseases or wounds. But…alternatives, consequences."

"What do you mean?"

"The vision," she says, her voice distant. "I think it never happened."

"A voice said that to me. You heard it?"

"Yes, the same as in the Scouring. I saw John, the man I ran away with. Remember? We had a baby and lived in a poor little hovel. He grew sick. He died. I'm sure of that. But in this vision I saw him as an old man. He was very much alive. He had children, grandchildren, even *great-*grandchildren. There was a portrait above the fireplace in the modest home where he lived. It was a beautiful portrait, and I knew it was his prized possession. It showed a woman in her youth. She was the woman he had loved for many years and had only recently lost in old age. And she…was not me." Emma clutches her knees tighter, looking away.

"I'm sorry," I say. "I can't imagine…"

"But you can," Emma whispers. "Tell me what you saw."

"Samantha," I begin. "She lived in the country, and she was making breakfast for her grandchildren in the kitchen. Her husband came in. She loved him so much. They had been together forty years. They were watching the grandkids so their own children could get away for a couple days. Her husband, he led the kids out to see the chickens. They'd met in the hospital. The same one where I'd worked, where I'd started secretly seeing Samantha. The voice said I'm the reason why this never happened."

Emma lets her head fall onto my shoulder, and I let mine fall onto hers, and we hold each other and cry. I think of what Rahab said about the tunnels and the glimpse into the pit. Even she feared the place. I don't need to know what it all means. It's clear enough. I didn't control my passions. I kept the children I saw from ever living. I filled the dark place with bones.

So much loss, so many lives never lived. The accusations drag me down, defeat me. Even those who didn't exist had the same ending I did: as bones buried underground. Maybe none of us should have existed at all. The thought spills over my mind like ink, blotting out the other visions.

But, no, that can't be right.

I'm still here, with Emma, with light and color, alive in some way in these five towers. We can still be better than we were. We have to keep moving, learning from what we see, no matter how bad it hurts. Otherwise the dark terrors of that bone-filled cavern—the knowledge of what might have been—will ruin us. That's why I have to find my Mom and Samantha and anyone else who knew me before and now is here. I have to tell them all: *I'm sorry*. I have to ask them to forgive me. No matter how bad it hurts. I'm not just bones yet.

I study the rigid lines of the Black Tower. It's too reckless, even for me, to stroll up to it and hope to somehow get inside. My power won't help. The girls here will shut me down. Emma and I could be caught, and our memories could be wiped.

As I look away from the tower and out over the hills, I wonder if my Mom or Samantha could be one of the workers. There's a worker on the nearest hill, facing the opposite direction from us and bending and rising, bending and rising, putting small, grassy plants into the ground in rows. There are two on the next hill, one on the terraces closer to the ridgeline. They're doing the same kind of work. I've counted thirteen workers when I first notice a darker cluster mid-hill in the distance. It looks like a few low buildings. Maybe the workers there are far enough away from the Black Tower to need a resting place. Everyone in Red and Blue lives in the tower, but there's no reason the other towers couldn't be different. The Black Tower could have a village for its farmers.

"You see that?" I ask Emma, pointing to the cluster.

She stirs from her quiet. "The buildings? I see three of them."

"Right. Maybe it's a village. Want to check it out?"

"You're the Alpha," she says.

"And I'm *your* pair."

She smiles, spinning her ruby ring. "I think we're past labels. But since I know how excited you feel, lead on…"

I can't help but smile back. She's riding my rollercoaster of emotions with me, as I did with her in the Blue Tower. She's choosing to trust me. As if I've earned it.

"We'll go to the village," I say. "Who knows, maybe

they'll welcome us as visitors and offer us dinner."

Emma rises to her feet. "Looks like they'll have plenty of rice."

# 37

MY LEATHER BOOTS were not made for this. From a distance the terraced hills of the Black Tower looked like a fine stroll. But as Emma and I descend from the tunnel opening, the mud deepens. I try to step lightly and evenly, on the driest places, but still each step down brings a swallowing *swelp* and *suck*, and each step up a *pop* and *slop* and *squelch* as my boot breaks free from the mire again. The sounds repeat a thousand times. My feet prune like shriveled raisins.

Emma had a better idea. With the first muddy encounter, she slipped off her shoes and carried them. She lifted her dress and tied it in a knot above her knees. Her calves are caked in grayish black goo, but at least her feet rise and fall easier.

"It's exfoliating," she says.

The first person to spot us doesn't run. It's a girl working on one of the terraces, barefoot like Emma, broad hat on her head, as she places thin green reeds, one by one, into the ankle-deep water. She looks up at us for only a moment before continuing her work. She is methodical.

Reed after reed in a clear pattern. Order and discipline mark the entire field.

This must be the Black Tower's way. Rice grows best in a place of order. Someone orchestrates the planting of seeds, then the replanting of seedling shoots into perfectly straight lines. Armies of workers harvest the grain by hand, gathering enough to fill the bellies of the hundreds here in Black. It couldn't be more different from Red, where the pigs only need a daily slop of food and a butchering knife.

As we crest another terraced hill, we see more hills stretching into the distance and a village in the valley below. The village has several low buildings with black-tiled roofs, wedged like lint in the fold of these dark hills. We descend, passing two more workers, and reach the thin cobblestone street running through the center of the village. The firm ground feels good. The street curves around several hills in the distance, leading toward the Black Tower. It looks like a half-day's walk to get there. Maybe more if there's mud to wade through.

Our arrival in the village is quickly noticed. People gather in doorways, staring at us. I expect to see families, mixed ages, coming to greet us. But they are all boys and girls around our age. No one seems to grow very old here, other than the leaders. These boys and girls wear dark, charcoal robes. They are mostly dirty, scrawny, and shoeless, with vacant eyes. They whisper in tight clusters as we walk along the cobblestones.

"She's from Red," one girl whispers, staring at Emma and her dress.

A boy spits at me. Another says something crude about Emma. I stay alert, ready to draw on our power, but no one tries to stop us.

Ahead a girl steps onto the center of the path, facing us with her arms crossed. She's dressed like the others, but I freeze in my tracks. Her eyes are narrow, dark as night, with flecks of gold like stars.

"*Kiyo.*"

"Why are you here?" she asks coldly.

I move forward until I'm a few feet away from her. She has no idea who I am. I hold out my hands peacefully. "I'm looking for my mother."

"There are no mothers here," Kiyo says.

This is a bad sign. Kiyo herself was a mother. She has been wiped and hasn't even seen yet what she saw in Blue. The villagers gather closer, enclosing Emma and me.

"You know that's not true," I say calmly. "You were a mother. Your sons would be looking for you, too."

Kiyo shakes her head. She shows no emotion. "I have no sons."

It makes me want to cry, to see her so blank. "You did before," I say. "You told me about them, when we were in Blue."

She grimaces like I've punched her in the gut. She looks away from me, at the group around us. Her crossed arms release and press down over her rough, charcoal robe, smoothing non-existent wrinkles.

"Those from Red cannot be trusted," she says. "Come, we will decide what to do with you."

Turning without another word, she enters a small wooden building beside us. The people around us step closer. A few of them point to the building that Kiyo entered. It could be a trap, but it's better than starting a fight now if we can avoid it. We could be wiped like Kiyo. Maybe I can help her remember. It's also still the best bet for finding my Mom and Samantha, if they're anywhere around here.

Emma and I exchange a glance. She knows about Kiyo, too. After Abram, Kiyo was the first person who came to me in the Blue Tower. Even without memories, she should have the same spirit—gentle and stoic.

"It's okay," Emma says. "Let's go."

We enter the building together. None of the other villagers follow us.

Inside is a single room, clean and simple, made of dark wood. The light is dim, the air still. Everything is still, as if this is a place where things move only in tiny increments, at their designated time and for their designated purpose. To one side, the floor is a sunken rectangle around a table on a mat of tightly woven straw. A candle, four small porcelain cups, and a steaming pot rest on the table. Kiyo waits for us with her knees folded and her robe blending into the dark wood below her.

Emma and I take seats across from each other at the table. I sit beside Kiyo so that I can keep an eye on the door. It's the only way in or out.

Kiyo pours steaming liquid from the pot into all four cups. I take the cup in my hand, feeling its warmth. The drink is pale green and smells like tea. It must be harmless. If she'd wanted to hurt us, she could have ordered the villagers to seize us outside. Unless she wanted to make it cleaner. Then she'd poison our tea.

She takes a sip. It was poured from the same pot.

"Drink," she says.

We do as ordered. It tastes good.

"Who's that cup for?" I ask, eyeing the fourth spot at the table. The steam from the cup rises in nearly straight lines through the still air.

"Me."

A boy's harsh voice comes from behind me. *Where did he come from?* Before I can even turn I feel the prick of something sharp at the back of my neck.

"Don't move," he demands. "Rice, why do you bring Red under my roof?"

There's something familiar about the voice. If only I could see…

As I try to turn my head, the sharp point presses harder into my neck, forcing me to look forward. I take a deep breath, staying still. Out of the corner of my eye I see Kiyo bow her head in an obvious display of deference.

"This boy claims to know me, Lord," Kiyo says. "Maybe he has not always been Red. Maybe he has been here before."

"Or maybe he is a spy. Or an assassin." The voice behind me sounds like an executioner's. "He must die."

The point pulls away from my neck. The floor creaks. Across the table, Emma's face twists in fear. Her eyes reflect a gleaming line, like metal.

*No, I will not go down like this.*

Things happen all at once. I summon the air into a wall behind me. The blade strikes it and bounces off. The boy shouts. A cloud of black smothers my mind, and my power slip away. I leap across the table to Emma.

We try to flee, but the boy is faster. He moves like a shadow and stands between us and the only door. The light behind him and the hood over his head make it impossible to make out his face in the dark room. As he closes on us, his sword rises through the still air. But then Kiyo is in front of us. The blade begins to swing but stops inches from her.

"He's harmless, Lord," Kiyo says. "I've shut him down."

"Good," the hooded boy says. "Now they'll be easier to kill. Out of the way."

Emma squeezes my hand. "Now," she whispers.

The surge of heat warms me before I even see it, blasting into the boy, flinging him back in a blaze of fire. His sword thuds against the dark wooden floor. I grab it and charge at the boy, but something trips me flat. The blade is yanked away from me. The boy and I are only a few feet apart, both rushing to our feet. The sword appears between us, separating us.

"Stop!" Kiyo demands, wielding the blade like she knows how to use it. "No powers. No swords. We will have tea. Then we will talk. Am I understood?"

"You will suffer for this," the boy says, scowling.

"I have suffered enough," Kiyo replies.

The boy moves toward her. Kiyo swings the blade to his neck, freezing him in place. "You know I'll do it."

The boy growls in anger, but he nods. "Fine. Tea."

He steps away from the blade and past me, toward the table. For the first time I glimpse his face. I should be surprised, but I'm not. It's Max, Axe, Lord, or whatever he wants to call himself now. It seems he'll haunt me wherever I go.

# 38

THE LUKEWARM GREEN TEA feels a lot better than steel in my throat. Kiyo sits beside me, still holding the blade that Max and I fought over. She keeps its long edge against the dark wooden table, pointed at Max across from her. In my mind he's more Max than Axe now. He looks like he did when I first met him in Blue, a little younger and without the beard that he somehow grew in Red. He seems to fit better here. His knuckles are as white as the porcelain cup that he clenches. He sips from the cup and grimaces.

"If the tea has grown cold," Kiyo says to him, "the Lord has only himself to blame."

"Rice should know better than to mock me," Max replies, fixing an angry stare on her. "The Masters will hear of this."

Kiyo bows her head calmly. "We will await their judgment."

Emma sets her cup down and leans forward. "Thank you, Kiyo, for keeping things civilized. I'm sorry that we have not been properly introduced. My name is Emma Chamberlain." She's smiling as if this truly is a tea party and Max didn't just try to kill us both. She must not remember him, or being his servant, because of what the link did to her. That's probably a good thing.

"Nice to meet you." Kiyo smiles back. "We do not have such grand names here. I am Rice."

"That's not your name," I say, but Emma gives me a look and shakes her head, blond hair swaying. It's clear she wants to do the talking. My heart is still pounding. She knows that. I lean back.

"What Cipher means," Emma says, "is that he remembers you from before. I also heard much about you."

"You were in Black?" Kiyo asks.

Her question reveals so much: she does not even remember everything in Black. She's been wiped here more than once.

"No, from another tower." Emma's voice is gentle. "We were once in the Blue Tower. I believe all four of us were. I was also in Yellow. In the same Scouring when Cipher captured me from Yellow, Black captured you, Kiyo. In another Scouring Cipher brought you back to Blue, but then you were caught again. It seems Black has a special interest in you."

"She is not Kiyo," Max says. "She is Rice."

"And you are Lord, it seems." Emma folds her hands on the table. "Tell us more about these titles."

"You are our captives," Max says. "We do not give secrets to spies."

"We're not spies," I snap. Emma's pleasant

conversation clearly isn't winning over Max. "We just want to find someone and leave."

Max sips his tea and grimaces like it's poison. "You're lying. Give me one reason why we should let you leave here alive."

*One reason.* There are so many. But if there's one thing all of us in the five towers want, it's to know who we were before this place. Marcus told me the Black Tower does not reveal much about the past. I have the advantage of knowing about Kiyo and Max.

"You lived in China," I say.

He waves his hand dismissively. "That means nothing. A lucky guess."

"So I'm right about you?" I ask.

He grunts. He doesn't deny it.

I lean forward, elbows on the table, fingers tapping silently on the white porcelain cup between my hands. "Wouldn't you like to know more about your past?"

Max breathes in deeply, then looks to Kiyo.

"Go on," she says, smiling encouragingly, "this can stay between us if you like."

He turns back to me. "Tell me what you know."

For the first time I feel sympathy for him. We're all the same here, desperate to remember, even if it hurts, even if we have to do it over and over again.

"I'm like you," I say. "I also want to know about myself. That's why we came here, to find two people I knew from before. One is Rose Fitzroy. She has brown eyes and long brown hair with a strand of white down the side. The other is Monica. She—" I hesitate, realizing I've never seen her full face here, only her eyes. Would she look like Samantha did as a younger girl? "She should have red hair," I say. "Do you know if Rose or Monica are here?"

"We're talking about *my* past," he says.

"Yes, if you help me."

"I could still kill you."

"Then you'd learn nothing." I meet his glare, steady. "Do you know if Rose or Monica are here?"

Kiyo whispers something to Max. It sounds like "number 9." He does not react.

"If you can help me find them," I say, "I'll tell you everything I know about your past, and Kiyo's. And I know a lot."

"This sounds fair," Kiyo says.

Max is shaking his head, but he doesn't say no. "If this girl you call Rose were here," he says, "what would you do if you found her?"

I want to say, *take her back!* But my mouth stays shut long enough to formulate a better response. "I want to talk with her, that's all. I don't know what comes after that."

He leans back and crosses his arms. "You infiltrated our lands to *talk* to someone? Again you lie. You will not capture anyone here. No one leaves this village without my permission."

"He's right," Kiyo says. "There are twelve of us here. The Masters would not look kindly on someone going missing. It won't do us any good if you tell us about our pasts, only for us to get wiped because we lost one of our villagers."

"So bring the girl here," Emma says. "You can guard her."

"This might work…" Max rubs his chin as he thinks. The rest of us are quiet, watching him. With his severe eyes and square jaw, he looks every bit like a leader, or a Lord, as they apparently call him here. He takes a deep breath, as if making up his mind. "Whatever. Maybe they wipe us. Maybe they don't. Tell us what you know, and if it's good enough, we'll bring the girl number 9 here and see what you would like to *talk* about."

"Yes!" Kiyo says softly but excitedly. "Thank you!"

"Rice, more tea," Max says. "And hot this time?"

"As you wish, Lord." Kiyo bows and excuses herself from the table.

We sit in quiet. She returns shortly with steaming cups.

I start with Max's story. I tell them everything from the Blue Tower, how he went by Max, but leave out the parts when I blew him out of his chair in my first class, beat him in the boat race, and when he shoved me off the pier into the water and got himself wiped. The rest of the story is not so bad. We were in the same class. He was a leader of our class in Blue, as he is here. But he was somehow captured by Red. With Red he rose quickly to Alpha, the leader of the tower. I say nothing of how he was captured by Black, and he doesn't ask. Instead he asks what I know about his past on earth. I tell him the little I'd gleaned from Marcus. He was a very wealthy and powerful man in China. He had four daughters. There had been a conflict with one of them, but I didn't know what had happened after that.

As Max listens, his expression slowly transforms from severe to distant to sad. "Do you remember their names?" he asks softly. "My daughters?"

"No," I admit. "I'm sorry."

"It is okay. I am glad to know what you have told me." Max gestures to Kiyo. "Your turn, Rice."

I give Kiyo's story as gently as I can. I tell her about her cold journey in Japan, fleeing from enemies, protecting her five children through the mountains and the snow, only to lose her oldest. As I speak, her eyes soften as Max's did. I think hearing the past gives them a glimmer of hope, reminding them that existence is more than this Black Tower.

The light outside begins to fade. A single candle on the table allows us to see each other dimly. I continue with Kiyo's story through our time in the Blue Tower, through our battles together in the Scouring. When I finish, it's quiet and dark outside.

"Thank you, Cipher." Kiyo stands, her face solemn and pale. "I will think on this," she says. "But first let's sleep. I would like to dream tonight."

<h1 style="text-align:center">39</h1>

EMMA AND I sleep on pallets in the dark room where I told Max's and Kiyo's stories. The next morning we wake to the smell of cooking rice and a rooster's crow. Max and Kiyo sit again at the table, along with a third person. My Mom.

I take the seat across from her, meeting her eyes, waiting, hoping. Emma sits beside me. She squeezes my hand assuringly.

"Good morning," Kiyo says to us. "We have brought who you wanted to see."

"I'm Villager 9," my Mom says, and her stiff, formal tone breaks my heart.

"I'm Cipher. This is Emma. We've met before."

"Oh?" my Mom asks.

Kiyo and Max watch me curiously. There's no reason to delay or avoid the topic, even if it tears me apart. "I'm your son," I say. "Or, I was."

"That's cute." My Mom smiles and looks to Kiyo. "Who is this boy?"

"I suspect he will tell you," Kiyo says.

"My name was Paul Fitzroy. Yours was Rose Fitzroy. You gave birth to me in 1978, in a city called Chicago, in a country called the United States of America, on a planet called earth."

She looks away from me, turning to Max. She's no longer smiling. "Lord, is this true?"

I answer before Max can. "He doesn't know. I know. I *was* your son. I've seen the past. You were in the Red Tower before Black caught you. They wiped your memories."

"What does he mean?" she asks, ignoring me and looking from Max to Kiyo. "Wiped?"

"The Masters ensure we start clean," Max says.

"Why?" she asks.

"It is not our place to question this." Max does not sound entirely convinced. "We have our roles here, and we must perform them well. The best will rise to the top. It is right. It is just."

This must be Black's mantra. I don't like it. "I've come from the Red Tower," I say to my Mom, "It's better there. You were one of the most powerful girls in Red. You had freedom, passion." I motion to the drab surroundings—dark wooden floors, charcoal robes, and rice. "Come back with me and you will wear a silk dress and eat like a queen."

"This is forbidden," Max snaps. "But even if it was allowed, going to Red would be a tragic mistake. Red lacks control. Go to them and you will only be brought back here, with your memories erased again."

My Mom calmly lifts her chopsticks and takes a bite of

rice, chewing slowly. Her face is beautiful as ever, but disturbingly empty. Before she was everything I remembered. Now she is only a hollow shell. I wonder again at why our memories must be erased. How does this process help anything? Do our minds have to be empty so that they can be filled a certain way and renewed? And if so, why haven't I been wiped yet? My Mom must be reeling to be rediscovering memories for the second or third or hundredth time. I would be.

"Mom," I say gently, "what are you thinking?"

"This person you say I was…will you tell me more about her?"

"I will tell you what I know. I think it will start coming back to you. You seemed to remember nearly everything when we last talked in Red. You filled in so many gaps for me."

She studies Max thoughtfully. "The Masters say that when our minds are properly disciplined and filled, then we may leave through the white light. This boy says he can help. Is that possible?"

Max opens his mouth to answer, but stops, as if surprised by his thoughts. "It may be possible."

"I see." My Mom turns to me. "I will go with you."

"No, this is *not* possible." Max rises to his feet, with any trace of uncertainty now gone. He glares at me. "You said you would only talk."

I shake my head. "I never promised that," I say. "She's coming with me."

He draws his sword faster than I can take a breath. It's

at my neck again, only this time it's at the front, the jugular.

Staying still, my eyes glance to Kiyo. She gives a slight nod, as if agreeing to stay out of this, maybe to let me go.

I seize the air and blast the sword out of Max's hands before he can move it. I coil air around him like chains and fling him to the floor, sliding until he hits the far wall, just as I'd done ages ago in the Blue Tower.

Emma hurries to my Mom. "Come, come," she's saying.

I hold out my hand to Kiyo. "Let's go."

She shakes her head.

"You can't stay!" I protest. "Come to the Red Tower with us. It is much better there. You will be welcome."

Kiyo doesn't budge. "I cannot leave," she says. "I am Rice. My place is here now. Someone must protect the others in the village."

"Let the *Lord* handle that," I say.

"No," she replies. "It is my responsibility."

Kiyo and I go back and forth like this a few more times, but she will not change her mind. Emma tells me we must go, that my power will be detected, that it could be stopped any moment. She's right. I give in, torn by getting my Mom back but leaving Kiyo behind.

We rush out without wasting more time. Outside, the whole village is gathered around, but oblivious to us. They look toward the Black Tower. When I follow their gaze, I see a cloud of smoke billowing out of the tower, except it's not like smoke from a fire. Its movements are too organized, too deliberate. The blackness flows like a river, racing straight at us.

"Come on!" Emma tugs at my sleeve. "We have to go!"

I begin to move after her and my Mom, but running won't work. The smoke is coming too fast, and I feel certain that when it reaches us my powers will be smothered. We will be caught. We will be wiped.

My eyes look up, to the ridge looming above. It's all that separates us from Red. It would be better than going through the tunnels and the terrible darkness there. If only we could get over the ridge…

"Stop, wait," I say, and Emma and my Mom turn back to me. Emma has powers from Yellow and Red. I have Blue. Maybe my Mom has some of Black's power already. That would be four colors, four powers. "I'm going to try something."

I concentrate and form a cloud of air. It begins to lift us off the ground, but the weight is too much. I won't be able to carry us all the way over the mountain ridge and down to the Red Tower.

"Let me have control." Emma does not wait for me to agree. She seems to know what I was thinking. She pulls the power away and begins to weave the four colors into a solid structure before us. She makes stairs leading up toward the ridge above, but they rise only twenty feet.

"Start climbing." Her words are strained. She grips my hand tight. "I can't make more, but it should be enough."

As we begin to climb the stairs together, with my Mom in the front, Emma begins to *move* the stairs, looping the stairs behind us to the front, over and over, like we're on a giant ball rolling up an invisible hillside. My Mom watches all this in shock, her face pale.

We rise quickly, far faster than our steps could take us. The view down is astonishing. The villagers' mouths hang open, but soon we are so high that we can no longer make out their expressions. Yet still the dark smoke races from the tower toward us, closing the distance.

Emma weaves and weaves, propelling us forward and up, faster and faster. The amount of power she holds is like nothing I've ever seen. She staggers from the effort. I brace myself against her, keeping her uneasy legs from buckling. A fall from this height would mean death. Would I wake up here in Black, or in Red? I'd rather not find out.

We're almost within reach of the ridge when the rolling stairs shimmer as if they could blink away any moment. Emma looks back frantically. I follow her gaze to where the smoke has closed on us.

"Take it," Emma gasps.

I seize the weave of power and continue forging it as Emma had. The effort of weaving four colors at once is monumental, debilitating. It's amazing that Emma sustained it so long.

My Mom steps off the top stair and onto the ridge, which falls steeply on both sides. She holds out her hand to us and shouts, "Jump!"

The smoke hits me. The power is gone. The stairs are gone.

Just as the surface beneath me vanishes, I take Emma's hand and we leap onto the narrow ridge. Our momentum makes us crash into my Mom, tangling the three of us as we slip on the icy surface. We slide down with nothing to grab, faster and faster, until we slam against a reddish boulder jutting up from the steep, snowy ground.

The boulder saved us. Past it, there's a cliff drop and open sky. The black smoke hovers above at the ridgeline but doesn't come closer, as if an invisible wall stops it from entering Red's lands.

We made it. But we can't stay here. The wind howls like madness. The air is thin as a sheet, making it hard to breathe. The cold bites, turning my sweat into ice. We huddle closer, with our backs to the boulder. The Red Tower is hundreds of feet below us. I feel completely drained. My power won't be enough to get us down.

"Can you carry us again?" I ask Emma.

Her gaze is distant. She shakes her head. She mouths the words, "Too weak."

A gust of wind blasts over us. It is so cold.

We really might die here. At least we'll wake up in Red. Maybe Rahab will have mercy on us and give us our memories back quickly.

"You are both very powerful," my Mom says, through chattering teeth. She still has blankness in her eyes, but she's also surprisingly calm. "We...walked on air. It has been good knowing you."

The words hurt. She doesn't remember.

Emma takes my Mom's hand. "I'm glad we met. Cipher has told me a lot about you. I was a mother, too, but...only briefly." Emma shivers and looks away.

We can't go down like this, not after what it took to get here. We'll hike along the ridge as far as we can. It will be a very long way, and very dangerous. But we have to try something. Freezing is no way to go.

I summon just enough air to dampen the wind's force around us. It batters at the invisible shield mercilessly. I already feel the power slipping, but I should be able to maintain it at least a few minutes. We won't get blown off the cliff yet.

"We have to move," I say. "We'll climb as far as we can. Stay close."

We begin inching our way up the slope from the boulder, crawling on our hands and knees. We've made it ten feet when Emma whispers, "What's that?"

She points down, toward the Red Tower, where a dark, soaring shape has appeared. It's a dragon.

# 40

THE DRAGON, BEHEMOTH, lands on the boulder that had stopped our fall. Its claws are even with my eyes. They're as long as my forearm and look as sharp as curved swords. Behemoth looks up the slope at the black smoke that still hovers at the border of Black and Red. It coils its neck back and breathes out a blast of fire into the smoke. The intense heat melts a line of snow and warms the air around us. The black smoke retreats, leaving only blue sky above.

Behemoth lowers its head and studies us with yellow, slitted eyes. "Climb on," it growls.

Emma moves first. She reaches up and takes hold of the top of Behemoth's neck. She pulls herself up, then scrambles to the middle of its back.

"You next," I say to my Mom.

She climbs on as Emma did. I follow after her. The scales are not as slippery as they look. They're dry and warm, like stones that have been resting by a fire. There are two rows of little horns running down the dragon's back. We hold tight to them as Behemoth rises on its perch and turns.

Without a sound, the immense dragon crouches and springs into the air. We begin to dive down the side of the cliff. It takes every ounce of strength to hold on as the wind whips around us. Wings unfurl to the sides and catch the air. Our descent levels and slows. Behemoth begins to circle the Red Tower, gradually spiraling down. For the first time, with my grip secure, the reality of this fantastic moment hits me.

We're flying. On a dragon.

We must have done something right.

The view below is mesmerizing. The Scouring looks like a perfect grey circle with a white circle at its center. The towers stand equidistant from each other, and their lands— or waters, for Blue—extend into the distance like five slices of a pie. I want the view to last, to study the terrain, but Behemoth draws closer and closer to the Red Tower. It lands smoothly with its claws clutching the parapet that surrounds the signal fire at the top of the tower. It lowers its head until it rests on the stone ground.

We climb off, one by one. Behemoth rises to a crouch on the parapet's edge. It sits still, like an oversized gargoyle. A flash of flame suddenly blazes beside me, then vanishes.

Rahab stands there, smiling. The fire makes her metallic red dress dance with life. "Welcome back! One hundred forty-*six*," she says. "We are most pleased."

"Thank you," I say, smiling at Emma and my Mom. I can't believe we survived, much less the way we escaped.

"No, thank you," Rahab replies. "It is one thing to

capture in the Scouring. It is quite another to capture one from Black's territory, especially *the very one* whose journey you can complete."

"Complete?" I ask. "What do you mean?"

"Look into the fire," Rahab says. "All of you. There are important things for you to see. And there will be a Scouring tomorrow. You three will go." She clasps my Mom's arm gently. "It could be a final Scouring for you."

My Mom only nods in response, her eyes turning from Rahab to the fire.

*Complete? Final?* These words are unusual here. And how could my Mom's journey be complete so soon after her memories were wiped?

I say to Rahab, "But the only way out of the Scouring is…"

"The White Tower," she finishes for me.

"That can't be possible," I say, glancing to my Mom. "She—"

Rahab stops me with a raised hand. "Look into the fire now," she repeats, "and you will see."

"Cipher?" Emma holds out her hand to me. "Shall we?"

The signal fire burns brightly in its ring of dragon teeth. The flames rise almost twice as high as the first time I came here, with Jafari's body. The Red Tower is stronger now. The warmth feels good, thawing my fingers and toes. I take Emma's hand, and then my Mom's. She doesn't resist even though she already seems lost in a vision. I stand between them and we gaze into the flames together.

It's a perfect September day. The sun shines in a blue sky and a breeze makes the warm air feel alive. I snap another picture with my phone. I can't stop taking pictures. Why would I? I've waited months for this day. I've finally made it to campus. My dorm building looks like a gothic castle, with ivy climbing up the walls. The plaque outside the front says, Chamberlain Hall, with a portrait of an old British man, Oliver Chamberlain, who donated the funds to build it centuries earlier. It's quite a legacy. So I snap a picture of it, too.

"Come on!" my Mom yells happily. "We've got a few more loads."

She waves for me to come. She stands beside a rusted blue pickup truck with a few boxes in the back. She's wearing jeans, a t-shirt, and flip-flops. She's not like any of the other parents around, who come in pairs and drive black and silver SUVs and wear loafers and blazers. But she's also much younger, and much more proud of me, I'm sure, than any other parent could be. She's worked hard to help me get here.

I bound down the building's front stairs and come to her side by the truck. "It's Chamberlain Hall, Mom! I had to take another picture. He founded this place. Can you believe how old everything is here?"

"Fine, fine." She tussles my hair playfully. "Did you find a spot for a picture of me on your shelf?"

I laugh and reach past her. Inside one of the boxes, at the top, is exactly the picture I had picked. It's in a simple, black frame. It's a picture of us a couple months before, when she dragged me away for a trip out to the beach for the day. Just the two of us. We cooked lobster and talked under the stars. She'd told me that night how proud she was of me, that she never deserved a son so smart or so good. She told me that she wanted things to go better for me than they had for her, and how she knew they would. She said I'd make a great doctor, a great husband, a great father someday.

"Here's the one!" I say, handing her the frame.

She takes it with both hands and studies it for a moment. She smiles even as she tears up, handing it back to me. "I'm sorry," she says, wiping at her eyes. "I promised I wouldn't cry."

I pull her into a hug. "It's okay. You know I'll call. When I'm not studying, of course."

"Of course," she sniffles the last tears away.

We go back to the boxes in the pickup truck. I carry two large ones, stacked on top of each other, through the front doors of Chamberlain Hall. I say goodbye to my mom, with a final hug, and start getting the room in order.

An hour later my phone rings. I figure it's my Mom, calling to check in on me already.

I'm laughing when I say, "Paul Fitzroy's dorm!"

The voice on the other line does not laugh back. "Is this Mr. Fitzroy?"

"Yes, why?"

"This is Officer Tom Williston, with the state police. Your mother had an accident."

<h1 style="text-align:center">41</h1>

THE VISION ENDS. Emma and my Mom still stand by my sides before the signal fire at the top of the Red Tower. It has grown dark outside, but the fire shows an immense, dark shape perched on the parapet across from us. The yellow slitted eyes, large as I am, do not frighten me as they once did. Rahab stands beside Behemoth, hand on its neck. They seem to have hardly moved.

"Come," Rahab says. "Tell us what you've seen."

Neither Emma nor my Mom hesitate. They move around the fire toward Rahab. I follow them, still disturbed by the memory.

"It was my son!" Emma says, stopping in front of Rahab and sounding as happy as I've ever heard her. "Oliver lived!"

*Oliver Chamberlain.* Emma has told me before that she was the daughter of Chamberlain. And her son's name in a vision was Oliver. She thought he had died in that hut with the man she had run away with. What she saw must have changed that. But how can she know which vision was right. "How do you know what happened to him?" I ask.

"I was with you!" Emma says excitedly. "The man on the plaque, at that building. He was my son, Oliver!"

"Yes," Behemoth rumbles. "He is here." The creature fixes its eyes on Rahab, as if waiting for her to speak.

"You have much more to see," Rahab says to Emma. "As do you, Dr. Fitzroy." She turns to my Mom. "But you have now seen all."

"You know the end," Behemoth says.

My Mom nods. Her serene face reflects the firelight so brightly that it almost shines. "I am ready," she says.

"Ready for what?" I ask.

She takes my hand and squeezes it tight. Up close, her face truly *shines*. It's not just a reflection. It's like there's light within her, blazing through the seams.

"Oh Paul, my little Paul," she says. "You will learn when you are ready. Thank you for finding me. Thank you for everything."

I smile. She knows me. She's back. "How much do you remember?" I ask.

"Everything, Paul. Everything."

*Everything?* How is that possible? She looked into the fire barely longer than I did. "What did you see?" I ask.

"I was with you, of course," she says. "Moving you into college, into your new life. And then I drove away, thinking of how everything had led to that point and the miracle of it. All at once I knew my story. Even the ending." She hugs me, then steps away. "I'm sorry I cannot tell you more. It's not so different than in the memory. You have to find your own way, as I go mine. But I would not have made it here without you. Thank you, Paul. I love you. I will see you again."

Without waiting for me to respond, she moves straight to Behemoth. A trail of light follows her as she goes, like the tail of a comet. What is happening to her?

"Wait," I say.

But she doesn't pause. In one smooth motion the creature dips its neck, and she climbs on. Behemoth's immense wings expand and flap. Wind gusts, and the two of them soar up, straight up. Suddenly, Behemoth reverses course and turns down. It flies like a dagger toward us. It dives right past us, *into* the fire.

And then it's gone. My Mom's gone.

My mouth hangs open. I try to ask a question, but I'm dumbfounded.

Rahab lifts my chin with the tip of her red-lacquered nail, as she has done many times before. She smiles warmly at me. "Rose is safe. You will see her tomorrow, briefly. She will be with you in the Scouring."

"Tomorrow?"

"I'm afraid you will have to trust us," Rahab says. "And if you love your mother, you will do whatever you can to get her to the center of the Scouring."

"Why?" I ask.

"I think you know," she says. "Now, you must come to the Feasting Hall. The Red Tower awaits you." Rahab does not give me a chance to say another word, as she bursts into flame and disappears.

I stand in shock. It has all happened too fast. The

retreat from Black, the vision in the fire, my Mom and Behemoth flying *into* the fire.

"Cipher," Emma says gently, coming to my side. It's just the two of us now. The fire lights up her face as she studies me. "You've never felt…like this."

"I know." She's right. There's so much confusion. But there's also…hope.

Emma smiles. "You don't want to lose her."

"Do you really think she'll go to the White Tower? How could she be ready?"

"I don't think we're supposed to know," Emma says. "It's her story. We should be happy for her."

"I am. I mean…if you're right."

Emma sits back on the parapet. "Your mother had been here a long time. Rahab and Behemoth said she'd seen everything, even the end."

*She had an accident.* That's what the officer told me in the memory. That's how I learned that my Mom died. Maybe she saw herself driving away in that blue pickup truck…then crashing…then dying.

"If you're right," I say, "why wouldn't my Mom have just told us?"

"You saw her. She changed," Emma says. "It was like she saw everything differently. Maybe she found a missing puzzle piece. I think I found one of my own."

"What do you mean?"

"I think we all started with the same vision, at that college building, but then we each went our own direction. When you were walking into the building, carrying two boxes, my vision froze on the portrait of my son, and then everything shifted. I still saw the plaque, but I saw through my son's own eyes. He was reviewing it, approving it, after he had decided to establish the school. He had the most lovely woman by his side, and would you believe it, two beautiful daughters!"

"You were a grandmother?" I say.

"Maybe, but I don't know if I lived to see them. I don't know how it ended for me. That might be what it takes to get into the White Tower."

"We have to learn how we died…"

"Yes," Emma says, "but until then, we have to press ahead with what we know. Now I know about my son, Oliver. I have to find him."

"I understand. That's how I felt when I learned that my Mom was here."

"People from our pasts must come here for a reason," Emma says. "There are brothers and sisters, like Jafari and Jacana. You have your Mom and Samantha. Now I have my son and…" She stops as if catching herself.

"And someone else?" I ask.

Emma gazes out toward the Scouring. "I haven't talked about this much."

"You can tell me."

"Do you remember, when we were in Blue, how we sailed to the Yellow Tower's land?" she asks. "And what happened when we reached the walls?"

"Of course," I say. "You shouted to the archers on the wall that you were the daughter of Chamberlain. They still wouldn't let us in. They shot me in the leg!"

Emma laughs. "I healed it. But I couldn't heal what it did to me. Those archers' words hurt more than arrows, because…my father is there."

"Your father? *In Yellow?*"

"He's a leader there, or he was," Emma says. "Not like Rahab, or Abram. But like the Alpha, except in Yellow's way."

"Why didn't you tell me this before?" I ask.

"A lot has changed since you first brought me to Blue, Cipher." She sighs and leans her head on my shoulder, a perfect fit.

I don't need to respond. She knows how I feel. There's no anger or disappointment about her hiding that her father is here. She needed time. She needed to trust me. And now we're together. It feels *right*. I don't want her to ever budge. I put my arms around her as we sit quietly by the fire. There are so many things I want to ask her—about her father, her son, the Yellow Tower, and us. But I wait. She doesn't need more questions now. Neither do I.

Eventually Emma breaks the silence. "I think someday I might go back to Yellow," she says softly. "But not until I find Oliver. He was not there. You saw the plaque. He was a very wealthy man. I have a feeling he's…with Green."

"Why?" I ask, thinking of Hank. He was captured by Green. If going there has something to do with being wealthy, Hank would not seem to fit. From what he told me, he had hardly more than a horse and a pair of boots.

"I talked to one of the girls, Zelle," Emma says. "A

memory showed her that she was in Green before coming to Red. The memory had to do with buying lots of things. Especially wine. She was rich. She did not sound happy about it. So, well…I just have a feeling.”

“But it’s only a guess,” I say. “Would you really go to Green?”

“I’m not sure. Don’t worry,” she smiles, “I won’t go without you. We’ve learned what happens when you go off alone, haven’t we?”

Her steady blue eyes and gentle smile lift my spirit. She knows what I have done, both here and before, and yet she is still by my side. I’m not worthy of such a friend. “It was a mistake,” I say. “I know that now. I’m sorry I left you.”

“No need to feel bad,” she replies. “But, from here on, let’s stay together, okay?”

*Stay together.* It makes me think of my wife, and of Samantha—the rowing tryout in Chicago, the hotel in Toronto, and the sidewalk covered in rainy petals. The memories do not hurt as they once did. Gaps remain, but what I’ve seen in the Red Tower’s fires has prepared me for this moment. Sitting with Emma, paired with her, I understand. I meet her eyes. “We *are* better that way.”

“You’re learning!” she says, laughing lightly and rising to her feet. “Let’s head to the Feasting Hall. The tower will want to see its leader before the Scouring.”

# 42

THE SOUND OF CHANTING engulfs us as the doors to the Feasting Hall open. "Alpha, Alpha, Alpha!" It takes my breath away. Fires suspended in midair make the cavernous room glow every hue of red. The Hall pulses with deep, steady drumbeats.

Rahab leads Emma and me through the crowd. Familiar faces watch us pass. They are smiling, cheering. A few of them pat me on the back or clasp my hand, as if I'm some kind of returning hero.

Seymour rushes up to me among the crowd. "Cipher, Cipher, I heard you captured someone from Black's lands!" he says. "That's amazing! You're a legend! And hey, look, I got my first pair! She's my sister!"

Beside him stands a girl who looks just like him—freckled and green-eyed and smiling. She was Axe's servant with Emma. Hayley.

"I hoped you would find her," I say.

"I'm starting to get memories back," Hayley says. "Thanks for setting me free."

"A million thanks!" Seymour says. "Now go on, go

on!" He nudges me forward. "The throne is waiting for you."

At the front of the Feasting Hall our Scouring group is gathered in pairs—Marcus and Boleyn, Jafari and Jacana, Khan and Apple, Seth and Zelle. Hank is gone. After we lost him and Seth's old pair, Zelle chose Seth. Despite the changes and those we've lost, it's good to be with these friends, to know something of their pasts, for them to know something of mine, and for us to fight on together.

I take the throne beside Rahab. The chanting fades as food is served. Bowls of bacon and beans. Rahab announces that the Scouring will be tomorrow, and new tasks have been assigned. The crowd goes to check the board, to find their number. It reminds me of my first night here, meeting Seymour and Marcus and getting task seventeen—*dragon teeth*. Tonight that task does not appear. Maybe it won't as long as Red is above equilibrium.

The Scouring group gathers as usual. A boy joins us and introduces himself as Monk. He says he worked his way up slowly through the ranks in Red. He's quiet and not much bigger than I am. He will probably pair with my Mom, if she shows up tomorrow. She must be coming, somehow. Rahab told me to do whatever I could to get her into the center of the Scouring. I have to make it happen.

The group wants to hear about our journey to the Black Tower. Emma does most of the talking, holding the group's attention. She stops the story with our return to the top of the Red Tower. She does not mention what we saw in the fire, or what happened to my Mom. I don't know how we could explain it anyway.

We descend the stairs to the Arena. My Mom still has not appeared. A new girl performs. She's good, drawing a dozen boys to drop to the sandy floor and race for her. When the competition ends, the boys leave for the Barracks, the girls for their rooms, and me for the Alpha's quarters.

I sleep and dream that I sit in a boat with Samantha. She watches me row. At first we wear the uniforms from our high school team. Then our clothes shift. She wears a nurse's scrubs, while I wear my white doctor's coat. Still I row. We pass over Lake Michigan and into a flooded forest. We get lost among huge trees. Samantha studies me silently, judging me, never looking away, as we go deeper and deeper into the forest's darkness. I wake up sweating in a pile of furs.

The next morning I make my way down through the Red Tower, joining with Emma and others along the way. Apple gives me an encouraging smile. Marcus, Seth, Khan, and Jafari each give me a friendly slap on the back. They know I'm ready, just as I know they're ready. We've been winning this battle for a while now.

When we reach the gate to the Scouring, Rahab and my Mom are waiting with their backs to us, looking toward the familiar, empty battleground. My Mom wears a red dress like the other girls from Red, but her skin glows like she can't contain some source of light inside of her.

They turn as we draw close. It's easy to forget how young my Mom looks here.

"You ready?" I ask her.

She smiles, but her gaze is distant, like part of her has already left this place. "Yes, Paul," she says, stepping forward and embracing me. Her voice drops to a whisper by my ear. "It's almost time. Thank you for all you've done."

"You're going to the White Tower, aren't you?" I whisper.

She nods, and squeezes me tighter.

I close my eyes and imagine her as I remember—grown into an adult, with wrinkles and flecks of gray in her hair, with the smell of roses and mint and cigarette. "Can't you take me with you?" I ask. "I want to go."

"Your time will come," she says. "I love you, Paul. Keep going. It will be worth it."

The iron gate begins to open. Metal grates loudly as draw chains rise.

"Let passion burn!" Rahab says, with her flames flickering above her hands.

My Mom gives me a final squeeze, then steps away. It seems like so long ago that I left Blue for Red, hoping to find her, to help her. We found each other. Now she could leave the five towers, forever. I am leading Red, with Emma by my side. My time will come. My Mom's time is now. I have to do everything I can to get her to the center.

Our group echoes the battle cry together: "Let passion burn."

We move into the Scouring in pairs. Emma stays close to me. No attacks come as we advance. Black moves along the wall toward Blue. Green and Yellow are inching forward slowly. We reach the middle of the Scouring before any other team is close. My feet stop at the line where the grey stone turns to white. The rest of our team positions around the circle's edge, facing out, ready to defend against any attacks.

My Mom takes my hand. She reaches her other arm forward, crossing over the edge of the white circle. Instantly, a shaft of pure white light beams up from the circle, basking her arm in brightness. The column of light stretches infinitely high, penetrating the gray sky above.

The sound of fighting is closer now, but I don't bother to look. Nothing could pull my eyes away.

My Mom squeezes my hand tightly. She still faces the light. My skin under her palm suddenly burns. I wince in pain, jerking back. But her grip holds firm. It feels like a red-hot iron brand pressed against my flesh, searing and sizzling. She lets go as she steps forward. The pain is instantly gone. She glances back and gives me a final smile before stepping all the way into the column of light. It covers her completely. Her skin glows.

"Whoa," Emma whispers by my side. She lifts the hand that burned. It has a criss-cross scar, matching the one on my other hand. "It's another one," Emma says, turning back toward the light. "Look at her now."

The light in front of us grows brighter and brighter. There's only a faint shadow of my Mom left, fading, fading, until I can't see anything through the light.

I reach forward, breathing fast, heart thumping. My

freshly scarred skin looks flat and lifeless as my hand hesitates at the edge of the dazzling pillar of light. I want to enter this light, to follow.

"Cipher! No!" someone shouts from behind.

But Emma is still with me, holding my other hand. "Let's try it," she says, knowing how I feel. "We'll do it together."

We both reach *into* the light. It enfolds my fingers, my hand, pulling me gently in and up and up.

The pull becomes faster and stronger. A rush of air and light and force draws my entire body up, feet lifting off the ground, like an ant sucked up into a vacuum cleaner. Emma clutches my hand, with her head tilted back and gazing up into the light. Inside the column, we can see my Mom above. She rises farther and farther above us, becoming smaller and smaller in the distance. She does not look down. Our ascent begins to slow. We will not catch her.

Something firm grabs me from below.

I try to ignore it, but it yanks at me. Reluctantly, I look away from my Mom and back down toward the Scouring.

A rope coils around my ankle, tethering me to the ground. Another rope has caught Emma beside me. As the rope tugs me down, the column of light continues to pull me up. Tension builds, like I'm being torn apart by the opposite forces. I writhe and fight to get free, but another rope slings onto my arm and tightens, like a lasso, entangling me more. I grab for the air, to blow the ropes free, but in my panic, awash in the pure white light, I cannot see any color. There's no blue or red. There's no thread to weave.

With a final yank, the ropes slam Emma and me to the ground. We land with a crash. My head hits the Scouring's stone, hard.

In a daze, with everything spinning, my thoughts drift away as if in a dream, and in the dream all that I can see is green, vibrant and alive and consuming.

J.B. SIMMONS is the bestselling author of the *Unbound* trilogy, *The Babel Tower*, and *Light in the Gloaming*. He lives and writes outside Washington, D.C. To learn more about J.B. and his books, visit **www.jbsimmons.com**.

Don't miss *The Green Tower*, the sequel to *The Red Tower* and the third book in The Five Towers Series, available on Amazon and more.